Secrets in Silicon Valley

A Miranda Marquette Mystery
Book 4

J.T. Kunkel

ISBN 978-1-950613-61-8
Copyright © 2021 J. T. Kunkel
Published by Taylor and Seale Publishing, LLC
3408 South Atlantic Avenue
Unit 139
Daytona Beach Shores, FL 32118

Cover design and layout by Chris Holmes

Publisher's Note: This is a work of fiction. Names, characters, places, and incidents are a product of the author's imagination or used fictitiously. Locales and public names are sometimes used fictitiously for atmospheric purposes. With the exception of public figures or specific historical references, any resemblance to actual people, living or dead, or to businesses, companies, events, institutions, or locales is completely coincidental. Any historical personages or actual events depicted are completely fictionalized and used only for inspiration. Any opinions expressed are completely those of fictionalized characters and not a reflection of the views of public figures, author, or publisher.

Acknowledgement

To Donna Pudick at Parkeast Literary Agency, my literary agent. Thank you for continuing to make me a better writer by knowing how to push me to the next level. You have helped me to develop improved writing and editing habits which I believe serve me better as a writer both now and in years to come. I continue to learn through your feedback and am very thankful to have you as an agent and a mentor.

To Veronica H. (Ronnie) Hart, my editor at Taylor and Seale Publishing. You continue to help me to hone my writing skills and to help me to understand the subtle differences between an acceptably written dialog and an exceptional one. I continue to learn more as a writer every day with your help and look forward to working with you more on the series as Miranda matures and grows.

To Mary Custureri, CEO of Taylor and Seale Publishing. I continue to be amazed at how many authors there are compared to how many published authors. I am thankful that you have chosen to publish the Miranda Marquette Mystery Series and I look forward to a long association.

I dedicate Secrets in the Silicon Valley to my gorgeous and brilliant wife Susan, the Love of my life, and my Marketing Director. When we met twenty-two years ago, we didn't have a clue the wild ride that we were in for, but we took the 'leap of faith' and jumped in with both feet. I have never had a day of regret. I look forward to getting old together, although that will be a long, long time from now, and spending eternity together thereafter. I will Love You forever.

Secrets in Silicon Valley

Chapter 1

May 2010

The aftermath of the murder trial last year was far-reaching. Sarah, my former upstairs neighbor, and her former boyfriend Bill ended up in Federal Prison—Sarah, for first-degree manslaughter and Bill as an accessory for killing her roommate, Jane.

Despite Sarah's confession in court and subsequent conviction, there was still a contingent of internet die-hards who insisted I was guilty. In a way, they were right. I wasn't guilty of murder, but I felt guilty about the murders of so many people near to me over the past three years.

My therapists have said that it was normal for me to feel responsible for the deaths of four people I had known within such a short period. I lie awake at night wondering if my recent past has prevented people I know and love, like Jason, from getting close to me because they fear for their lives.

Maureen, my present therapist here in Santa Clara, had been working with me to help me to reconcile my role, or lack thereof, in the murders. There were a large and growing number of internet rats dubbing me the Princess of Death, who continued to express a desire to see me in jail, even though the legal system had declared me completely innocent.

History had a place for people who found themselves in the wrong place at the wrong time. The Salem Witch Trials were a perfect example. The fact was, those convicted witches were just regular people caught in a struggle between two prominent families in Salem: The Porters and the Putnams. When all was said and done, of the two hundred accused of witchcraft, they executed twenty innocent women. It took intervention by law enforcement from Boston for the insanity in Salem to end. Much of the time these days, I was feeling like a modern-day Salem witch.

When would this insanity end?

#

The alarm went off at 7:00. I turned on the shower as hot as it would go. The water stayed warm forever, but it was never quite hot enough. I thought about asking the landlady to turn up the water heater, but she had given me such a great deal on the apartment, I hated to bother her with petty requests. I vowed to find the water heater and turn it up myself, but I hadn't had the nerve to venture down into the basement to find it. This house was the first property with a basement I had lived in since moving to California, so I feared if I ever ventured downstairs, an earthquake would pick that time to rumble through. After some consideration, I decided the water temperature was tolerable.

I toweled myself dry and looked in the full-length mirror on the wall. My daily running was paying off. A few weeks ago, I could tell I had put on a few pounds, which was understandable with the number of stress factors I had endured over the past year. I had lost my company, which was closed down by the government. I had lost all my assets, also courtesy of the government. I found a job in Santa Clara and relocated from my ocean view ranch in Malibu to a furnished apartment in Santa Clara, usually reserved for students at Santa Clara University.

Amazingly, I had adjusted remarkably well to those changes. On the other hand, a source of constant frustration was my boss, Jason. When we first met nearly two years ago, he seemed interested in me, but then made it clear that he wasn't ready for a relationship as he was still recovering from a bad break-up.

Then last year, in a sweet gesture, he left me a note that he was ready to take the plunge. Since then, he had changed his mind no fewer than five times. We dated once every week or two, and it always seemed to me that we had a good time, then he suddenly became awkward and distant. Then we went out a few weeks later with the same result for days afterward.

I was getting a complex, so on the advice of Tea, my co-worker, I saved for weeks so that I could go shopping and update my wardrobe. Everything I had been able to salvage when I moved was too formal for work or too conservative. More than ten years my junior, Tea felt like I needed to update my closet if I couldn't get his attention. Or perhaps I could garner some of his co-workers' attention and make him realize just what he was missing.

With that in mind, I slipped into my new Victoria's Secret bra and shimmied into my matching panties. I surveyed myself in the mirror with no complaints. It was risky to wear a mini skirt when it was as likely I'd be standing on a ten-foot ladder in the warehouse as sitting at my computer entering orders. I decided to ask one of the guys for help if I needed something off the top shelf in the warehouse.

After my first couple of weeks of employment, I had made a strategic error when I started dressing for comfort in jeans and tee-shirts. My recently updated wardrobe represented an

3

upgrade of my original strategy of dressing for success, but with improved clothing options. It felt right as I zipped my newly acquired miniskirt and left my blouse's top two buttons undone.

Although, after a few days of my new strategy, I wasn't sure if my newfound popularity with the opposite sex was everything I'd hoped it would be. After all, I was trying to get Jason's attention, and he was as oblivious as he had ever been.

Suddenly two new product development engineers found a critical need to show up at my desk at all hours of the day. Rick and Barry couldn't have more different in their styles or alike in their intentions.

Rick was the quintessential ladies' man. He was a mid-forties divorcee with slightly graying hair and a boyish look and charm to go along with it. Knowing that women found him attractive was his most annoying quality. He lacked that slightest amount of humility. He was also too much of a man's man to be appealing, to me at least. He gave me the impression that he'd much rather go to a dive bar with a couple of guys after work with the intent of ogling women all evening than ever date one.

Barry, on the other hand, was a woman's best friend. 'Friend' being the operative word. He would bend over backward to do women favors, which made my skin crawl. He offered to move my car into a shadier parking spot once the sun had crossed the sky. He begged to grab my lunch from the fridge and deliver it to me. He would almost break his leg to get in front of me so that he could open the door. He was more of a puppy dog than most four-legged ones. But worse than that, his habit of calling me 'Miss M' made me want to crawl into a hole and never come out, like nails on a chalkboard.

Another noticeable change for me, with several construction projects going on outside and adjacent to the employee parking lot, was an occasional whistle from several workers on my way in or out. I chose to ignore them. They didn't need to know I always appreciated the compliment.

About a week into my new dress code, I got an idea. I would arrange a follow-up meeting with Bob and Jason regarding my system recommendations. Nearly a year ago, I had suggested some computer network and software upgrades, which I promised would save the company hundreds of thousands per year. As Jason had warned would happen, I had received only platitudes from Bob. After all this time, his pessimism about getting Bob to take any real action seemed justified.

After my usual morning gossip with Tea on Monday, I slipped out of the customer service suite and headed to the main offices. I was hopeful that Jason was at his desk. As usual, computer printouts littered his desk. I often wondered if he really gleaned any information from those reports or was just trying to look busy for Bob, but I never let on.

Evidenced by the fact that he nearly jumped out of his skin, I startled him when I entered. "Hi, boss! Good weekend?"

He noticeably blushed, either because I startled him or because he noticed that I wasn't wearing my typical sweats and an 'I Heart Venice Beach' tee-shirt. I held his glance noticeably longer than usual, so I figured my wardrobe change was a hit. He stammered just a touch, "Miranda, h-how nice to see you. Long time no see. Well, you know what I mean."

I smiled. "Sure, I do." I paused for effect. "Hey, want to get back together with Bob to do a follow-up on my presentation? I've never heard anything back from him. I honestly thought I had him convinced."

He glanced at the calendar on his desk. He seemed a little disappointed that I was here on business, or perhaps that was wishful thinking. "How about Thursday at two?" he responded looking more at me than at his calendar.

I'd left my cell phone in my cubicle. Even though I knew I had nothing on my calendar, I didn't want to seem unimportant. "Let me check my calendar," I said with a slight smirk.

His perplexed look told me he didn't know if I was kidding or not. "Okay, Miranda, let me know." I got up from the chair in front of his desk and started toward the door.

Before I could reach the door, he softened his tone, "Miranda?"

I paused and turned around, hopeful and anticipating, but let down again.

He spoke in a lower voice so that no one outside his office could hear. "Have you noticed anything strange about Rick lately? He seems different."

I almost asked, 'How should I know?' but he and I were already in a weird place, so I did everything I could do not to sound sarcastic. "Gosh, Jason, I don't know. He seems fine to me. In fact, better than fine as far as I can tell." I winked and headed back to my workspace. I wasn't sure I had accomplished anything, but if he was jealous of him, that should have kicked it up a notch.

When I returned to my desk, I sat, wondering if I should give up on Jason. There was no question he had issues. Sure, I had problems of my own, but I had learned through years of therapy not to chase a lost cause.

Tea had been pretty quiet so far today, and I had learned to leave her alone when she got like that or risk some snippy comment and no talking for a day or two. I had a feeling there was trouble in paradise with Mike, but she wasn't sharing. I had finally met him when her car broke down a few weeks ago, and he came to pick her up. One thing I immediately picked up on was that he was a major flirt. I wasn't old enough to be his mother, but I was old enough to think of him as a child. But I could see the hurt in Tea's eyes when he joked around with me, so I was cautious not to give him any mixed signals.

She had been cordial since then, but it felt like there was an underlying issue. Part of me wanted to address it, and part of me thought it might blow over.

So, I was surprised when she strolled over to my desk and said, "Miranda, can I talk to you for a minute?"

I smiled and turned from my screen to give her my full attention. "Sure, sweetheart, what's up?"

She inhaled like it was her last breath. "Um, something's been bothering me the last couple of weeks. You know when Mike picked me up from work?"

I would be happy to have this conversation behind us. "Uh-huh," I said casually.

She seemed to search for the words. "You didn't *like* him or anything, right?"

I bit my lip. "Well, sure, I liked him. He seemed like a nice guy." I was pretty sure that wouldn't satisfy her, but I had to admit I was playing her a little.

She insisted, "No, I mean, were you *attracted* to him? After you two met, he couldn't talk about anything but you for days: how smart you are, how pretty you are, how funny you are. You know I think you are amazing, right? But this was over the top." I sensed there were underlying issues in their relationship far more significant than this.

I decided it would be unkind to torture her any further. I put my hand on her arm. "Believe me, Tea, you have nothing to worry about. He was a bit of a flirt, but I was just playing along to be nice. Sorry if that got misinterpreted. He was like a wise kid who sits in the back of the class, and I was the substitute teacher. It was all harmless banter."

She still looked worried. "I'm not sure that was how Mike took it. He was taken with you."

I took her hand. "Tea, it was nothing. Do you want me to talk to him?"

She took a step back. "No! That would only make it worse."

I thought for a minute, considering what I would do in her circumstances. "Have you talked to Mike about it?"

She bit her lip. "No. He'd just tell me that my imagination is running away with me like he always does."

I didn't know what to do, and she was getting more worked up by the second. I had to ask because this seemed an over-the-top reaction based solely on our interaction. "Is everything okay between you two?"

She half nodded and then burst into tears. I held her, and she buried her face in my shoulder. When she stopped sobbing, she spoke in broken sentences sniffling in between words.

"I ... think ... he's ... cheating ... on ... me!" I didn't know how to respond, so I held her until she could speak without gasping for air. "He's been acting strangely for a while now. I can't put my finger on it. He's vague about where he's been. He's on his phone at all hours of the day and night and gets angry when I ask him what he's doing."

I didn't know him at all and didn't want to meddle. It sounded like Tea could be right. I didn't have the best track record in managing my own relationships, but I couldn't resist trying to help her.

"I think the best thing to do is to sit down and talk to him. Tell him what you're feeling and let him explain what is going on with him. Men are strange animals. They hide their feelings. They can be ashamed to admit when they need help. So before you jump to any conclusions, give him a chance. Then if he either admits that he's cheating or is evasive, you'll know that you did everything you could."

She smiled weakly. "I know you're right, Miranda. I've just been so afraid that he wouldn't give me the answer I wanted, I've avoided it completely, which makes me more miserable. I'll talk to him tonight."

I wasn't a therapist, but I had had enough sessions in my lifetime to know what advice they would probably give, and I thought I nailed it. She went back to her desk and looked more hopeful than she had in a while. I prayed to God for her sake that he wasn't cheating, but, either way, it was always better to know the truth.

Chapter 2

I lived close enough to work that I could walk home. I had done it a couple of times in the year I had worked here. As long as I had lived in California, I didn't take for granted the gorgeous weather we had much of the year. I had always loved early Spring and late Fall growing up in New Orleans, so Northern California's cooler temperatures suited me fine.

I kept a pair of ASICS running shoes at work for when I felt like getting some exercise. I didn't care how I looked with my sneakers and miniskirt. The weather was perfect, so I decided I was walking.

After nearly an hour of dodging oncoming cars and ignoring gestures of all kinds, I made it home. Lost in my thoughts, I hadn't noticed someone sitting on my front steps until I was a few houses up from mine. Before it registered who it was, she had already jumped up and started running toward me.

Even before she reached me, I knew it was Patricia by her perfect facial features, jet black hair, and alabaster skin. She was my only remaining FEAST (First Extreme All-Girl Sports Team) teammate. Tara and Annika had died at the hands of others, but I still felt responsible. While she and I had butted heads as teammates, we bonded in Switzerland during the murder trial of her baby's biological father. He was convicted and now in prison for the foreseeable future.

Her original plan to move in with me in Malibu was short-lived when the government shut down my internet-based company. The idea of relocating her infant son, Nate, to Northern California while trying to figure out my next move had been too much for her. So she moved back in with her parents in

Colorado. I hadn't seen her since I left Malibu. I returned the enthusiastic hug she gave me even though she nearly knocked me off my feet.

Then I held her at arm's length. "Well, look at you! Aren't you a sight for sore eyes? What are you doing here?" After giving birth less than a year ago, she was back to her pre-baby model weight.

We walked arm in arm back to the porch. I unlocked the door, and we went in together. I said, "Let's sit down and talk! It's been how long now?"

She smirked. "Tell me you don't know the date you left your other world behind! It's been almost a year, but it seems like at least a decade."

Her shoulder-length black hair fell in front of her jet-black eyes the way it always did when she got animated, which had been more and more the longer I knew her. She used to be reserved and moody, but motherhood agreed with her. She flipped her hair back without missing a beat. Then she put her hands on her hips and mock-scolded me. "Hey, I thought you told me you were going to keep in touch. You could text me once in a while. There's also this new thing I'm trying called Facebook. You should sign up. We could communicate that way."

I wasn't too enthusiastic about being even more tied to my computer or my phone. "Oh, I don't know. I'm still not over that MySpace disaster." I changed the subject. "So, you haven't told me what you're doing here." I hit her on the arm.

She laughed and flipped her hair again. She had a devilish look on her face and looked like she was going to burst. "*We're moving here!*"

I looked at her like she was from Venus, Mars, or another planet. "What? No way!"

Her expression turned sheepish. "Um, don't get mad, but I was hoping I could stay with you until I got settled. I'm not bringing Nate out until I get a place to live. My parents are the ultimate grandparents and, I swear they would take him full time if I'd let them."

I dragged her to the couch. "Okay, now tell me everything. Why are you moving here? Did you get a job here? Did you get run out of town?" I giggled at the last one, knowing that it wasn't likely since her parents were pillars of the Denver community.

She sat, facing me on the couch. "Okay, here's the story. It was fine for a while with my parents and Nate. He adores them, and they adore him, so it has been a good situation for all of us, for the most part. But they say you can't go back, and I guess it's true. I had grown in ways I didn't realize until I moved home and realized I had so much more to give to the world. And my parents, God love them, can't figure out how to stop parenting me." She grimaced like a cockroach had just crawled over her hand.

I knew just what she meant. I'd had years of dysfunction with my mom that we had only recently resolved. "I completely agree," I said, nodding my head.

She sat on the edge of the couch. "So, anyway, I started applying for jobs all over the place. Granted, I might have exaggerated my experience, especially where working for you was concerned, but I figured you'd back me up if I needed you to."

I shook my head. "You are so darned modest! You did a great job after Heather left town. You were a natural."

Patricia smiled. It was so good to see her smiling again. I felt so bad when my company folded, and I had to relocate quickly, leaving her up in the air. She continued. "Anyway, I applied for a job at Karma Electronics. They were a start-up a few years ago, and now are giving Apple a run for its money. It was all about developing relationships with community businesses, and I thought I could handle it and that it might even be fun. I figured it was a long shot, but I interviewed last week, and they called yesterday and offered me the job!"

I jumped up in excitement. "Get out! I'm so excited! The dynamic duo is back. So have you figured out where you're going to live yet?"

She bit her lip. "Well, I kind of used your address on my resume so they would think I was local. So technically, I live here."

I reassured her. "You are always welcome here as long as you need to stay, but let's face it, it's probably too small for two in the long run. But I have a *great* idea. The apartment upstairs is vacant, and the landlord's been having trouble renting it. I guess the fact that the college student who lived there was killed by her roommate could have something to do with that."

She suddenly looked consumed by guilt. "I know. I watched it all on T.V. I'm sorry I didn't come to your rescue when the internet turned on you. I felt horrible. I just wasn't in a good place at that point. I knew I had to get out of there, but I had no idea how or when I could make that work."

I didn't like to think about my notoriety as the Princess of Death, but it ended okay. "It wasn't your responsibility to come up and take care of me. It wasn't as bad as, I'm sure, the press made it seem. They are not my friend."

She shook her head. "They clearly don't have a clue who you are. I used to get so angry; I wanted to jump inside my laptop and take some of them down. People who live their life online need to get real." Her fiery and intense side had revealed itself during the week she and I spent in Switzerland. It suited her well.

I was so sick of talking about my last year; I wanted to change the subject. "So, Patricia, I really think you should talk to the landlord about the upstairs apartment. She's tired of renting to students, so you would be perfect."

I thought she would be thrilled, but she immediately got more serious. "Can I be totally frank with you, Miranda?" We sat knee to knee on the couch, and her eyes were burning through me.

I nodded. "Always."

She continued. "There's one thing about my move I didn't mention earlier. Things weren't all peaches and cream in Denver before I left." She hesitated, like part of her wanted to tell me, and part of her didn't. "I was being stalked by some crazy guy."

I grabbed her hand, "What? Who? How do you know?"

She snickered sarcastically. "Oh, believe me, I knew. There was no mistaking this." She took a deep breath. "I met him one evening when I was jogging. I took a break in a park, catching my breath and stretching before running the second half. He was sitting on a bench nearby and started up a conversation with me. I was lonely, living at home with my parents, and he was really charming and kind of sweet. In retrospect, I probably paid too much attention to him."

After we talked for a while, he asked if I wanted to get a drink. There was a bar across the street, and I didn't see any harm. We talked for a couple of hours. I had texted my parents, so they didn't worry about where I was. Toward the end, his questions started getting kind of personal, about where I lived, other relationships that I had had, and stuff like that. He was nice enough, but I wasn't ready to share that information.

"He was putting the shots of whiskey away, but I only had one glass of wine. When he ordered one more, I saw that as an opportunity to make a break for it. But when I told him I had to go, he started getting belligerent and angry. I tried to calmly explain that I had to go, then our waitress picked up on my predicament and tried to intervene. That was all it took for him to get downright nasty."

I could feel her anguish. "That must have been horrible!"

She frowned deeply. "Oh, it gets worse. The waitress called the police, and when they got there, he refused to leave. They practically had to carry him out, and they arrested him on a bunch of drummed up charges. Okay, the guy was drunk, so make sure he gets home and call it a night. But no, they charged him with being drunk and disorderly, a public nuisance, resisting arrest, and I don't know what else."

Her face turned pale, reliving what clearly was a nightmare. She continued in a low and slow cadence like she was giving her statement to the police. "I nearly forgot about the guy after a few days. Then, one night, maybe a week after the whole thing happened, I got home to find red paint on my parent's front door with a heart painted on it with the word 'DIE' inside the heart."

I was horrified. "Oh, my God! What did you do?"

She continued, staring past me. "My dad painted over it, and I just tried to forget about it. I convinced myself it was some random kids being kids. But then a couple of days later, he did the same thing, only worse. Much worse." She choked on her words. "I'm embarrassed even to tell you what he wrote, but it was ugly—horrible. So finally, I decided I had to call the police. They took my statement but, without proof that it was him, let me know it wasn't likely anything could or would be done. They said that I should just go on with my life." She looked me in the eye. "How can I just go on with my life?"

I couldn't relate from my own experience, but I'd handled many similar circumstances when I was a cop.

She closed her eyes briefly, willing herself to finish the story. "Well, a couple of days later, I went downstairs to get in my car to drive to work. Somebody had spray painted threats and obscenities all over it. You could barely recognize it. On the sidewalk next to the car was a red spray-painted heart with 'SOON' inside."

She continued, "I called the police again, and they took another statement. This time, the damage was so extensive, they couldn't ignore it, so they arrested him."

I felt some encouragement. "Oh, so that's good."

She shook her head. "Within a short time, they released him for lack of evidence."

Tears ran down her cheeks, and I grabbed a box of tissues and handed it to her. She seemed determined to get everything out. "That was when I decided to get a new start out here. I haven't been able to eat or sleep for weeks. My parents have been super supportive, but there's nothing they can do either."

I did everything in my power to be a positive force. I hadn't realized I'd been hunched over, leaning toward her as if afraid to miss a word. I straightened up, slapped my hands on my thighs, and said, "Well, this is your lucky day. I'm here, and I won't let anything bad happen to you. You can stay here as long as you want. And when you're ready, you can find a place of your own, whether it's upstairs or somewhere else nearby."

She hugged me. "Thanks, Miranda. I knew you would know just what to say. Thank you so much!"

I was embarrassed by her praise, so I directed it back to her. "You're the strongest person I know. Don't you ever forget that. With all this on top of Larry's conviction, I'd be a basket case if I were you." Larry was the father of her child.

She smiled through her tears. "I feel like everything is going to be okay now that I'm here."

I forced a smile. "I'll make sure it is," knowing I was probably as powerless as anyone in Denver had been.

Chapter 3

We talked until at least midnight when she finally fell asleep on the couch. Knowing the trauma that she had been through, I wanted to make sure she was asleep before I went to bed. When the alarm went off at 6:30, it took two cups of coffee before I even started to wake up.

She stirred several times but didn't wake up before I left at 7:30. Since I walked home last night, I had to take the motorcycle and now had two vehicles at work. That was poor planning on my part, but I hadn't expected a surprise visit from Patricia, which was worth the inconvenience.

I had tons of work backed-up and hoped that arriving a half-hour before my official start time would give me a jump on it. But due to system issues and the fact that my computer was continually rebooting itself, I only got four orders of the twenty I had on my desk processed. I decided to compose an email to Bob and Jason regarding my continued frustration with the system. I figured that I had nothing to lose by asking for a response to the proposal I had made months ago.

While I assumed the answer was 'No' since they hadn't responded, I wasn't giving up. In the middle of completing the email, Tea arrived, her typical five minutes late. She pushed everything in her life to the limit. When I jokingly mentioned that, she just glared. I guessed this wasn't one of her good days.

She continued through my area to the break room to make coffee without comment. Ten minutes later, she emerged with a half-empty cup of coffee and an apologetic smile on her face. Our cubicles were close enough to one another so we could speak, but we rarely did unless we physically approached the other's workspace. That was our unwritten rule about creating personal space.

However, this morning, she broke it. "Sorry, Miranda. I didn't sleep so well last night."

She didn't know the half of it, but I wasn't going to bring Patricia's issues into the office. So, I replied, "That's fine, Tea. I'm a little tired today too." I thought she might ask why, and I didn't have a good answer, so I was happy she didn't pursue it. I really liked Tea but having Patricia around even for a short time made it evident to me how much more work it was to maintain my friendship with Tea.

Due to my computer issues, I had to work until seven to get caught up. I suddenly felt guilty for leaving Patricia alone in the apartment all day, so I texted her just before leaving. "On my way home."

She responded. "Okay."

I wasn't sure if she was an emoticon user and purposely omitted a smiley face when she responded or if she had relished her alone-time. Either way, I hadn't followed up with her once today. I felt like a horrible friend. I guess sometimes I was, but hopefully not all the time. My therapist had told me to work on not centering solely on myself after two people from my past, on the same day, had blamed me for ruining their lives. I'd have to think about that later.

I decided to ride my motorcycle home, and maybe walk back to get the car. Otherwise, I was stuck with two vehicles at work indefinitely. Maybe Patricia would ride back to work with me on the back of the bike and then drive my car home. It would probably depend on how abandoned she had felt by me being so absorbed with work all day.

I was relieved when I got home and found Patricia relaxing on one of the lounge chairs on the front porch. She jumped up to meet me when I pulled up. She seemed to be feeling better and bursting with news. "Guess what!"

I was so glad she wasn't mad at me. "Um, you met the man of your dreams?"

She put her finger on her chin. "Well, in a way. I met your landlady today."

I chuckled. "Okay, now that's really a stretch since she's a woman!"

She grinned. "Perhaps I should say, 'Our landlady'! I'm going to be your upstairs neighbor! You were so right. The opportunity to rent the apartment to a non-student was too much for her to resist. She didn't even care if I hadn't started my job yet and had no pay stubs."

My mouth gaped open in stunned amazement. "So, when do you move in?"

She reached into her pocket and pulled out a key. "I'm moved in. I thought I'd do the neighborly thing and let you know before you found out some other way, like from the landlady."

We hugged. "I'm so happy. I can't believe it. I've been feeling really lonely here since all the excitement with the murder trial ended, and now my bestie is right upstairs."

I was surprised when Patricia's mouth dropped; she let go of me and ran inside my apartment. I followed her in, asking, "What was that?"

Patricia was white and shaking. "It was him. I'm sure it was him."

I asked, "What was him? Who?"

She paced around like a caged tiger. "Him, that James guy from Denver! Somehow, he followed me here. How can I ever get away?"

I looked through the screen door to the street. "Are you sure it was him? "

She was indignant. "Miranda, I see this guy every day and every night in my nightmares! I know what he looks like."

I was still skeptical. "Did you see him in a vehicle?"

She was getting frustrated. "Yes, he was in a vehicle! Do you think he's just going to stroll down the street and say 'Hi.'?"

I hesitated, seeing that she was getting aggravated, and I wanted to be supportive. "Do you know what kind of vehicle he owns?"

She stopped pacing and stood stone still and spoke quietly. "No, Miranda, I don't. It was probably a rental. I just know he's here. And now he knows where I live. Where *we* live, and now he's seen me with you, so he knows that I know someone here in Santa Clara, and where we both live. I've ruined everything!" She buried her face in her hands and sobbed.

I had to get this under control quickly before Patricia had a meltdown. "Okay, let's assume for a minute that it was him." She glared at me. "I'm not saying it wasn't, but we don't know that for sure. So let's say it was him. So far, he has a pattern of spray-painting things to scare you. If he's here, he will probably do the same thing."

She looked like she was going to throw up. "*Or* he'll be furious that I tried to escape him, and he'll carry out his threats."

I thought for a minute. "Well, you have your own apartment, but I think you should stay here for a while. I honestly think this guy is a lot of hot air and just wants to scare you. If he really wanted to hurt you, he probably would have already."

She looked at me like I was crazy. "So you're trying to tell me that every crazy in the world that torments and intimidates someone *never* carries out their threats? I've read plenty of police accounts of cases like this since this all happened. They *often* carry out their threats! They just need to get angry or frustrated enough. That's when it goes from being a game to

21

something more serious. And that's when people get hurt. Or killed."

I couldn't argue with the facts. No-one knew them better than I did. When I was on the force, I had worked very closely with several criminals with a similar M.O. None of those situations had happy endings. On top of everything else, the odds were that this perp suffered from emotional or mental illness, which made the situation even more complicated.

Finally, I said contritely, "Okay, I've been trying to paint it with rose-colored glasses. I don't want to believe that you are really in danger. And now that you're here, I don't want you to keep running. We will deal with this together."

She smiled, but I could tell she was still frustrated. "I appreciate that Miranda, but I don't want to put you in danger. This guy is my problem."

I punched her on the arm affectionately. "Now you stop that crazy talk. I won't have it. I would never leave you to deal with this alone. You remember in Thun when we said we'd be friends forever?"

She nodded.

I directed her to the couch and sat next to her. "You will stay here until we know it's safe for you to be alone. That's non-negotiable. Now, you have this guy's name and everything, right?"

She reached into her pocket. "Yes, I have it right here. If he ever gets me, I want the evidence on my person. It's James Rich. I'll text it to you, so you have it on your phone."

I stood up. "Let's go to the police station so we can put them on alert. Unfortunately, I left my car at work, so I only have my motorcycle. Are you good with that?"

She laughed. "I thought you'd never ask."

Chapter 4

I knew it was unlikely that the police would do anything since the perp hadn't broken any laws in their jurisdiction. Still, it could give the police a head start if he continued threatening Patricia here in California.

I had become familiar with Detective Wanda Marshall, a tough but compassionate black woman, probably mid-forties with straight black hair and a face with plenty of miles on it. While we weren't exactly friends, we had developed a mutual respect during my last run-in with the law.

Coincidentally, she was just coming into the building as we were. "Marquette?" She had a way with words. "I thought that was you. What brings you back to our humble station?"

Actually, it was one of the most beautiful, state of the art police stations I had ever visited, but if she thought it was humble, who was I to argue?

"Detective Marshall, this is my friend Patricia. She wants to report a potential nuisance."

She motioned us to follow her. "I was just gonna do some paperwork, but that can always wait."

She walked us to a familiar-looking interrogation room. Instinctively, I sat with my back to the two-way mirror and motioned Patricia to sit next to me. The detective faced the mirror, perhaps knowing from experience that I preferred my back to the two-way. She smiled and attempted to engage Patricia as opposed to getting my version of the story. "And your full name is?"

She smiled and shook the detective's hand. "My name is Patricia Ann White. I'm new in town. I guess you could say it didn't take me long to find trouble."

The detective laughed. "Well, if you're a friend of this one, I'm not surprised. She was somewhat of a celebrity around here for several months and not in a good way. We're hoping things have calmed down a bit now, so don't tell me anything that will increase my stress level."

She winked. Clearly, she enjoyed her job, which was something to be envied in this day and age.

Patricia spent the next half hour filling the detective in on the man who stalked her. As it turned out, per the detective's database, his name was John Blake. James Rich was an alias he had used in several states. There were no open warrants for his arrest, but he had a rap sheet a mile long. Coincidentally, Colorado and California were two of the three states he had committed crimes in. Hawaii was the third.

As Patricia and the detective talked, I wondered if she had really seen him on the road passing my apartment or if it was her imagination. I tried to imagine a scenario where he could have figured out this quickly that she was here. I couldn't come up with an explanation without some expensive navigational tracking equipment, and that seemed unlikely.

As I had predicted, there wasn't much the detective could do other than taking down the information. When we left the station, Patricia seemed calmer and more grounded, sharing her story with the detective. As an ex-cop, I figured it was a futile exercise, but I didn't let on to Patricia.

We rode back to the house in silence. When we got there, I asked, "Do you want to stay with me tonight until you feel more comfortable?" I wanted to offer my place but also respect her privacy, and I thought she might relish her first night in a new apartment.

She waved me off. "I'm feeling a lot better. Honestly, now that I went through all of the detective's questioning, I'm not completely sure I saw him. So, I'm going with that until I find out otherwise, which hopefully is never." She walked to the door and exited without looking back, with a wave behind her back.

I was happy she was at least willing to try her new place. I knew it was essential for her recovery from the trauma of being stalked and threatened.

#

I woke up exhausted in the morning, having tossed and turned all night, dreaming about Patricia's stalker. I hoped that she slept like a baby after everything she had endured the past few weeks. I downed two mugs of coffee before leaving for work at 7:30.

I was happy to have a few minutes in my space before Tea came in. The orders were arriving fast and furious, and I was barely keeping my head above water. With Patricia moving in upstairs, I wanted to spend some time with her and not every waking hour at work.

I was disappointed and disillusioned when Jason let me know he hadn't been able to get an appointment with Bob to follow up on my system proposal. It appeared that neither of them had taken me seriously. Sure, Jason had warned me that Bob would reject it, but I doubted Bob would dismiss the idea out of hand.

Luckily, I had developed some of my own workarounds for their antiquated systems, but I still hated being thought of as just another pretty face.

I sat feeling sorry for myself until Tea came in. I immediately knew something was wrong. First, she had a scarf around her head, which made her look like a fifty-year-old motel housekeeper. Second, she didn't go to the break room for coffee; she just signed onto her computer and stared straight at the screen.

Eventually, she removed the scarf and ran to the ladies' room. When she returned, she was significantly more made-up than usual. I had a bad feeling, but I didn't want to be too intrusive. I tried to sound casual. "Hey, Tea, are you okay?"

She mumbled something, then burst into tears. "I'm fine." She managed to say between sobs.

Well, I knew she wasn't okay, but I didn't want to call her a liar. So I asked, "Did you and Mike have a fight?"

She stood fast. "No." She stared at her computer screen.

I said, "Well, if you want to talk, I'm here."

It took her thirty seconds to come clean. She slinked over to my workstation. "Mike was drinking last night, and I said some things that made him mad. At first, he screamed at me like he had before when he's been drinking, so I didn't really think much of it. Then he started taunting and toying with me. He started pushing me around. I told him to stop, but the more I resisted, the more serious he got. I'd never seen him like this, and I was terrified and tried to push him away. Then he got furious and started pummeling me, first on the arms, then in the stomach and finally on my head." Her voice was without emotion and matter of fact. Tears were still running down her cheeks.

I stood up and pulled her close. She flinched and gasped. It was apparent that she had pain all over her body. I had no idea how badly she was injured because she was fully covered, but I wanted to get her to the emergency room.

"Honey, you need to get checked out to make sure you're okay."

She eluded my grasp. "No! I'm not going to the hospital!"

I pleaded with her. "But you're hurt. You could have broken something."

She said, "No. Do you know what happens in California when there is suspected abuse? They arrest first and ask questions later. I can't afford to live without his income while they figure this out in court. The state doesn't even need me to press charges. The consequences are automatic and I'd be bankrupt in a matter of days. He didn't mean it. I just made him mad. I learned my lesson not to do that again."

I stood with my hands on my hips, not believing what I was hearing. "You have got to be kidding! Are you just going to let him get away with this? You two aren't even married, and you don't have kids. It's time to get out."

She stared at me like I was crazy. "I love Mike. He's a good man. He just got drunk, and I made him mad. We're fine. He apologized this morning. I'm not going anywhere, Miranda, and you can't make me."

I suddenly felt like I was going crazy, but I decided this wasn't something I could do anything about right now. It was too fresh. "Okay, Tea. But if you ever need me, call me. I'll step in, and he'll wish he never lifted a hand to a woman."

She didn't even acknowledge my statement and went back to her desk.

#

We didn't talk much for the rest of the day, just work-related stuff. I felt absolutely horrible about what he had done to her, but more so about her reaction. She was setting herself up for a life of abuse and didn't even know it.

I had ridden the motorcycle in and decided to jog home. I had dressed casually today despite my new dress code and wanted to take advantage of it. I ran a couple of extra miles in an attempt to get Tea and Mike off my mind. I was a sweaty mess by the time I got home. There was no sign of Patricia outside, so I went inside to shower. I hoped that later she would help me again with my vehicle situation.

The hot water—I wondered if Patricia had asked the landlord to turn the temperature up—revived me, but also made me feel tremendously guilty. My two best friends, Tea and Patricia, were being tortured, and all I could think about was my own comfort. What kind of friend was I? What kind of person was I?

My therapist was understating when she told me I *might* want to work on my self-centered nature. What I think she meant was that I was utterly self-absorbed or possibly even a borderline narcissist. She didn't have to tell me; it was evident in the reading material she assigned me. *Trapped in The Mirror* was a dead giveaway. Great book, but it was hard to admit to myself that I was that non-empathetic.

My goal was to make a new friend every month now that I was settling into Santa Clara. I'd never had many friends; in fact, I purposely avoided friendships and relationships when I was in school. My teen years didn't lend themselves to bringing friends home. The household I grew up in was unadulteratedly dysfunctional. At times, I was surprised that I turned out as normal as I had.

I sat on the stool in front of the mirror and revved up the blow dryer. It was rare these days that I took any time to think. I had been running non-stop since the government had ripped my life in Malibu out from under me. I wondered if it was mentally healthier to tell myself everything was okay or stay mired in anger and regret. I could hear my therapist implying that perhaps neither extreme was the answer. I was an expert on extreme behaviors. I was happy, though, that I hadn't had a full-blown anxiety attack in nearly a year. That seemed like progress to me.

After my hair was sufficiently under control, I put on a shorty robe and strolled out to the kitchen for some sustenance. I hadn't been to the store for several days, so there wasn't much. I opened a can of tuna, mixed it with some light mayo, cayenne pepper, and a dash of sea salt, then sat at the kitchen table eating my version of dinner.

I was half-way through the tuna when there was a knock on the door. I had never lived anywhere where there was more activity at my front door. It was unnerving at times after living a solitary life in Malibu before Heather, and then Patricia moved in.

I opened the door half expecting Patricia, but it definitely was not her. A bronzed man around thirty with dimples on his cheeks, dark blue, almost midnight, eyes, a perfect head of dirty blond hair, wearing a purposely ripped tank top and tight, low-slung jeans, stood staring at me. I stared back, and for a moment, time stood still.

Finally, he broke the spell. I watched his perfect mouth as words seemed to tumble out. "I'm so sorry to bother you, but I'm a friend of Patricia's."

I continued gaping at him.

"Your upstairs neighbor? Do you know when she's coming home by any chance? I knocked but got no response."

First, I couldn't believe Patricia had already found this guy, and she had only lived here for five minutes. Second, where was Patricia? She knew no one here and didn't start her job until next week. I had expected her to greet me again upon my arrival, which was, admittedly, not a reasonable expectation.

I suddenly realized that I only wore my short robe and felt extremely exposed. I came to that conclusion at the same moment I realized we were still standing in the doorway, and I hadn't invited the Adonis in.

I briefly thought of bolting to my room while slamming the door, but another glance at his amazing face made me impulsively ask him if he wanted to come in. Luckily, I was retaken by sanity at the same moment. I yelled to him behind me that I'd be right back, as I nearly ran to my room and locked the door behind me.

My instincts were kicking in, and a sixth sense was telling me to run. But there was nowhere to go, so I decided to create some space between us in the name of clothes. I threw off my robe, ran to the dresser for my most conservative bra and underwear. I grabbed a button-up white shirt, put it on, buttoning it to the top, and threw on some Lee Riders. This was not a skinny jean moment.

I rushed through the dressing process, not wanting to leave him alone in the apartment for too long. Not that there was anything exciting for him to get into, it just creeped me out that he was out there alone in my space.

As I dressed, I had worked myself into a frazzle, picturing him rifling through my drawers and cabinets. But I was surprised not to see him anywhere when I came out of the bedroom. Then I lost consciousness.

Chapter 5

"Hello? Is someone there?" I woke with a start. Everything was black, my head hurt intensely, and I couldn't move.

I thought I had heard a female voice, but maybe I dreamed it.

Then I heard it again in a whisper. *"Hello? Is someone there?"*

There *was* someone somewhere to my left if my ears weren't deceiving me.

I tried to whisper in response since I figured there must be a reason she was whispering, but nothing came out but a grunt.

I wondered if I was still in my apartment or, if not, where I was or how I had gotten here. I was groggy, and it hurt to think. Then I remembered the face. The face that made me let my guard down while innately knowing it was wrong and dangerous. How could I have been so stupid to have allowed him in my apartment? Hadn't I learned anything in my thirty-six years?

I wanted to communicate, but somebody covered my mouth with a gag. I tried again to move my hands, but they were secured behind my back, and I could barely move them back and forth. They were either tied, zip-tied, or handcuffed. I was sitting on a hard floor. and my butt was asleep. Somebody, probably the same dreamy guy, had secured my feet together through a similar means as my hands. A strong odor filled my nose, a chemical of some sort. I thought I must be in a factory or a warehouse, but definitely not my apartment.

I wondered how it was that this other woman's mouth was free so that she could whisper. And how could I communicate with her? Was she free to move around or bound like I was? I also wondered if my legs were bound to something or just to one another. If this guy only tied them to one another, then maybe I could get up off the floor and hop, or scootch along the floor somehow. I wasn't sure what that would get me, especially since he covered my eyes, but it seemed like a better idea than just sitting here in the dark. My imagination started running wild. How was I dressed, or was I even dressed? Had anyone touched me or worse? I needed to free myself now.

I tilted my head and felt the collar of my shirt against my neck. It wasn't too difficult to feel the jeans I'd put on just before I left the bedroom. I was briefly relieved.

I leaned against a wall, pushing my feet against the floor with the intent of working myself up the wall, trying to push up with my hands. I tried and tried and was only able to get up the wall a couple of inches. Defeated, I slid back down. In frustration, I slammed my legs down. That made me realize I wasn't as immobile as I had first suspected Even though my hands were tied behind my back, I figured I might be able to scoot forward on my butt and tried again.

The unknown woman hadn't whispered in a few minutes, and, since my mouth was securely fastened shut, I couldn't ask where she was. I assumed that she couldn't move and couldn't see, so we were in somewhat of a stalemate. I didn't want to scare her, but I figured that this same creep had kidnapped her, so if we could figure out how to work together, we might get free.

I kicked myself again for letting the guy into my apartment. With all my police training, it was hard to believe that a pretty face had weakened me. But I didn't have time for negativity right now. I would have a talk with myself later when I was free.

I tried to remember where her whisper came from, wondering if she was still there or could move around. She *had* to have heard me shuffling around, moaning, and whining as I struggled to move, so she might have been too scared to say anything else. I also considered the fact that she might no longer be in here. I opted for the former because I figured that I would have heard her escaping or being forced to go with our captor.

I inched along another five feet toward where I thought her voice had come from. I had to be careful since our captor blindfolded me. I didn't want to hurt myself on something sharp or hot. Suddenly I hit something hard in front of me with my foot. It was a wall. I then turned left with my foot feeling along the wall for an opening. The sounds I made as I moved echoed as if I had just entered a much larger space. I wondered if I had entered a separate warehouse or manufacturing space where the other woman was held.

My instinct told me to go as quickly as possible without putting myself in any more danger than I was already in. I sensed that I was close, but I didn't hear anything else from her. I stayed along the wall around the corner and went another five feet until I felt what seemed like the leg of a cheap aluminum kitchen chair like we had when I was a kid. I nearly jumped out of my skin when she yelled, practically in my ear, "Don't touch me!"

Clearly, I was within a foot of her. I suddenly felt a rush of relief because it was clear from her voice that I shared the space with Patricia. There was no doubt in my mind. I had to somehow communicate to her that I was me despite being gagged.

While I inched, whatever secured my hands and wrists behind me had loosened up. The fact that I was nearly able to get myself free told me we were working with an amateur. I pulled and pulled, and finally, my hands were free. I wanted to scream with delight, but my mouth was still covered.

I reached up and pulled the blindfold from my head. Now I needed to get my mouth free so that we could communicate, and I could breathe. As I untied the bandana covering my mouth, I had a sinking feeling that we weren't going to get free before our kidnapper came back. Similar to the ropes around my hands, the bandana was another amateur move. I figured Patricia somehow shimmied out of hers. If so, she was a lot more creative than I was.

I said in a quiet voice, "Patricia?"

She responded quietly. "Miranda?"

I wanted to hug her, but that wasn't happening. There was so much I wanted to say. Whether she knew what we were doing here or where 'here' was, whether she thought he was coming back anytime soon or if he was still here somewhere. I shifted into police mode. "Patricia, are you okay?"

She laughed, which made me feel so much better. "I'm okay for being abducted, but otherwise, I'm having a super-di-duper day."

I tried to stifle a laugh. But it came out involuntarily. I knew we were wasting precious time, so I pulled it back together. "Can you move anything, like your hands or legs? How'd you get your mouth free? We need to get each other free quickly. So what are we dealing with?"

Patricia exhaled loudly. "I got my hands free first and was able to get my gag off pretty quickly, but everything else is so tight I can't move."

I continued working on my ropes. They seemed to be more doable than Patricia's. I worked on freeing my legs, which was now a piece of cake with my hands and sight. Within five minutes, we were both free, but the last thing we wanted to do was run into John or anyone else. It was surprising that we had been allowed to get this far, and I was hoping that we weren't being monitored remotely, only to be snatched up and re-tied, or worse. My mind was moving a mile a minute as we talked and surveyed the space we were in, evidently a warehouse.

"Was it John or James or whatever his name is? Did you see him? Did he hurt you?"

She responded slowly. "I don't know. I woke up like this. I guess you did too?"

I wasn't proud of my next response. "He knocked on my door, looking for you, and I let him in."

Patricia responded breathlessly, "That has to be John. No-one can say 'No' to him at the beginning. Even after everything he's put me through, he has a face that I don't want to forget. Sitting in that park, he looked like the typical Colorado ski bum that I knew I should steer away from, but I didn't."

I would never forget that face either. "He looked like a surfer to me, but I could imagine he might have looked like a skier with Colorado as a backdrop. All I can say is that your description didn't do him justice. His looks caught me off-guard."

I wanted to talk further with Patricia to see if she had seen John again since she saw him passing our house or anything else that had happened to her yesterday, but safety and speed was the order of the day.

I took a page out of my police training and attempted to scope out the rest of the building, confirming that we were alone. We stayed away from the few windows so that nobody could see us from the outside. I was surprised that it was daylight—that must have been some knock on the head.

Getting a good look at the space, I confirmed that we were in a working warehouse with several offices on the building's perimeter.

I was just about to declare the building 'safe' when I heard voices outside. We were twenty feet from the only door anywhere near us, and the source was heading this way quickly. I motioned for Patricia to follow me, and we slipped into a nearby office that had a door inside, either a closet or a bathroom. I didn't care which at this point. We opened the door and found out quickly—it was a small bathroom with a closet.

She closed the bathroom door, and we squeezed into the closet. The shelves dug into my back and we couldn't completely close the door. We were sitting ducks if they came in here.

I put my finger to my lips as Patricia was about to say something. We could still hear voices, but not as clearly as earlier. They were probably at the other end of the warehouse, and they didn't sound happy.

Then it sounded like they reversed direction and were headed back toward us.

We both held our breath as if that would prevent them from opening the door.

Two men were arguing.

"I told you we should stay with them." The first one had a high, whiney voice.

The second one was more of a baritone, definitely John. "I told you we should use zip-ties and not make-shift ropes and bandanas. Well, at least they didn't see us." He corrected himself, "Didn't see you, I mean. Now they both know what I look like."

I strained to hear more as they moved further away, both to my relief and disappointment. I was relieved they didn't seem to be interested in searching the building for us but disappointed that I couldn't hear anything more incriminating.

#

We waited for a half-hour and sneaked out the back, hoping our luck held out. We slipped behind the tennis club next door and found ourselves on Calle De Luna up toward the bay, across from the stadium.

Having no idea if our abductors were still in the neighborhood, I called 911. Within a few minutes, a patrol car pulled up. We safely climbed in the back seat, which was my primary goal. They took a report, although they seemed somewhat skeptical of the whole story. They did ask if we wanted to seek medical treatment, which we both refused.

In the end, they dropped us off at the house, promised to put out an APB, and to cruise by the house periodically. I got this idea the younger of the two was more interested in dating Patricia than anything else, but they were pleasant and at least gave us a ride home.

I invited her in when we got out of the patrol car. Neither of us had said much since we escaped our captors. We were probably in shock.

She sat staring at the wall while I talked about everything except what had happened today, bustling around the apartment, wiping off counters, changing paper towel rolls, washing some dishes in the sink, anything to burn off this nervous energy.

Finally, she motioned for me to sit next to her, patting the seat. It felt like a role reversal since I was usually the one trying to get her to talk while she avoided it like the plague.

She folded her hands in her lap, looking like a schoolmarm. "I think we need to talk about this, don't you?"

I responded cheerfully, "I guess so. Not sure what there is to say. We were abducted. We got away. End of story."

She took my hand and looked me directly in the eye. "And I know the police said they would keep an eye out, but they have limited resources, so what if they come back?

Obviously, they know where we live." She thought for a minute, then continued. "And who are they? From your description, I'm sure the guy who visited your apartment was John—that certainly sounded like him in the warehouse;

besides, he admitted that we both knew what he looked like. But who is the other guy? I also got the impression that they are working for someone else, like they aren't the brains of the operation. Who could possibly want to abduct us, and for what reason?"

I thought for a minute. "Great questions. The strangest thing is that John isn't working alone. When you described him earlier, he sounded like a loner to me, a psycho loner. It raises all sorts of questions about what happened in Denver and what his motivations were. Also, how did he find you so quickly when you moved out here?"

Patricia chewed on her lower lip like she did when she was thinking. "Hey, you were a cop. There must be ways that people can be tracked without their knowledge, right?"

I thought for a minute. "Yes, you're right. I hadn't considered this when I thought he was just a loner who had chanced upon you. But, if he were part of a bigger plot, it would make more sense. Did John give you anything? A gift? Something that you would keep with you?"

She thought for a second. "No, nothing."

I considered their interactions after their first meeting. "But he obviously knew where you and your parents lived. Did you park your car on the street, in the driveway, or the garage?"

She responded, "I parked in the driveway until he ruined my car with the spray paint."

I grumbled, "Oh, yeah, I forgot about that. Did you get a new car soon after that?"

She wasn't comfortable talking about this topic, but I thought it was critical. "Yes, the insurance company replaced it a couple of days later."

"And how much time was there between you getting your new car and coming out here."

She took out her phone to look at a calendar. "At least a month. He was arrested then released during that time."

The picture was clear. "I'll bet he planted an electronic homing device under your car somewhere. I'll take a look at it. It's the only thing that makes sense."

She lay back on the couch and stared at the ceiling. "But why? It wasn't just a coincidence that I met this guy in the park, was it?"

I shook my head. "The whole thing was a setup. He didn't care if he got arrested. In fact, he wanted to. All of this is part of something much bigger."

She started pacing between the living room and the kitchen. "So, it doesn't matter where I move or what I do; he's going to be there. And now I've gotten you involved."

I couldn't think of a good comeback but knew we needed to take action. "Okay, we're going back to visit Detective Marshall to let her know what happened. I know we reported it, but I'm not sure those two won't just shelve it. I know she can make sure some action is taken. Granted, we don't know who John is working with, but we have an eye and earwitness account that he was involved in this." I jumped up from the couch. Her pacing was driving me crazy.

Patricia hugged me. "Thanks for keeping your head. Maybe we can finally get this guy behind bars. I don't know why, with his record, they released him the first time after threatening me and trashing my car."

"Resources are short, demand is high, and there's pressure to get a conviction or let them go. It's not right, but I expect it's still true."

We drove in my Rover to the police station. I had visited there way too often since moving to town.

Chapter 6

The detective welcomed us warmly into her office. It was my first time meeting with her that wasn't in an interrogation room. She'd already heard about our experience and immediately offered to get us medical attention, which we both declined.

Surprisingly, she seemed remorseful about not protecting us after we reported our concerns yesterday.

She took notes and shook her head. "So you were both abducted while unconscious? And you said you heard two voices in the warehouse?"

"Yes, it should all be in the report," I said.

"You know I need to hear it for myself."

I hoped this would result in more than a pat on the head and instructions to get back to them if anything else happened. "Detective, I can even understand why our initial visit didn't result in an arrest, but don't tell me nothing's going to happen now."

She gritted her teeth. "Oh, you can be sure something will happen now. This abduction was on my watch in my jurisdiction. They have no idea who they are messing with. No offense, but this isn't Denver."

Patricia responded quietly, "No offense taken."

Detective Marshall stared intently at her computer screen. Her voice showed a hint of frustration. "As far as I can tell, this guy has always worked alone. And, Marquette, your contention that he used a tracking device to follow Patricia out here from Colorado suggests that he's stepped up his game."

I scratched my head. "Yeah, when Patricia first told me about everything that happened in Colorado, I figured it would all go away when she moved out here. Usually, a guy like him will find his next victim and move on."

The detective nodded. "I agree. Something happened between their initial contact and her departure from the state." She addressed Patricia directly. "You said that your parents are wealthy, correct?"

She seemed uncomfortable talking about it. "Well, yes, I guess you could say that. I don't really think about it that much."

I wanted to see if the detective and I were on the same page. "Here's what I'm thinking. This whole meeting in the park by this John guy wasn't random. He knew who she was and that her parents were wealthy. He tried to get her to trust him so that he could carry out whatever he had planned, but it went wrong that first night in the bar. So he improvised and tried plan B, scaring her. I don't know what the motivation was for that, but I'm sure there was one. Then when she skipped town, he went to plan C—following her and abducting her, probably for ransom."

Detective Marshall responded while studying the screen. "So, where do you think he picked up accomplices, before or after she left town?"

I chewed on the end of a pencil. "I think it was some time after they met, but before she left town. He figured out that he couldn't do it alone and, if they kidnapped Patricia, there would be more than enough ransom to go around."

The detective continued, "So, based on his record, we have no idea who he is working with. But we can tell from the conversation you overheard in the warehouse; they're not calling the shots. He and this other guy are working for someone else."

Patricia had been sitting silently. "I can't believe this is happening," she said, resting her forehead in her hands. "Why

41

not just leave Miranda alone? If they want my parent's money, all they need is me."

Detective Marshall conjectured, "Maybe for insurance. Maybe for protection. They probably figured she knew the story of why you left town and didn't want any loose ends."

Patricia stood up and started pacing the detective's office. "I thought it was weird at the time that they didn't search the warehouse after we got untied and attempted our escape. Had they done a thorough search of the building, we were sitting ducks."

I laughed, "Yeah, they were far more concerned with which of them had messed up with the big boss than searching for us. He must be one bad character." Then I realized there wasn't much to laugh about. "Of course, unless we relocate very suddenly and either remove the homing device on your car or just take mine, we'll be found in a matter of minutes."

Patricia sat down after she realized there was no place to go.

The detective addressed both of us. "Well, at least we can take some action now. We'll issue an APB today for John Blake. We'll also stake out your property in an unmarked car twenty-four hours a day for at least the next week. The odds are if they are going to strike again, it'll be within a day or two."

We both stood up and shook her hand. I was feeling like she was wrapping things up. This had been one of my more satisfying trips to the police station, even though Patricia and I were still in imminent danger.

#

We sat on the couch in my living room. Judging from Patricia's wild-eyed look, she felt as trapped as I did. I said the six words that had made me the happiest since moving to the west coast, "Want to go to the beach?"

Patricia seemed to snap out of her mood. "Yes! I'd love to! Let's take the motorcycle!"

I jumped up, wanting to do anything but sit around waiting to be abducted again. It was in the mid-70s, so I put on my leather for safety. Patricia wanted to wear her bikini, but I convinced her that skinny jeans and a leather top I could never fit into would give her some minor protection in case of a crash. We both wore bathing suits underneath so that we wouldn't have to fuss with the changing room once we got there.

Half Moon Bay Beach was still my favorite in the Bay area even since before moving here. With traffic, I parked the motorcycle in the State Park Parking lot in less than an hour. The rear seat was a bit cramped, but we had a fun ride over La Honda Road, one of my favorite riding routes in this part of the country.

Hoping for the best, we just left our clothes, boots, and helmet sitting on the bike and scampered up the beach in our bathing suits. I found that most people will leave a motorcycle alone, so I hoped that would be the case today.

After walking for a half-hour or so, talking about pretty much nothing, I felt relaxed for the first time in a couple of days. The fact that Patricia and I were able to escape our captors made both of us feel momentarily in control of our world, even though we knew they could come back at any time.

We sat for a while, about a mile up the beach toward Dunes Beach and Miramar. Most visitors to the state park never got up this far, so it was relatively secluded even though it was a weekend. We sat staring at the ocean, and my cell phone rang. It was the Santa Clara Police Department.

I answered it, hoping for good news. "Hello, this is Miranda."

The detective was on the other line. "Miranda, Wanda Marshall."

I was surprised she used her first name. I hoped that meant she had good news. I wanted to sound hopeful. "Yes, Detective?"

She did have good news. "We have apprehended your perp and, it appears, his partner. They were in the vicinity of your apartment this afternoon, actually at your door."

I was surprised they had either the nerve or the stupidity to show up the next day. "Wow, you caught them that fast? Impressive. Is there anything we need to do?" I already knew the drill, having been a cop.

She responded quickly, "Yes, you two need to get down here so that you can identify the one you know in a line-up. We also will do a voice test so that you can identify the other one."

Patricia was interpreting the conversation from my end of the call and jumping up and down on the sand.

We needed to get moving. "Okay, Detective. We're at the beach right now, but we'll be in within a couple of hours." I hung up.

Patricia pouted at my response, but I knew she'd want to get this taken care of as soon as possible.

I felt her pain. "I'd love to stay here all day too. This was the most relaxed I've felt in a while." I winked at a couple of cute guys who seemed to be scoping us out on their way up the beach. I was happy to feel good about myself again. That hadn't always been the case.

Even though we had a deadline, we strolled casually down the beach to the motorcycle, talking about Patricia's new job, which started on Monday. We were so thankful to have this abduction behind us and have the suspects behind bars. At least that was one less thing to worry about.

It was early evening when we pulled up to the police station. We considered going home first but I wanted to get the identification of the perps over with. Patricia seemed reticent, but after what we'd just been through, I chalked it up to nerves.

The detective seemed a bit harried when we arrived. I remembered from my days as a cop, a million things she needed to take care of once she got a suspect behind bars: booking the suspects, questioning them, and taking their statements, reviewing their arrest records, making arrangements to have them transported to another holding facility when necessary, and then endless paperwork. There was also the adrenaline rush of a successful stakeout, which often lasted for days.

After she greeted us, she rushed us into the line-up review room. "Thanks so much for coming. I'm going to have to pass you off to my partner, Detective Jared Connelly. He'll take good care of you. I'll check in before you leave."

I remembered Detective Connelly, although I don't think I knew his first name at the time, from last year, when I found my previous upstairs neighbor dead in the cemetery near the house. That set in motion a series of events that got me more notoriety on the internet than I had ever asked for. Thankfully, they didn't arrest me for her murder, but there were times when I thought they might.

Jared shook both of our hands and directed us through the process of identifying the suspects. "You are looking through a two-way mirror. In a few minutes, we will escort in several people. I understand that you both have had visual contact with one of our suspects and possibly heard the voice of the other. We'll ask each suspect to speak a simple sentence so you can evaluate whether or not you recognize their voice."

This was nothing new to me, but Patricia was a rookie to police procedures. She immediately shifted into her shy and insecure mode, deferring to me with the detective. I could only imagine she didn't relish seeing the guy who had threatened her in Denver and then followed her to California. I knew one thing. I would never forget that face.

Jared explained, "You will be doing this one at a time, so Patricia, you will be just outside in a waiting area while Miranda identifies her suspect, then you will change places." He led her out.

Within about a minute, they led in five suspects. My guy was number two. I let Detective Connelly know my choice and stood to retrieve Patricia. She looked pale as she passed me. I smiled my encouragement.

Detective Connelly asked me to return to the room while he took notes on a pad. "Now, we will have each suspect make the same statement since neither of you has seen one suspect but had heard him. Patricia, please wait outside again." She left the room, making eye contact with me as she left.

Each of the suspects repeated the statement, "My name is John Smith, and I am in the Santa Clara police station."

The statement confirmed for me that number two was the right pick for the first suspect. The suspects had unique voices. The second was number four with a distinctive, high, and whiney voice. I was sure of it.

They then asked me to leave and to come back in, in a minute or so.

She whispered to me. *"It's number four."* He looked the complete opposite of his voice. I would have pictured him with red hair, freckles, ghost-white skin, and a hundred and fifty pounds soaking wet. He was six-three, at least, muscular in a good way, and a perfect head of dirty blonde hair. He could have been John's brother, or at least surfing buddy, except for his sea-blue eyes. She confirmed, "And of course John was number two."

I nodded.

Detective Connelly took some additional notes. He then spoke to both of us. "I want to thank the two of you for coming in. I know you already provided statements relating to your abductions and the other interactions Patricia had with the suspect before she left Colorado. Is there anything you want to add?"

Patricia, who had become even paler than usual during the identification process, regained her color, so I was relieved. She stood up, which I saw as a good sign. She responded to the detective, "Nope, I'm good. How about you, Miranda?"

I had nothing further and shook the detective's hand. "I think we are done here. Thanks for calling us in and let us know if you need anything else from us in the meantime."

Chapter 7

Patricia was quiet when we got home, even though she opted to come to my apartment instead of going to hers. I didn't want to pry, but I wanted to help her with what she was going through.

I asked her quietly, "Are you okay?"

She turned to look at me but appeared to be looking through me. Her voice was far away. "I guess so. Seeing John like that wasn't good for me. Now I'm starting a new job. I don't know what I was thinking. I don't know the first thing about community relations."

I moved closer to her and touched her arm. "You'll be great! I'm sure they teach you everything you need to know. Think about how quickly you picked up Heather's job. I didn't have to show you anything."

She smiled slightly, "Yeah, but that was working for you. *This* is Karma."

I motioned her to sit opposite me on the couch. "I don't think it'll be a bad thing to get out of this house and do something. John and his friend are behind bars. At this point, we don't know if there is anyone else involved, so I'm assuming there isn't until I hear otherwise."

Patricia grabbed my hands. "You're probably right. I'm nervous about the job, and it'll probably be fine. I need to concentrate on what I need to do between now and Monday morning. I haven't thought about what I'm going to wear, whether or not I'm going to take a lunch, what route I'm going to take to get there, or a thousand other things."

I was happy she was getting her attitude turned around. "That's great. You concentrate on the positive, and I'll worry about the rest."

Patricia turned her attention to her cell phone. She appeared to be reading a text or an email. She immediately jumped up looking like a caged animal, walking between the living room and the kitchen as she talked.

"Oh my God, my parents and Nate are coming later this week. They're worried about me and want to see how I'm doing. How can I concentrate on a job when I'm going to see my son? I've missed him so much."

She took a breath, and I took the opportunity to break-in. "Whoa! Slow down! This is great news. You'll get to see your little pumpkin and your parents. That'll keep you busy for sure."

Just then, my cell phone vibrated. The Caller ID read, 'Santa Clara Police Department.' I hit my phone button. "Hello."

It was Detective Marshall. "Miranda, I just wanted to update you regarding your visit with us today. You could definitively identify the two suspects, John Blake and David Miller, in the line-up. That will be very helpful in court. They're two small time thugs known as the Surf Brothers. I wanted to thank you both for coming in."

I beamed and gave a thumbs up to Patricia. "We were happy to help. As their court dates approach, let us know what else we can do. I'd be happy to testify, and I think Patricia would be also."

She gave me a panicked look, but I figured I could convince her later.

When I hung up the phone, Patricia started talking a mile a minute. "Miranda, I can't possibly testify in court. I would be a terrible witness. There's a part of me that still thinks James got a bum rap. Besides, you have to admit he's gorgeous."

Sometimes she amazed me. "Okay, the guy's got a face that could stop traffic. I'm with you there. But, after he threatened you, spray-painted your car, and followed you from Denver, you still feel sorry for him?"

She bit her lip. "We talked a lot that first day we met. He was an orphan like I was, but he wasn't one of the lucky ones. He got passed from one foster home to another."

I stared at her in disbelief. There was more going on with Patricia than I knew. "I agree the guy needs help, and maybe that'll happen as a result of them arresting him, but he made some awful choices when it came to dealing with you and your family. I can't help but think he has at least some level of responsibility for his choices."

She wouldn't relent. "I'm surprised, Miranda, with your struggles with anxiety disorder, that you don't have more compassion."

I suddenly felt like she was attacking me personally. "Now, wait a minute, Patricia. The asshat assaulted and kidnapped me. You think I care what he looks like?" I felt my face growing hot and red.

She could tell that she had struck a nerve. "Okay. Okay, I'm sorry. You're right."

I did my best to put her comments behind me. "Thanks."

I knew, though, that I hadn't completely convinced her. "I'm just not sure that prison is the right place for John. He needs help."

I chose to agree to disagree, "Okay, Patricia, I can see we aren't going to see eye to eye on this completely, but please think about testifying against him when the trial comes. It's up to the court to determine if he needs some sort of mental help rather than incarceration, right?"

We hugged, and she whispered. "You're right, Miranda, and thanks for being my friend, even when we disagree. I haven't had a lot of friendships that could pass that kind of test."

I whispered back. "Me, either." I hugged her tighter. "How about we order a pizza and I'll open a bottle of wine?"

#

She spent the night on my couch and on Sunday we spent time talking about our high school days. Her background fascinated me because, in so many ways, we were opposites. She participated in beauty pageants with her mother, and they were very close. My mother and I rarely saw eye to eye during my teen years. She dressed to impress every day, usually wearing skirts or dresses. I'd preferred grunge, ripped jeans, and black tee-shirts to match my black dyed hair, black fingernails, and toenails and piercings. She was quiet and reserved. I was outspoken and bold.

On the other hand, Patricia and I both had an overriding fear of our peers. We were loners. We were aloof and hard to nail down. We wanted to be anywhere else but where we were. But when we graduated, we ultimately went in different directions. Patricia stayed at home in Denver with her parents. I left Louisiana and moved half-way across the country.

Any way you looked at it, we were unlikely friends. If you then took into account that, when we were teammates, she and I butted heads on multiple occasions, it was even less likely that we would end up where we are were now. I also thought for some time that she was responsible for Annika, our third teammate's death. I couldn't have been more wrong.

I tossed and turned most of the night on Sunday, got up a couple of times, and heard Patricia pacing the floors upstairs. I think I was as nervous as she was for her first day. My therapist had me working on empathy, and it was paying off.

51

She left for work at 7:30, a few minutes before I did, although her start time was 8:30. With any luck, she would make it. I waved out the window but didn't stop to talk because I was sure she was nervous enough without me holding her up.

I left at 7:45 and got to work at 7:50. My commute was so un-California-like, and I loved it. I was sipping on my first cup of coffee when Tea sauntered in. She had a way of communicating everything she was feeling with her walk. Depending on her mood, she would slink, slide, ramble, stroll, plod, trudge, or wend her way in. Mike had to be blind if he didn't know how she felt at any point in time. I'd only known her a year, and it was nearly always apparent to me.

I was happy to see that Tea was having a good day. With only two of us in the workspace, one depressed, upset, angry, agitated, worried, or sad person could easily rain on the other's parade. She was beaming as she passed my workstation.

She set her backpack on the floor by her desk as she came over to talk. "Have I ever told you that you're a genius?"

I took my pen from my mouth. "As a matter of fact, no."

She pulled up a chair, so I knew she was in for the long haul. "Remember when you told me that I had to tell Mike what to do because he was a guy and couldn't possibly figure it out for himself?"

I thought for a minute. "Well, I didn't exactly say that, but yes, I remember."

"Well, Saturday, I was starting to get frustrated. We were playing the 'What do you want to do? Oh, I don't know, what do you want to do?' game. Well, I had already told him on Friday night that I wanted to grocery shop on Saturday morning, so he either wasn't listening, forgot, or was utterly ignoring my needs."

This was a familiar story from my past life.

She continued, "But rather than getting angry, I just said, 'Oh Mike, I know you're pulling my leg. Which grocery store did you want to go to?' At first, he looked confused, like he had no idea what I was talking about, because he didn't. But, in an attempt not to look foolish, he said, 'How about Safeway on the Alameda?' Well, of course, we were going to Safeway on the Alameda! That's the only place we've shopped since we moved here, and it's the only grocery store within a couple of miles. My point is that I didn't get mad or say anything derogatory; I let him think it was his idea. And we had the best shopping trip we've had in a while because I didn't feel like I was forcing him into it."

I couldn't take full credit because my therapist, two therapists ago, taught me this trick. But at least I retained it. "Well, that's great, Tea." I high fived her. "Here's to small victories."

She wasn't done, and I knew it. She held up her hand. "Wait, there's more! We were so relaxed after not fighting about grocery shopping; he took me out to brunch at Bill's Café. I had the crab cake benedict, and he had the bread pudding French toast. But that's not the best part."

I was all ears. "So, what could be better than crab cake benedict?"

She shifted from thrilled and excited to solemn and serious. "Well, we got talking at the restaurant, and he apologized for hitting me. My first inclination was to accept his apology and move on, but we were on such a roll, I had to chance it." She paused for dramatic effect. "I told him that this was the last time; that my father was abusive and that I wasn't going to live through this again or watch him ruin our children's lives. I told him that he needed to go to counseling, or I was leaving him."

My mouth stood open, which I suppose was a little rude, but I couldn't help myself. She had been so defensive and closed to my pleas; I thought that she would just continue to sweep his behavior under the rug. I hugged her, and tears streamed down her face. "I am so proud of you. That took guts, and I love to see you believing in yourself. When you have that, you can do anything."

She squeezed me with her head buried in my shoulder. "I was so ashamed, and I just wanted it all to go away. But when I was sitting and eating with him, it hit me that it was then or never. I had to bring it up when we were in a good place so that neither of us was speaking out of anger or defensiveness."

If I left this job today, it would have made it worthwhile because I would have felt like I made a difference in her life. That was all you could ask of this world when it came down to it. My mouth was starting to hurt from smiling so much. "You'd better get to work before we both get fired." Then I whispered, "I'm so proud of you."

She beamed and sat down at her workstation.

The day flew by as my time was filled entering backlogged orders. I was getting used to being behind, which I knew wasn't right, but it was the reality I lived in. I needed to come to terms with the fact that Bob would never upgrade the computer system. I was usually so busy trying to catch up or keep up; I didn't have time to make things any more efficient than I already had. I had developed some shortcuts and done away with some duplicative procedures, but I had a feeling that with just the tools at my disposal, I could still make things much more efficient. I promised myself to work on that while I plodded along as things were.

Tea left around five and hugged me again on the way out the door. I stayed only until five-thirty because I couldn't wait to see how Patricia's first day had gone.

I was thrilled to see her sitting on my front porch, waiting for me to pull up. She sat rocking in one of the two old white wooden rocking chairs that looked like they had been there since the house was built. I parked the car and climbed the three steps to the wraparound porch.

She was holding her cards close to the chest. If Tea wore her emotions on her sleeve, Patricia hid hers under her coat. The corners of her mouth were just slightly curled up, which I thought was a good sign.

I sat down in the chair next to her, and we both rocked for a while.

Eventually, she started to talk. "How did I ever let you convince me that this job was a good idea?"

I thought about it, realizing that I had nothing to do with it. She already had the job when she moved out here. So in her way, I knew she was kidding. Besides, knowing Patricia as I do, if she had a bad day, would be upstairs trying to figure out her next move in solitude. The fact that we were sitting down here together meant it went well.

Realizing that she was waiting for an answer, I improvised. "Well, I just happen to know that you are one of the smartest, prettiest, best employees that anyone could ever have. So, I had to share you with Karma. I know I'll have my own company again someday. And when that happens, I want you back. Deal?"

I extended my hand, and she gave me hers. "Deal."

I finally gave up and asked her the question that needed to be asked. "So, how'd it go?"

She flashed her best smile, "Oh, Miranda, it was pure heaven. I just love my boss. She's maybe five years older than I am and has been there for three years. She started as a customer service rep and made it to Managing Director in two years. Karma has gotten so big so fast; it's had some growing pains. They haven't been the best neighbor. They've caused traffic jams like never before because of all the employees. They've nearly tripled in size in the last five years. It's Susan's job, my boss, to take a fresh look at Karma the company, Karma the employer, Karma the neighbor, and Karma the huge campus on Valley Green Drive in Cupertino.

"It's her job to make the people of the Silicon Valley proud of Karma, like they were when they started up. In a few years, they plan to build a new headquarters and house all of us in one massive circular building with over two million square feet on nearly two hundred acres. It's Susan's job to make sure that we're ready, that the government is in our corner, that the neighbors welcome us, and provide a sustainable workplace for decades to come. And I'm her personal assistant.

"But she wants us to be more like partners. She wants to bounce ideas off me and for me to come up with ideas too. This is my dream job, Miranda, and I didn't even know it. Here's something crazy. Do you want to know why she hired me over the other fifty, yes, fifty candidates that they interviewed?

I stared at her blankly.

She laughed. "Come on, Miranda, step it up. You're usually good at this kind of thing."

I tried my hardest, but I still had nothing. "Um, because she liked you?"

She playfully glared at me. "Yeah. This was an easy one. Isn't it obvious? Because of my perky personality. And I apparently did really well on the aptitude and typing tests and I have no idea because everyone else probably did as well."

"Well, congratulations. Good job."

She laughed under her breath. "I'm just glad they chose me. It seems like a perfect fit. By the end of the day, I was finishing Susan's sentences."

I felt an unwelcome pang of jealousy. I pushed it down. I didn't have many friends, and I wasn't sure I wanted to share this one. "That's great, Patricia. Just don't forget about us little people when you take over Karma."

She gave me a curious look. "You're not making fun of me, are you?"

I looked her in the eye. "I'm working on being as honest as I can. I'm not sure I'm ready to share you yet. You just got here."

She smiled broadly. "That's so sweet, Miranda. But don't worry about losing me. I'm loyal to the death. Besides, you have Tea in your life too."

I nodded, "Well, that's true, but I almost think of her more like a daughter. She's got a lot of growing up to do."

She touched my arm. "When I agreed that we were friends forever in Switzerland, I meant it."

Chapter 8

The next day went pretty routinely until I got home from work. After I took a hot shower, I heard voices upstairs. It sounded like a man and a woman arguing. On second listen, it was a man and two women. After a few minutes of trying to decipher the few words, I remembered that this was the day Patricia's parents were scheduled to arrive.

It sounded less and less like a social call and more like an intervention. I was able to put together several statements that made things clearer.

"You can't possibly want to stay here!"

"Why not?"

"This place is a dump and I don't want my grandson living here. We've bought a vacation house in Cupertino."

Patricia was a bit more soft-spoken than her parents, although I had heard her find her voice a couple of times in Switzerland. She was a touch more intense during her pregnancy, which would have worked to be an advantage right now. It sounded to me like her parents needed to be yelled over.

This yelling match went on for at least an hour until I heard several sets of footsteps stomping down the stairs outside my apartment. I spied out the window a couple in their late fifties or early sixties carrying a baby, obviously Nate. As she had described to me earlier, Patricia's mother had the same alabaster skin and jet-black hair as she did. She also had a very athletic build, especially for a woman her age. Her dad appeared to be about 5'10" and two hundred pounds, pretty average with salt and pepper hair. They were strapping Nate in a black Mercedes, climbed in, and sped away to places unknown but likely closer to Cupertino.

I hesitated, not wanting to appear like I was eavesdropping. Within two minutes, Patricia flew down the stairs and knocked on my door.

I opened it to flashbacks of my previous neighbor, Sarah, whose moods were all over the place, depending on the day. Patricia rushed into my apartment, talking a mile a minute. "Can you believe those people? I can't even call them my parents right now. I am so angry. They basically said I couldn't be trusted to take care of Nate; they accused me of falling in love with a lunatic, and you'll love this—they accused you of being in on this whole abduction thing."

I had to decide to either be appropriately outraged or admit that I had overheard much of their argument through the ceiling. I opted for the truth. "Um, I have to admit it was loud enough that I heard most of it." I tried to put a positive face on it. "They certainly are protective of you and Nate, so that's a good thing, right?"

She sat on the couch with her head in her hands. "They don't trust my parenting. Especially after that mess with James, they don't think I am mentally fit to make my own decisions. Yes, I do believe that James really needs help, and I'm not sure, even now, that the best place for him is in prison. Somehow, their concern has diminished because my father now has political aspirations in Colorado."

I was starting to see their point concerning her parenting. She hardly ever even talked about her son. "After everything James did, threatening you, and now abducting us? He probably does have some behavioral health issues, but we should let the courts figure that out."

There was something behind her eyes that I couldn't read. Maybe her parents were right. Perhaps she had fallen for him. I knew from our conversations that she had never had a serious relationship before Larry, Nate's father. And that relationship didn't last long since he was convicted of murder and in prison. I needed to find out. "So, Patricia, is it possible that you have feelings for James?"

She blurted out, "No! I mean, I don't know. I don't know what I feel."

I didn't like the sound of that. He must have been some charmer and wormed his way right into her head and possibly her heart. I had gotten the impression that she was afraid to testify against him in court, but now it seemed it wasn't fear at all. It could be a manifestation of Stockholm Syndrome.

Patricia fought back tears. "I wanted to hate him when I identified him in the line-up, but I couldn't. He has a hold on me that won't let go."

I bit my lip before saying something I might regret later. "Okay, I understand. Mixing the head with the heart can get very confusing. I face a little bit of that every day at work." My face reddened at the admission that I still had a thing for Jason.

Patricia focused on the problem at hand. "So what do I do about my parents? Why do they always have to control everything? I love them, but they are going to have to let me grow up at some point. One, they are not going to hold Nate hostage. And two, they are not going to convince me to move to Cupertino. I'm staying right here."

I thought for a second. "Hey, maybe you and I could go see your parents together. Right now, I'm a stranger to them, and that's not a good thing for someone who likes to control everything around them."

Patricia hugged me. "That's a great idea. Once they meet you and see how together you have it, they won't be so nervous about Nate and me living above you."

I smiled to see her back to her old self. "Well, just let me know when you want me to meet them, and I'll do my best to make an excellent first impression."

She headed toward the door. "I'm going to get a good night's sleep and not do anything rash. Maybe that'll give them some time to come to their senses."

She turned and looked at me from the doorway. "Thanks for being there for me, Miranda. I could never successfully take my parents on by myself, but with you, I have a chance."

It felt good to have a positive impact on her life. "Well, thanks for being my friend. It means the world to me."

Patricia looked more energized and self-confident as she headed out the door, much as she had after her first day of work. My opinion was that she should keep her distance from her parents, but I was withholding judgment.

#

Just after Patricia left, I received a call from Wanda who told me the court freed the two suspects who abducted Patricia and me on $100,000 bail each, which I thought was an outrage. I tossed and turned much of Tuesday night. I felt like everything around me was unresolved. Jason and I hadn't spoken in several weeks, even though I thought our last date went pretty well.

I dragged into work on Wednesday morning, hoping for an uneventful day. Tea didn't notice my mood, which was fine with me. I didn't want to talk about anything; just get my work done and go home. She was having a string of good days with Mike, and I was thankful that things seemed to be turning around for them.

When I finally made it home at 7:30, I was exhausted, looking forward to a hot bath and a glass of Cabernet. As I pulled in front of the house, visitors dashed my hopes. Patricia's parents were seated on my front porch. Patricia and Nate were nowhere in sight. Perhaps they were upstairs sharing some quality time.

Rather than approaching them warily with the complete apprehension I felt, I strode confidently toward them with my hand thrust forward. "Hello, I'm Miranda Marquette."

Her father stood first and shook my hand, which surprised me a little. "We're Charles and Antoinette, Patricia's parents."

Her mother smiled demurely. "Call me Toni. All my friends do."

I couldn't help but stare at her, with her Cleopatra-like straight jet-black hair and beautiful pale complexion. Patricia was nearly a carbon copy of her, and yet, they had adopted her. I smiled, and she approached me with open arms. We hugged. I was surprised by how well this seemed to be going, but I knew they had a plan, and this was not a social call.

"Please, come in. I've been so excited to meet you," I said, trying to sound sincere. The fact was that I had been dreading it. I knew they disapproved of my friendship with their daughter, and I knew I was just about to find out why.

They followed me into my apartment, and I motioned them to sit on the couch. "Can I get you something? Coffee, iced tea, water?"

They declined. "No, thank you. We just wanted to have a little chat," Patricia's father said as he motioned me to sit on the love seat. I could tell he was on a mission, so I just sat quietly. "Now, Miranda, we appreciate everything you have done for Patricia. You have really helped her to come out of her shell. She's always been painfully shy but has transformed into a much more self-confident woman since meeting you."

Believing that was a good thing, I responded, "Thank you." Though, my gut told me that there was a 'but' or a 'however' coming at any moment.

"But we are very concerned about her. Her life has been spiraling out of control since she became more independent. And to a certain degree, we blame ourselves. We have always been very protective of her. She had a tough start to her life, and we've always wanted to do everything we could do to make that up to her. Her mother and I couldn't have children and adopting her was truly a dream come true."

I nodded. "Yes, Patricia shared that with me."

They both nodded, but this was clearly not my time to talk. Her father continued. "Unfortunately, from the point that Patricia joined your Extreme Team, things have gone out of kilter. Until joining you, she had been anything but an adrenaline junkie. She didn't even learn to ride a bike until she was ten, and that was only because her classmates made such fun of her for not knowing how. So, when she first joined you, we saw that as a good sign, that she was finally branching out on her own. But then your first teammate, Tara, died. Then Patricia fell for that terrible man who got her pregnant—"

Her mother interrupted, "Now, we love Nate with all our hearts, but that relationship was horrible. It changed her, and not in good ways. We nearly lost her forever during the pregnancy. Thank God she came to her senses while she was in Switzerland for the trial."

I wanted to remind them that I encouraged her to stay with them until after Nate was born, but this wasn't the time. I nodded, remembering the change in Patricia when she was with Larry.

Charles closed his eyes briefly as if he were trying to remember a well-planned out speech. "So, it seems now we have a dilemma. Patricia is dead set about moving out here permanently with Nate. As much as we'd love to move here to close to her, I'm going to be a late Republican entry into the Colorado governor's race. The Republican Party has no consensus candidate, and I have been asked to enter as an independent. I will need to be in Denver as much as possible over the next six months."

This was a lot to take in. I had no idea he had immediate political aspirations, but I really didn't know much about him, just what Patricia had told me.

Her father looked briefly at this wife and then directly at me. "We had a knock-down-drag-out fight with Patricia last night, and I thought we were going to lose her again. She made some valid points and attributed much of her newfound confidence to you."

He paused, so I knew he was probably getting to the hard part.

He cleared his throat. "Quite honestly, when you had a multi-million-dollar mansion in Malibu, we were far less concerned about her relationship with you. However, you seem to have had some business reversals, which now appear to be impacting your ability to take care of yourself, much less Patricia. Anyway, call it what you want; you seem to have a knack for getting the people around you killed."

I rolled my eyes at the apparent reference to the 'Princess of Death' tag the press and the internet had given me. "Don't tell me you believe all that garbage," I said without thinking.

His face softened. "Actually, I don't give it much credence. My brief experience with the press has taught me to have a thick skin or go home."

He paused briefly, and Toni took over, "Patricia is an intelligent, beautiful woman. But, I suppose, thanks to us, in many ways she's still a child. We need to know if you will be able to watch out for her on top of everything else you have going in your life. We were very impressed with how resourceful you both were when those lowlife thugs abducted both of you, and we can't help but feel that much of that came from you."

I blushed slightly at the compliment. "Thank you." I thought back to our time in Switzerland. "Patricia and I bonded when we went to Thun for the murder trial. We have only become closer since then. She is my priority. You have my word on that. As you mentioned, my life has been turned a bit upside down recently. Having Patricia here even a short time has been as good for me as I hope it has been for her."

They paused and looked at one another, appearing to be satisfied with my responses. Charles spoke again. "We will give you our contact information, and please, contact us at any time should you need anything. We couldn't have been happier about the arrests of the suspects in your abduction case but aren't happy that they have been let out on bail. Please be careful."

They stood up, and I followed them to the door. "I have a good relationship with the local police, and they are watching us very closely, which can be a little unnerving at times, but it's all good."

Toni hugged me, and Charles shook my hand. Toni smiled and said, "We really hope to get to know you better, Miranda. I know Patricia considers you to be family, and we would like to also."

I was surprised by how well this had gone and felt total relief. "You can never have enough family."

They headed to the stairs to Patricia's apartment and left a half-hour later with Nate. They hadn't mentioned taking care of Nate, so I had to assume they were taking him back to Colorado.

About fifteen minutes later, after taking a brief shower and dressed down from my workday, Patricia showed up at my door. Tears streaked her face. "I don't know if I can do it, Miranda. Seeing Nate again only reinforced how much I've missed him and how much I love him. I want him with me so he can know I'm his mother."

We sat on the sofa with my arm around her shoulder while she sniffled and tried to catch her breath. Just as she seemed calmer, my cell phone vibrated in my pocket. I pulled it out. 'Santa Clara Police Department' showed on the screen.

I immediately recognized Detective Marshall's voice. "Miranda, this is Wanda Marshall." I was surprised that she called me 'Miranda.' She usually called me 'Marquette' when she was in a playful mood. So, this call was an odd combination of more personal and more serious than usual. "I have some news on your case, and I wanted you to hear it from me before you saw it on the news. I don't quite know how to soft-peddle this, so I'll just say it." She hesitated briefly, then blurted out, "Both of the suspects in your abduction case have been found dead."

I let out a deep breath, realizing that I had been holding it in anticipation of her information. "What? How? When? Where? Do you know who did it?"

The detective spoke cautiously. "Because this is an open case, I am unable to comment any further regarding specifics relating to these suspects. I guess it wouldn't do any harm to let you know they were found in the warehouse where they had taken you. Someone killed them execution-style. We are following several leads, but I can't comment any further."

I was surprised she gave me as much as she did. "Well, thank you so much, Detective Marshall. Should you need anything from Patricia or me that might help your case, let me know."

"Well, hopefully, this will help you sleep better at night, at least knowing that these guys aren't out on the street. I will definitely be in touch as the case progresses. Thank you. Bye." She seemed relieved.

"Bye, and thanks."

Patricia had been listening carefully to the call, but she didn't have much to go with. "What was that all about?"

It seemed inappropriate to smile since two human beings were dead. On the other hand, I could already feel my stress level falling. I hadn't realized how much the abduction had affected me until now. I decided to take the detective's direct approach. "They're dead." I purposely didn't use their names because I didn't want to humanize them. Plus, I knew that Patricia still had mixed emotions about John, so I didn't want to mention his name.

The blood drained from her face. I watched her quietly for a few minutes, but I was unable to read her. Finally, she jumped up. "Oh, thank God, Miranda. I felt horrible about getting you involved in my issues. And I couldn't seem to resist James, as bad as I knew he was for me."

I finally felt like I could really express myself and went to the fridge for a couple of bottles of water. I threw one to her. "I'm so thrilled that you aren't sad about that guy. He was on the wrong road for whatever reason, and there was nothing you could have done to help him. We are safe now, and so are your parents and Nate. And you've got the job of your dreams!"

Patricia perched on the edge of the kitchen table, pondering. "Now, all I need is to get my son back."

I hoped this development would make her parents act more reasonably. Nate was, after all, Patricia's son first and their grandchild second. I was in her corner. "Well, let's get you settled into your job, and we'll tackle that next."

We spent the rest of the evening, celebrating quietly and planning how to navigate Patricia's rich, connected, controlling parents.

Chapter 9

I was drifting in and out of sleep, aware that it was nearly time to wake up on Thursday, for work. My cell phone vibrated on my bedside table, signaling that I had a phone call.

I glanced at the screen. It was a number from Long Beach that I didn't recognize. Long Beach had a familiar ring to it, but in my just-waking-up state, I couldn't place who it might be. I took a chance and answered. "Hello?" I sounded nearly as asleep as I was.

The voice came through the phone like a steamroller, "Don't tell me I woke you? Not on a beautiful, gorgeous, wonderful day like this." I wracked my brain. It wasn't my mom, my sister Sabine, or a co-worker. No-one at Ion was that enthusiastic except Anna, the receptionist, and it definitely wasn't her voice.

She continued as if she'd already been up for six hours. "This is Miranda, right?"

I kicked myself for not being able to figure out who it was.

She laughed, and that brought back a hint of recognition. It was all coming back, the flight to Switzerland, and the talking and laughing and wine we had had. Now, if I could just come up with her name. M, it started with M. Martha? No. Margaret? No. Margo! I felt redeemed. "Margo Prentice! How are you? And why are you calling me at this God-forsaken hour?"

She was still on a roll. "Well, I was planning on being in your neck of the woods, and I thought I'd look you up."

I hesitated. "Hmmm. Well, you know I don't live in Malibu anymore, right?"

Margo sounded like my oldest and most familiar friend, and we had only spent a flight to Switzerland together. I was comfortable with her and her over-the-top personality both then and now. "Gosh, yes. Are you kidding? You were somewhat of a cult hero in my neighborhood last year when most of the internet and press were bashing you. I followed you every day on Facebook and CNN to find out what lies they were telling about you next. I should have contacted you then, but I thought you might be a little busy."

I scratched my head. "Wow, I never really thought that many people were paying attention, although it was hard to miss the ones demonstrating and carrying signs in front of the courthouse. I'm glad to have that behind me. So when are you coming to Santa Clara?"

Margo continued, "I'll be there this afternoon. I have a business meeting of sorts. Any chance we can get together? Are you working?"

I smiled with the memory of having my complete freedom and wondered, briefly, why I hadn't enjoyed it more. "Yes, I'm working, but we could get together around six." I gave her my address.

She seemed excited to see me. "I'm so glad that your phone number hasn't changed! I am so looking forward to seeing you. Can I bring anything? How about a bottle of wine? Red, wasn't it?"

I laughed, "Yes, I'm still a huge Cabernet fan, but don't go out of your way." I could tell she was getting ready to get off the phone. "I'm so excited to see you, Margo, and hear about all your capers since Switzerland."

Her voice took on a hint of seriousness, "Well, I'm not sure I can share *everything,* but it'll be fun. See you then! Bye." She hung up.

I hung up and glanced at my watch and scolded myself, "Miranda, you're going to be late if you don't get out of here." I ran to the bathroom to take a shower. Washing my hair would have to wait. I brushed my teeth, dressed in jeans and a tee-shirt, breaking my own dress code, and ran to the Rover.

I was pulling into the parking lot just as Tea was getting out of her car. She blocked the sun from her eyes as she watched me drive in, probably thinking she couldn't possibly be seeing what she was seeing. She waited for me to park and giggled, "To what do I owe the pleasure of Miranda Marquette running late? I think this is a first," she teased.

I jumped out of the Rover, half intending to race her to the door, but I thought better of it, realizing just how juvenile that would have been. "I got a call from an old friend, and I lost track of time."

Tea tossed her hair playfully out of her eyes. "I wasn't aware you had any long, lost friends. Do tell."

Even though I knew she was kidding, she had struck a nerve, "Oh, I have plenty of friends, believe me." I bit my tongue as I got to my workspace.

She gave me a questioning look as she continued to her desk and then to the break room to make coffee. She brought me a cup on her way back. Unusual. I figured she was making amends, and I smiled up at her questioning face. I said, "Sorry, I'm a little sensitive about the lack of friends thing."

She placed a hand on my shoulder. "And I'm sorry about my lack of sensitivity. It's not my best trait, but counseling has helped me to identify it."

I wanted to ask her how her counseling was going, but I decided to stay on topic. "That's great! Anyway, I met Margo on my last trip to Switzerland. She was eccentric, outspoken, colorful, loud, and fun. We met at the airport and talked and laughed all the way to Zurich. We swore we'd get back together again, but I was pretty sure it would never happen."

71

She chewed on her lip, which she often does when she thinks, "So, she just called you out of the blue?"

I nodded. "Yes, she said she had some kind of meeting, which seems odd. I'm pretty sure the woman doesn't work. She's a professional ex-wife, and she does exceptionally well. I'm not sure if she married again since we last met. She was single then and just getting used to reclaiming her maiden name. If I were her, I'd just keep it, married or not. You can get away with that these days."

Tea seemed to want to work something else into the conversation. "Hey, speaking of getting married, how's it going with Jason?"

I felt my face get hot. We had gone to the movies on a Saturday night a few weeks ago, and it was nice. He seemed more attentive than he had in the past. But I had pretty much written him off as anyone to have a serious relationship with, so I decided just to enjoy whatever it was that we did have.

After our date, he walked me to my door as he had every other time we had dated. I hadn't even bothered to ask him in for months since he always had some excuse or another not to. So, I was just going to turn to the door to unlock it, and he kissed me. He immediately said, "Good night," turned and walked to his car, so I had no idea if this meant something, if it had been pre-planned, an impulse, or what. I often ran into him at work, but I hadn't seen him since then. So, I was a little on-edge when it came to Jason.

Realizing that I was replaying our date in my head over and over instead of responding to Tea, I laughed and said, "He's such a nice guy, but I just don't see it going anywhere."

She gave me an odd look but didn't ask anything further and settled into her workspace.

I had been keeping thoughts of Jason in th
but now they were front and center. I couldn
if he was avoiding me. Except since that date
in the same place at the same time during the
busy last week, I didn't think about it all that much, but now that
Tea had reminded me, it was driving me crazy.

Without saying a word, I got up from my desk and walked
out of the office door on the way to the administrative offices. I
was on a mission and didn't stop to chat with Anna on the way
through the lobby. When I reached Jason's office, he was buried
behind a stack of paper as usual. He glanced up and smiled as I
approached his desk. I was not smiling.

"Okay, Mister. Am I not pretty enough? Not smart enough?
Am I too much of a smart mouth? Have you decided that you
don't date employees? Am I—"

He put his hand up. "Whoa, at least give me a chance to
answer."

I sat down on the right side chair in front of his desk. I
drummed my fingers impatiently on the arm of the chair.

He had a distressed look on his face, and I had no idea what
it meant but figured it couldn't be good. I forced my negative
thoughts down as my therapist had taught me. He seemed to be
trying to remember a pre-planned speech.

Finally, he looked me in the eye. "Miranda, you're the most
beautiful girl I've ever been out with. You're smart and funny,
and you can dish it out as well as you can take it. You are sincere,
tell the truth, are independent, and not needy. As far as I can tell,
you're perfect."

I started to say that no-one was perfect, but he put his hand
up. He continued, "Wait, let me finish. It could be the last time
I'm feeling this brave."

quieted my mouth and my mind. The situation was starting to feel surreal after having lived it so many times in my head.

He closed his eyes, searching for the words. When he opened them, I thought I saw tears glistening in them. "I know that I've told you about my relationship issues."

I nodded.

"I also know that I have told you that I was ready to move forward and then have given you mixed signals."

I couldn't help but add a touch of sarcasm. "Really?"

He gave me a quick little smile and then got serious again. "I know it. I know I'm the problem. So when we went out last week, I made myself a promise that I would take a risk with you. I knew I wanted to kiss you, but I couldn't figure out how or when through the whole dinner and movie. So I finally just did it, and I didn't stick around to see your reaction."

I couldn't stay quiet any longer. "Jason, you are the exact opposite of the guy I thought I met in that bar in San Francisco a couple of years ago. You appeared to be so self-confident and in control, but that was all a guise. You shouldn't have to ask me how it went when we kissed. You should have been able to tell, to feel it deep in your heart. I know that I felt something. I also know that your avoidance of the situation has hurt. I told you from day one. I'm either all-in, or I'm all-out. I have been ready to be all-in with you for a while, but quite honestly, I'm not even sure what it is that I'm in with you."

He sat staring straight ahead, barely breathing, nearly paralyzed by something I assumed was fear. I felt like I had done what I needed to do, and I was ready to move on. There is a point when pride just takes over, and this was it. I stood and turned toward the door.

Suddenly, he blurted out, "I want you to be my girl."

I stopped in my tracks and turned to face him. I said, "It's about time," and walked out, not looking back. I nearly ran to the outside door and the parking lot. I'd have to apologize later to Anna, since I'd already come and gone twice without chatting with her.

I stood in the parking lot, just breathing in and out. I replayed the scene through my mind over and over. His girl? I felt like I was in a nineteen-sixties Bobby Darin movie, the kind my Grandpapa and I watched over and over again.

I spent at least fifteen minutes out there, just living in the moment like my therapist always told me to, then returned to the customer service suite and my workstation. I was relieved that Tea wasn't at hers.

I spent the next hour composing an email to Jason asking just what he meant by being 'his girl' and what I could expect from him.

Two hours later, he sent me this:

Dear Miranda,

Here's what you can expect of me:

1) I will always be true
2) I will be your best friend
3) Your needs will always come first
4) I will let the whole world know how I feel about you
5) I will stop looking
6) I will always listen to you
7) I will write songs for you
8) I will do everything else I can't think of right now.

Love,
Jason

I printed it out and slid it under my keyboard, where I could always take a peek at it. I spent the rest of the day entering orders and reading the email over and over again. By the time I was ready to go home, I was walking on air.

Until I got out of my Rover and headed toward my front porch. And there was Margo sitting in wait, with a suitcase and a couple of other bags stacked around her. She was a heavy packer just like my sister, Sabine. She immediately stood and strode toward me. "Aren't you a sight for sore eyes? You'll have to tell me how all of this happened." She made a broad gesture to include the apartment and Santa Clara, probably referring to my business reversals.

I grinned. "You know what, Margo. After the wonderful day I had today, none of that even matters." We hugged, and I led her into the apartment. "Here, let me grab a couple of those bags."

She insisted, "Oh, I've got it all. I'm used to traveling the world for months at a time." Then she smiled and asked, "So what happened today to make your life so special?" She surveyed the room and chose the loveseat to sit on after she stacked her bags against the wall. Maybe because it had the newest throw on it. Despite my loving my apartment, seeing it through a stranger's eyes, I had to admit it was a bit shabby.

I couldn't resist saying in a sing-song voice, "I've got a boyfriend! I've got a boyfriend!" After all, I kind of felt like I was fifteen, and I was going with it.

Margo rummaged around in a cloth bag from her stash by the wall. She pulled out several bottles of California Cabernet. There were so many great vineyards with new ones opening every day. I hadn't tried any of these labels, so I let her pick one to open. As she opened the Dominus Cabernet, which I knew to be one of the best low-elevation vineyards in the Napa Valley, she said, "Well, that's something to celebrate! At least I hope so."

Still reveling in the feeling, I leaned back on the couch. "Oh, yes, it is. I've been working on this guy for several years since we met in San Francisco. At that point, I was at the top of my game financially, but my social life was a mess. Since then, I've learned to live more frugally, but I've also learned to appreciate what I have instead of always wanting more and more but feeling empty inside."

"I don't remember if I told you my life story on that crazy flight to Switzerland."

I thought for a minute. "You told me lots of stories about marriages that didn't last. I can't remember how many times you've been married, but it's a lot. Right?"

She pretended to be counting on her fingers. "Yes, I guess five is a lot. And, should all go right, I'll be done with this one soon. I thought I could do it, get married, and stay married, but it's just not in my DNA. This one's been a bit of a problem because he required a prenup, and he's sticking with it. My meeting today will hopefully solve that problem."

I figured she was meeting with an attorney, but she didn't expound on how she planned on solving her problem.

A few minutes later, there was a knock on the door. I wasn't expecting anyone, so I was surprised to see a giant of a man, probably in his mid-forties, with a ruddy complexion and a three-piece suit. He blinked when he saw me. "Is Miss Prentice here?"

I frowned, "Just a sec. Let me get her." I wasn't too excited about letting this thug into my house.

I called for Margo. "Margo, you have company."

She bolted for the door carrying a briefcase that had been resting on her one of her suitcases by the wall. "Oh, I'm so sorry,

77

I never expected that he'd show up here. I'll just meet with him now, and I'll be right back."

"Are you sure? You could meet in here."

"It's okay. He's a friend."

I watched them walk up the street and get in the back of a black Cadillac limo.

I figured that she might be a while, so I took the opportunity to peruse the wines Margo had brought with her. There was a Spottswoode "Family Estate" Cabernet, which I had heard about but never tried. At $150 per bottle, I wasn't likely to buy it now, so I was happy Margo had brought it.

The other three bottles, the Cliff Lede Stags Leap District, the Arrowood, and the Laurel Glen Sonoma Mountain Cabernets, all came very highly recommended. When my *Food and Wine* magazine subscription expires at the end of the year, I'd have to renew it despite my considerably lower budget. I love wine, whether I have the money to buy it or not.

After finishing the open bottle, I opted to jump in the shower, so I could relax when Margo returned. I had just finished blow-drying my hair and emerging from the bedroom in exercise shorts and a t-shirt when I saw Margo emerge from the back of the limo without the briefcase. She walked onto the front porch and retrieved her cell phone from her pocket.

I strained to listen, but she was too far out of range for me to hear. I could tell she was having a heated exchange with the person on the other end of the line but nothing more. I wondered if it was her husband since she had implied that they probably wouldn't be married much longer.

After she hung up, she lit a cigarette and smoked it with such intensity, I wondered what it had ever done to her. She pulled out her phone again and had a far more intimate conversation with lots of giggling and whispering.

One thing was sure. I really didn't know this woman very well and had no idea what she was up to. As I finished combing out my hair, I decided it didn't matter. We had connected at a time when we both needed someone to talk to en route to Switzerland. We could certainly enjoy a few harmless bottles of wine without knowing intimate details about each other's lives.

Her body language was far more relaxed as she entered the house after the second call. "Hey, you didn't even open the second bottle yet? Girl, you disappoint me!"

I grabbed a wine opener and the nearest bottle. "You don't have to tell me twice." I pulled out the cork and tossed it in the trash.

She sat, staring into her glass after I poured it. I didn't want to pry, but her mood seemed to have changed since her meeting. "Are you okay?"

She snapped back to reality. "Oh yeah. I'm fine. I just had a tough phone call."

I touched her arm. "Well, if you want to talk, I'm here. If not, I'm here too."

She smiled, "Thanks, Miranda. I'm fine." She straightened her skirt. "Now, where were we?"

We spent the rest of the evening talking and laughing. After the third bottle of Cabernet, she asked if she could sleep on the couch. I had expected her to stay because neither of us could have possibly driven after three bottles of wine.

#

We hugged as I headed out to work on Friday morning. She said she'd lock the door on her way out.

Chapter 10

Friday was a whirlwind of activity at work. Tea describing, in excruciating detail, her most recent fight with Mike. It seemed like they were back to square one. Thankfully, he hadn't gotten violent with her, but I think it was only because he had been too drunk to accomplish landing any punches. In my opinion, he was a ticking bomb just waiting to explode. She had learned that as long as she allowed him to control her, she could keep the peace at home, but as soon as she exerted any independence, he resisted. There was no way for both of them to be truly happy.

On a happier note, Jason asked me out for Saturday night. I would have to get used to dating, which was not something I had done a lot of recently. My heart and body were ready to go full steam ahead, but my mind was ready to take it very slowly.

I was taking a lot of orders from new clients at work which was more than I could possibly process in a day. Sales were picking up, but with Ion providing me with no additional resources. I was still working on a strategy for the company to hire some extra help, but if that went as well as my proposal for a new computer system, I was in trouble.

I dragged out of the office at just after five, determined not to be a slave to my job. And while I had come to love my job more every day and was well-respected by my co-workers, requested by name by our customers, and generally considered the most upwardly mobile person in the company, I wasn't advancing. I was just taking on more and more in hopes of eventually being recognized but never was. This frustration was something I needed to discuss with Jason.

Patricia was just climbing her stairs as I parked the car. I yelled to her. "Hey, good lookin,' wanna come down for a beer?"

She waved and gave me the 'give me a minute' signal to let me know she'd be right down. Knowing I probably wouldn't have time for an after-work shower, I ran to my room to find some casual clothes before she arrived. I found a pair of terry shorts and a tank top that I hadn't worn in ages at the bottom of my drawer. I whispered, "Note to self: go through your drawers to see what you actually have in there."

Patricia was perched on the couch when I came out of the bedroom, sipping on a Michelob Ultra, seemingly bursting with information. "You will never, in a million years, guess what happened at work today!"

I put my hand on my head as if that would magically give me access to the secrets of the universe. "Um, let's see. You got a delicious salad for lunch?"

She rolled her eyes. "God, Miranda, that is so *last week.*"

I absolutely loved having Patricia as a neighbor and best friend. She had become so self-confident and downright fun to spend time with within such a short time.

I grabbed her beer and took a swig. She responded with a mock-disgusted look. "Now, I have to get a new one, so I don't get your cooties."

I drank the rest of it and threw the bottle halfway across the room into the recycling bin as she grabbed two more from the fridge. She carried them to the kitchen table but didn't hand either of them to me, then sat on the chair at the end of the table. "I'm holding this hostage until you let me tell you what happened at work today."

I sat at the other end of the table, pouting, "Okay, have it your way."

"Oh, no big deal, I only got a promotion," she said, trying to sound casual.

I put my hands on my hips as I stood up. "No way! You've been there for five minutes, and I work and slave my life away to get ten cents an hour raise."

She sat back in her chair with her hands behind her head. "And my boss, Susan, says that this is just the beginning. She's been held back because she's had too much work to do and had to work sixty-hour weeks just to keep her head above water. Well, now that she has me, the sky's the limit. She wants me to build a whole department handling all community relations related to the new headquarters. That's small potatoes for her. I'm sure she'll be a VP by then. It's supposed to open in 2017."

I had no idea what any of this meant, so I had to ask. "So, what sort of community relations do new headquarters require?"

She loved to talk about her work and glowed with pride. "Well, if it were anyone but Karma, it wouldn't be a big deal, but we're talking two point eight million square feet on 175 acres. This building and grounds are going to be bigger than many towns."

I had only paid moderate attention when she told me about this the first time, but now I finally got it. "Wow, talk about being in the right place at the right time." She gave me a hurt look.

I tried to dig myself out of my gaff. "And the fact that you are by far the best person for the job. I'll bet you have a perspective that no-one else who's been at Karma for their entire career could possibly have."

She pounded her fist on the table for emphasis, "That's right, Miranda. I know nothing about Karma, which, oddly, makes me the perfect person for the job. I don't have the typical slanted view that many of them have. Thank God, Susan was able to recognize that."

I went to her end of the table and hugged her. "I'm so happy for you and proud of you. It makes me so happy."

She handed me my beer. "Thanks, Miranda. You know how much that means coming from you."

After we spent the next hour discussing how she was going to get up to speed at Karma, out of nowhere, she asked, "So, now that we've discussed my news, fill me in on what's new with Jason."

I'd been so busy at work and hadn't seen much of Patricia this week, especially with my surprise visit from Margo; I hadn't had a chance to give her the good news. "Well, to be honest, I finally got sick of riding the middle ground with Jason. You know me; I'm an all-in or go home kind of girl. And he's been avoiding me since he *finally* kissed me goodnight after all this time. Part of me figured it was over. He didn't feel the spark, and that would have been okay," I lied.

Patricia was on the edge of her seat.

I searched my memory bank. "As it turned out, he was waiting for me to come around, afraid that maybe I didn't feel it. Well, he couldn't have been more wrong. I nearly died in his arms that night." I felt like there was a song in there somewhere, but I couldn't place it.

Patricia smiled broadly. "Oh, Miranda, I'm so happy for you. So, what's next for you and Jason?"

I wasn't entirely sure where Jason and I were going, but it was definitely out of the friend zone. "Well, I don't honestly know but he did ask me to be his girl."

She laughed. "Is that really what he said? It's romantic in a quirky beach movie kind of way."

I giggled, "You and I think so much alike. He's so sweet and I'm so ready to have someone in my life, but I know I ought to be careful."

Patricia's face became serious. "I know just what you mean, and I have a child to prove it. I made the same vow, should I ever start dating again."

I reached out for her hand. "I have a feeling now that you're working with a gazillion people, you'll have them lining up to ask you out."

She smiled, "You're probably right, and that kind of scares me a little. I've already noticed guys checking me out. It kind of makes me a little nervous to date again."

My phone vibrated in my pocket, I looked at the screen, and it was Jason. I gave Patricia the 'give me a second' sign. "Hi, stranger," I gushed.

It was nice to hear his voice. "Hey, gorgeous."

The affectionate name-calling was a little weird since we'd spent so little time as dating friends, but I figured I could adjust. "Hey there. To what do I owe the pleasure of your call?"

Patricia rolled her eyes, and I shrugged,

Jason sounded nervous. I thought it was cute. "Listen, I'm taking a few days to visit my parents and—um—wondered if you'd like to join me. You can see where I grew up, you know?"

All of a sudden, a thousand thoughts ran through my head. "Really? Your parents? And you want me with you?"

"Well, if you want some time to think about it—"

I cleared my throat. "No. You just took me by surprise, is all. That sounds great. Where are your parents? New York? When would you want to go? How—"

He laughed. "Okay, take a breath. I haven't arranged anything yet. I just wanted to bounce it off you."

I smiled. "Thank you, Jason. I'd love to go. I don't have much planned except for work, but I think I might be able to get a couple of days off."

Having gotten my okay, he seemed ready to get off the phone. "It shouldn't be a problem. I'll talk to your boss if I have to!" He chuckled at his joke. "Well, okay, Miranda, I'll pick you up tomorrow at six."

I had nearly forgotten we had a date tomorrow night. "That's right! Hey, what movie are we going to see anyway?" This was a test. If he chose another action or military film, I'd have to reconsider.

He was on top of his game. "I thought *Like Crazy* looked good."

I smiled, "That sounds great! I was sure you were going to say *The Darkest Hour* or *Haywire*."

I could hear a smile in his voice. "I got the message last time we saw an action film, even though you are an action kind of girl, you like romances. You don't have to tell me twice."

It was nice to be heard. "Thanks, Jason. I look forward to tomorrow. Talk to you then."

We hung up.

Patricia had been typing on her phone while I was talking to Jason. She completed her typing just after I hung up. "So, that sounded serious. You're going to meet his parents?"

I blushed a little, not expecting Jason to step up so quickly, "I guess we are lunging forward and hoping for the best."

Patricia was more perceptive than I ever would have thought a few months ago. "I'm sure you're excited but have mixed emotions about meeting his family. So, enjoy it, be gracious, and relax. After all, he hasn't given you a ring or even implied that's the direction he's going in."

I wondered if Patricia had missed her calling as a therapist, but she loved her Karma job. I decided not to bring that up. I responded, "That's what I'll do. I'll meet the family and just do what I do. I'm sure his parents will love me."

I reminded myself that I only needed to be true to who I am, and the rest would work itself out. It would do me good to get out of California. I also reminded myself to take a couple of days in New Orleans with my family soon. I wondered if we could work that into these plans or if that would be too complicated.

I felt good that since my mom was diagnosed with breast cancer, I called her at least once a week. We were closer now than we ever had been. I couldn't wait, though, to be with her again. She would love to meet Jason because she worried that I was going to die an old maid.

My sister Sabine would love to meet him too. She was a much harsher critic than my mom because she not only wanted me to be with a man but also with the right man. She would put him through his paces in the most loving way possible. I wasn't sure if I had ever met a man who Sabine thought was good enough for me, but this could be the first time.

The more I thought about it, the more I decided that New Orleans needed to be a separate trip from seeing his parents.

Patricia and I had a couple more beers and called it a night.

Chapter 11

I awoke with a start on Saturday morning. My first thought was that I was late to work. I needed to get a calendar where I crossed out the days like I did while growing up. I had already inadvertently shown up to work on Saturday more than once because I had no idea what day it was. I glanced at my phone for the time: 8:35 a.m.

I had promised myself I would do some domestic chores today: clean the kitchen and bathroom; sweep the floors, dust, do my laundry, change the bed, and generally straighten things out. I had found about living in an apartment, smaller than the great room in my house, that things got messy quickly. After I cleaned, I showered, shaved, plucked my eyebrows, and painted my fingernails and toenails. It had been forever since I'd had a mani-pedi, and it was likely to be much longer before I could afford one.

By the time five o'clock rolled around, I was collapsed in a kitchen chair with an iced coffee. I am addicted to Starbucks Vanilla Sweet Cream Cold Brew but have had to settle for a homemade version since my financial situation changed. I prayed for Dunkin' Donuts to make it to California, but my prayers remained unanswered. I could get a large, iced coffee there for half the price of Starbucks, but they had, for whatever reason, forsaken the Golden State.

Realizing that Jason would be picking me up in less than an hour, I ran to the bathroom to get cleaned up. Within forty-five minutes, I had gotten my hair to a far more amazing place than it usually arrived. My blonde hair fell softly around my shoulders. I applied the tiniest amount of make-up to cover the hairline scars on my face, a leftover from being shot when I was a cop. I rarely thought about that now unless I saw my face in the mirror in a particular light.

I opted for a black mini-skirt and white button-up blouse with white gladiator sandals. I stood in front of the full-length mirror on the bathroom door and realized I needed some color, so added a jade earrings and necklace. "You clean up pretty good," I said out loud, not sure who I was trying to convince.

Jason was punctual, knocking on my front door at precisely six. He looked sharp in a pair of khaki shorts and a golf shirt, dressed better than he usually did for work. He came through the door, giving me a soft kiss on the cheek. He whispered, "You look incredible."

My usual reaction to a compliment was to deflect it, but my therapist had worked with me on this, and I said quietly, "Thank you."

He said he made reservations at a seafood restaurant right on the beach and asked me if that was okay. After he parked, we walked down the pier to a cozy building draped with fairy lights reflecting off the water. Inside, the tables were covered with white linen tablecloths and set with sparkling glasses and silver. We both ordered lobster bisque and the grilled catch of day. We shared a bottle of sauvignon blanc. The movie was a perfect romantic end to the evening. As we rode in his car back to my apartment, I felt like I had to make my intentions clear before things got awkward as we saw one another more. I sat back in the bucket seat, trying to sound casual. "I really enjoyed this entire evening—the dinner, the movie and especially your company."

He smiled. "Me too."

I bit my lip, "But I wanted to talk about something to make sure we're on the same page."

He took my hand and said, "I'm sure we are."

I wasn't going to be deterred. "Well, I wasn't sure exactly what you had in mind when you asked me to be 'your girl.'" I hesitated to see if he would clarify it on his own.

When he had waited as long as I felt appropriate, I jumped in. "Well, here's what it means to me. You want me to be your exclusive girlfriend, and I'm good with that. And we won't see anyone else, right?"

He nodded. "That's kind of what I meant."

I worked on finding the right words, and they just weren't coming. I wanted to be kind, direct, and straightforward. My tendency to be overly blunt had hurt many feelings over the year, so I was turning over a new leaf. "Okay, just so we're clear. I saved your note, but there's just this one little thing that kind of bothers me."

He grinned. "You saved the memo I sent you?"

"I did. And as much as I love what you said about us being exclusive and all that, it kind of felt a little too much like, I don't know, ownership or possession."

"I don't get it."

"You know. Exclusive. All the promises almost like married people make and, to be honest, I'd like to take this slow."

"Slow?"

Had I assumed too much? "Just what I said, let's go slowly. I want to take it slow—really slow and enjoy every moment."

He maneuvered the car around double-parked cars in front of a movie theater that was letting out and simply said, "Uh-huh."

We rode silently for the rest of the way to my apartment. Staring straight ahead, I wasn't sure what he was thinking. He opened his car door and walked around to open mine. He offered his hand to help me out of the car. He held my hand while we walked to the apartment. When we got to my door, he put his arms around me, pulled me close, and we kissed, this time a real deep and enduring kiss.

My body responded on its own, not recognizing my own personal rules. His hands slid under by blouse. My breath came in short gasps as I reached for his wrists and gently pushed him away. "I'm—I'm not ready for this, Jason."

"I thought—"

"Like I said before, can we just take this slowly?"

He took my hands in his. "I'll wait for you forever if that's what it takes."

And just as quickly, he let go, headed toward his car, and he was gone.

Ah, Jason, if you only knew how hard it was to send you away just now. I unlocked the door and stole silently into my apartment. I laid down on the bed, trying to get a handle on what just happened. I'd almost made a liar out of myself when I said I wanted to go slow.

I dressed in my favorite Hello Kitty pajamas and lay awake in bed for a while. I giggled at the thought of what he would say if he could see me in these p.j.s.

#

The weeks flew by, and before I knew it, we were embarking from the San Jose Airport to Buffalo. I was surprised to find out that the flight would be fourteen hours, including two layovers in Phoenix and Orlando. When all was said and done, it would be a sixteen-hour day because we still had to drive another hour and a half from Buffalo to Jamestown. Then there was the time change. Having never been to New York, I guess I fell into the stereotype that we'd be seeing the Empire State Building and Yankee Stadium.

90

We drove on highways for a little while but as we left Buffalo, I was astonished at the lack of traffic on the roads. I had gotten so used to riding on eight-lane roads with bumper-to-bumper traffic, the concept of a two-lane country road was utterly foreign. The bright moonlight displayed fenced fields and the silhouettes of barns and herds of cattle.

Jason and I rode silently in the rental car. We had talked so much on the plane, there wasn't much left to say. He had told me about his family so that I was completely prepared. His parents were simple country people. His father owned a small hardware store, and his mom was a wife and mother. They went to church every week, lived for family holidays like Thanksgiving and Christmas, and worked hard every day of their lives.

Jason has three brothers, two older and one younger. They were less than five years apart. He also felt like an outsider, born to the wrong family. When he left for LA right out of high school to pursue a singing career, they were sad but not surprised. Now he'd been gone twenty years and tried to get back home a couple of times a year but wasn't always successful.

When we pulled into the driveway of the large farmhouse on a couple of acres, it looked like a postcard of the American Dream to me. There was a camper parked next to the two-car garage, a motorcycle, a pickup truck, and a Ford Explorer in the driveway.

Jason led me into the house without knocking. The aroma of chocolate chip cookies hung in the air, and I could hear laughter coming from what I guessed was the family room. The house appeared older but nicely remodeled.

When his mother, a jolly, matronly looking woman, probably near sixty, realized that we had arrived, she dropped everything and ran to hug Jason. She held him until he started to squirm.

She said, "You were always the one who was hardest to hold down."

After she released him, she suddenly realized that I was standing there. She released him and opened her arms to me. After a warm, welcoming embrace, she said, "You must be Miranda. It's so lovely to meet you after all this time. He's been talking about you for years."

I gave him a sidelong glance. "Oh, really? I had no idea. Years? What's he been saying about me?" I poked him in the ribs. "I'll have to have a heart to heart with your mom, so I can find out how you really feel."

Thrilled that I was playing along, she smiled broadly. "Oh, Miranda, you have no idea. We'll talk."

I laughed. "You've got a deal, Mrs. Wall."

She waved me off. "Please call me 'Greta' or 'Mom' if you'd prefer. Everyone does."

"You've got a deal, Mom."

She shifted gears. "Now, Miranda, I've got the guest room at the end of the hall all ready for you. And Jason, you can have your old room. There have been a few changes, but it should be comfortable."

Jason asked, "So how's Dad doing?"

She shook her head with a sad smile, "He's up and down. The doctors keep running tests, but they have no idea. He's just tired all the time. But we're keeping positive thoughts."

I was so tired that I was relieved when she let me know that she was heading up to bed.

I was beyond exhausted when I finally laid my head on the feather pillow. I was asleep within minutes. I slept a dreamless nine hours, which was nearly unheard of for me. The three-hour time difference was irrelevant at this point. I felt refreshed and energized. I was pleased to find that my bedroom had its own bath, and I luxuriated in the oversized tub far longer than I should have. I imagined the upstairs had been completely gutted and rebuilt at some point. It was modern and very well done.

When I finally ventured downstairs, a man, the spitting image of Jason twenty years from now, worked the griddle, making pancakes, bacon, sausage, and eggs of all varieties, scrambled, fried, and poached. He dropped his cooking utensils and gave me a warm handshake. "I'm Jerry Wall. And any friend of Jason's is a welcome guest in our home." Based on Mrs. Wall's comments last evening, I had expected him to appear ill and frail, but he seemed healthy.

His mother sat at the kitchen table, nursing a mug of coffee. "I trust that you slept well. I didn't expect to see you down here until at least ten. It's still five o'clock your time."

I smiled. "I prefer to ignore time zones and go with how I feel. That oversized tub upstairs was just what the doctor ordered."

Jerry pointed at the griddle and the plates piled with food. "What'll it be? Pick your poison."

I was dying for caffeine. "I'll tell you what. I'll have a cup of coffee and then decide."

Greta motioned for me to sit next to her. "I knew I liked you! I do the same thing. Don't ask me to decide anything without at least one cup of coffee. Now, Miranda, I understand you work with Jason."

I corrected her. "I work *for* him, actually. I had some misgivings about dating my boss, and he wasn't too keen on the idea either. I guess that's why we kind of had a slow start."

She smiled at her husband. "I was a cashier at Jerry's dad's hardware store. His dad had him filling in as supervisor, teaching him the business, so I guess you could say Jerry was my boss too."

Jerry chuckled. "But I guess we all know who the boss is now, right, dear?"

They smiled affectionately at one another, and I could feel the love radiating between this sweet couple. I wondered if they knew how lucky there were. I had a feeling they did.

I saw snippets of Jason's personality in his parents. He was a hard worker, had a good sense of humor, and loved to cook. I wasn't sure yet about his capacity to love. If he was able to learn that from his parents, he would be a great catch. Only time would tell.

#

Jason and I spent an adventurous weekend in his old stomping ground. I learned a lot, but most surprising that Lucille Ball was born and raised here. Since she was one of my Grandpapa's favorite people, she was also one of mine. We visited her childhood home/museum and spent several hours there.

I was concerned that Jason might be bored, but he admitted he had never visited the museum before. I was appalled. "Are you kidding me? If I had lived here, I'd go there every time I came back here to visit. There was so much to see. I'm sure you'd see something new every time."

I had to admit had I grown up here, that I might never have left. It felt like home to me. Jason was starting to feel like home to me too. The more time we spent together, the more compatible we were.

By the time we got back to Santa Clara, I was exhausted again. We took a red-eye from Buffalo and arrived at the San Jose Airport at seven in the morning on Monday. I planned to rest all day and wake up fresh for work on Tuesday.

Always the gentleman, Jason, walked me to my front door. We were both barely awake enough to stand and held one another up with our arms around each other as we walked. When we got to the door, he wrapped me in his arms and kissed me like there was no tomorrow, even though I was pretty sure there was a tomorrow for us. I hoped so, anyway.

I watched as he walked to his car and drove away.

Upon entering my apartment, I knew immediately there was something very wrong. I had been exposed enough as a cop and quite a bit since, and I recognized the stench of death. I started searching my apartment. I found nothing in the kitchen, living room, or bedroom. I glanced into the bathroom and saw nothing initially, but the smell was getting stronger in that part of the apartment. So I walked into the bathroom and pulled back the shower curtain.

Sitting in the tub was the man who came to my door looking for Margo. He had a single gunshot to the forehead.

My mind and heart rate started racing. My ears were ringing, and I became increasingly lightheaded. I sat on the floor, bent my knees up, brought my face down to my knees, and tried not to lose consciousness.

Chapter 12

I was so proud of how my treatment for anxiety disorder had been working. My symptoms had been less and less evident, even in stressful situations until now. I hadn't felt any anxiety at all during the trip to meet Jason's family. I truly believed that if I could altogether discontinue the practice of finding dead bodies, I might be cured.

But now I had to come to terms with my situation. It was just me and a dead body, again. That was the bad news. The good news was, for once, I had a rock-solid alibi. There was nothing better documented than airline travel. And on top of that, I had Jason and his parents who could vouch for me.

Our weekend trip would hold a lot of water with the police, which I needed to call. I just needed to gather my thoughts first. Since I already had a relationship with her, I opted to call Wanda directly instead of 9-1-1.

I dialed her number, which was already in my contacts.

She answered after the first ring. "Wanda Marshall, how can I help you?"

My mouth went dry, and my throat tightened. I hadn't even thought about what to say. Did I know the guy? How did I know him? Had he been to my apartment before? I nearly hung up but thought she probably had me on caller ID and knew that it was me calling her. I did my best to sound concerned but not guilty.

"Detective Marshall, I went away for the weekend, and when I returned home, I found a dead body in my bathroom." In spite of my resolve, my voice sounded shaky even to me.

Maybe it was my imagination but I could have sworn I heard her mumble, "The Princess of Death strikes again."

But when I responded, "Pardon me?", she replied in full voice, "We'll be right there," and hung up.

I steadied myself with the wall as I stood up from the bathroom floor. My legs were a little like jelly. I flopped on the couch to prepare for the onslaught of humanity which would likely follow this call.

The trickiest part of the interrogation would be my relationship with the victim. If asked directly, there was no way to respond truthfully without throwing Margo under the bus. The more my head cleared, the more confused I became. Just who was this guy, why was Margo meeting with him, and why was he dead in my apartment?

Margo had said some things that seemed like she was just joking on our trip to Switzerland, but she sort of implied that she killed at least one of her husbands. She even gave me some advice about how she got away with it. She was so eccentric, I figured she was trying to be funny, but now I wasn't so sure.

While a part of me wanted to protect her, I couldn't do it at the expense of my freedom or credibility. We barely knew each other. I was certainly fond of her, but I wasn't taking a murder rap for her. I debated telling the detective I had never seen the guy before, but that would surely come back to bite me at some point. Honesty and credibility are critical, especially now that the detective saw me as more of an ally than an enemy. A lie on my part would blow that permanently.

I was satisfied I had a game plan when they arrived only a couple of minutes later.

When I opened the door, the first thing Detective Marshall did was the obvious. She asked me where the body was. I pointed to the bathroom. She told me to sit in the kitchen.

First responders showed up and she directed them to the bathroom. They came out pretty quickly and then chaos reigned for two or three hours as the medical examiner and a Crime Scene Unit were called in. Investigators wore white suits and booties as they prowled around spraying and painting everything the perpetrator might have touched or walked on. It crossed my mind that someone was going to have to clean up the mess.

As everyone worked at their designated tasks, Detective Marshall came into the kitchen with Detective Connelly. They sat at the kitchen table. He operated a tape recorder. Marshall took notes on a regular note pad.

She started gently enough, certainly far less aggressive than when we first met in the cemetery last year. "Miranda, please tell me in your own words what transpired to get us to where we are today."

I was caught a little off guard, expecting some more specific questions, but I recovered quickly. "Well, I was off on a trip for the long weekend with my new boyfriend."

The detective looked at me over her glasses. "Good for you, Miranda. I hope it works out for you."

I blushed, wondering if I appeared that desperate for a man or if she was actually being supportive. "Thanks. I went back East to meet his family. They were very nice."

She smiled but seemed to realize that we were getting off track. "When did you come back from your weekend?"

I straighten in my seat. "We took the red-eye, so it was around seven this morning when I arrived. I planned to go to bed and sleep a good portion of the day, but I knew instantly something was very wrong when I got inside. That smell is unmistakable. So I searched for a dead body, thinking I'd discover a rat or maybe a racoon, instead I found that man in the bathtub." I decided not to go into detail about my panic attack unless I absolutely had to. I paused, making sure that everything I'd said was accurate. "And that's what happened."

She wrote feverishly despite the recorder. She paused briefly and put the end of the pen in her mouth. "And did you know the victim?"

She stared straight into my eyes, looking for a hint that I was lying. "Well, I didn't know him, but I had seen him before. A friend of mine came into town about ten days ago for a meeting with this man. He came to the door to pick her up."

I got her attention with this detail. "The guy you just found dead in your bathtub came to your door to pick your friend up for a meeting? Tell me a little more about that."

I could feel my underarms starting to sweat. "Yes, and they had a meeting in a limo parked on the street outside the apartment."

She put down her pen, so she was free to talk with her hands. "Girl, you're telling me that you had a friend here who met with this man in a car outside, and you didn't think that was kind of odd?"

I stuttered a little. "W-well, she didn't give me any details about the meeting, and I didn't pry."

She pounded the table. "Marquette, you used to be a cop! Did none of your instincts kick in even once?"

I was surprised that she was getting so animated, especially since I had done nothing wrong. "We were having a good time and a couple of bottles of Cabernet, so I was not in cop mode."

She wrote some more notes then continued, "So, are you telling me you don't know who this guy was?"

I shook my head. "No idea."

She looked like her head was going to explode. "He's Tony 'the Shark' Sansone." She continued to glare when I didn't react. "You really have no idea who that is, do you?" Her voice softened slightly.

I had no idea. "Nope, not a clue."

She couldn't help but let me know, and I figured I'd find out soon enough on the news anyway. "Tony's on the FBI's Top Ten Most Wanted List and has been for decades. He's the hitman's hitman. He's as slippery as an eel. He's been in and out of custody for years, but his raps just don't stick despite ironclad evidence.

"I can't believe he's been terminated on my watch and in my district. This might be great or a total disaster, but my gut tells me the latter." She stopped talking as if she realized she was sharing far too much with a witness in a murder case.

I suddenly realized that Margo was in big trouble. Had she been meeting with this Tony guy to arrange knocking off her most recent husband? She intimated that she was having some issues with him about the divorce. I was sure that the detective could read my mind and I wanted to change the subject as soon as possible.

"I think this is going to be a big feather in your cap that somebody murdered him in your district. I'm sure you can spin it in your favor."

I thought I had her distracted enough to not pursue any further questions about Margo, but I was wrong. I could see the wheels turning in her head.

"So, your friend meets with a most-wanted hitman in a limo near your apartment, and he winds up dead in your bathroom. How could that be a coincidence? Did she have a key?"

I responded quickly, "No, she didn't have a key."

She jumped on that. "But she might have taken yours somewhere to get a copy, right?"

I thought back on her visit. "No, I was with her the whole time."

She wasn't letting this die. "How about when you fell asleep? Couldn't she have gone somewhere and gotten a key made and snuck back in?"

My head was beginning to hurt. "Well, I guess it's possible." I couldn't lie. "I honestly don't know what to think anymore. I really don't know her very well. We met on a flight to Switzerland a couple of years ago."

I could see a thousand more questions running through Wanda's mind, but she didn't ask them, at least not yet. "Well, maybe you can give me her contact number, and I can ask her directly."

I wasn't sure it mattered at this point, but I said, "My gut says that she's not the type to either hire a hitman or kill one."

A gurney rolled past the kitchen door with a body bag on it. Mr. Sansone's last trip. Hopefully, the swarm of crime scene people would leave as well.

I provided Wanda with Margo's contact information. I hoped that she could straighten this whole thing out. The police had falsely accused me of murder at least twice in my life, and I knew it was a horrible place to be. And, since the body was found in my apartment, I couldn't be too careful even with an ironclad alibi.

"We're nearly done here for now," Wanda said and Detective Connelly dutifully turned off the tape recorder and stood up. "This is still a crime scene so you're going to have to find some place to stay for a few days."

"How fortunate for me I haven't unpacked from my trip yet. Now all I need is a someplace to go," I said.

"What about your upstairs neighbor?"

"She's at work. I suppose I could ask her when she gets home." I felt fidgety. Maybe I ought to let Jason know what was going on. Then again, maybe not. With my history, another murder attached to my name might scare him completely away. I needed some time to think and sort things out.

I pulled out my phone as I considered who I might call. My news feed flashed a bulletin. I clicked on it and waited while a video downloaded and then watched and listened in stunned silence.

"A prominent businessman from Long Beach, Malcolm Wilson, who had been reported missing by his wife two days ago, has been found dead, shot in the head. His body was discovered under a lifeguard chair on Hermosa Beach, in an enclosed storage container. We have been unable to reach his widow, a local philanthropist named Margo Prentice, for a comment."

I had no idea that the detective had been watching as she stood behind me. "You have got to be kidding me," she muttered under her breath.

This situation was going from bad to worse. Wanda chose her words carefully. "Miranda, did you know about any of this?"

I shook my head. "No, I didn't even know who her husband was. She did mention that they were going through a divorce but didn't go into much detail."

She stared directly into my eyes. "Do not contact this woman. Leave this up to us. Do you hear me?" She continued, "And just so we're clear, if she contacts you, you will let me know immediately, right?"

I smiled, even though I felt like she was treating me like a three-year-old. "Right. I will contact you immediately."

She studied me long enough to make me squirm. "We will be in and out of here for the next couple of days. Have you considered where you can stay?"

I nodded, "Right now, I'm hungry and tired. I've got a headache. Is it all right if I sit on the front porch until I figure it out?"

"Sure."

She and Connelly left soon after that. I sat on the front porch flipping through all the newsfeeds on my phone, trying to pick up as much information about the Malcolm Wilson shooting as possible, but they were all reporting the same thing. The media, though, appeared to be camped outside Margo's impressive house in Long Beach, hoping to pounce on her if she showed her face. I felt sorry for her, whether she was guilty or not. Feeling trapped in your own home was a horrible feeling. Part of me wanted to call her to get her side of the story, but I couldn't afford to have a record of a call to her on my cell phone.

Just as I decided I probably ought to go get something to eat and find a place to say, Patricia showed up from around the corner. I double-checked my phone and saw it was already five-thirty. No wonder I felt famished.

"What's all that?" she said, looking at the crime scene tape crisscrossing my front door.

I turned her around and headed her upstairs. She just looked at me but didn't resist. "We need to go up to your apartment. I'll explain there."

She looked at me like I was crazy, "I can hardly wait to hear what this is all about," she said as I followed her up the stairs.

I briefly changed the subject. "While you've been happily ensconced in your posh job all day, I've been downstairs engaged with the police."

She stretched her arms and yawned. "I wasn't at work. My parents came for a surprise visit, and I got to bed way later than expected. I called Susan this morning, and she was fine with me taking the day off." She then did a double take. "Wait a minute. You what?"

Patricia stretched out on the couch, yawning. She still appeared oblivious to what had been going on right under her apartment for the last several hours. "Do you want some coffee?"

She had a full pot, and I poured her and me a cup and sat on her love seat. "I have to say, it's been an interesting day."

She yawned again. "So I expect you'll tell me all about it."

She amazed me sometimes. "Are you trying to tell me you didn't see an ambulance with a crew, the police, and the medical examiner coming into my apartment?"

She sat up. "What? No. I slept in the back room last night because my parents used my room. I can't see or hear anything from back there. They left at some ungodly hour this morning and I've been shlepping around all day drinking coffee and watching TV. What happened?"

She could be so oblivious. "Well, first of all, I came home from my weekend with Jason, which was awesome, by the way."

She brightened, "You'll have to tell me all about it."

I longed for the peace I felt at his parent's house right now. "I will definitely give you all the details. I really enjoyed myself. But, anyway, when I got back early this morning, I found a body in my bathroom."

Patricia gasped in horror, "Oh my god! That must have been horrible. What kind of body?"

"A man. It was someone I recognized, a guy that Margo met with when she was here."

Her face twisted in confusion. "Well, that makes no sense. Margo lives hours from here, and although I've never met her, I can't imagine a friend of yours being involved in foul play."

I explained, "I don't know what to think. Nothing else really makes sense."

She smiled. "Well, at least you have an alibi. I'm not sure that'll be enough to keep the internet trolls from reviving your Princess of Death title."

I closed my eyes. "Oh my god, I hadn't even thought about that with all the excitement I've had so far today. I'm sure they'll figure it out. And probably the press will follow their trail. I may have another unplanned news conference in my future." I sat down next to her. "So, anyway, I called Detective Marshall and went through the typical questioning and everything that happens when a dead body is found. I'm getting way too used to the process if you ask me."

She touched my arm. "All kidding aside, I can't even imagine. I would have totally freaked out."

I confessed, "Well, to be honest, I had a bit of a panic attack and had to recover before I called the detective."

She bit her lip. "How did the detective react? I got the impression that she can be tough."

I thought back. "Considering there was another dead body in my vicinity, she wasn't bad. Turns out, though, that this guy is on the FBI's most-wanted list. She knew him by sight. He was, evidently, an infamous hitman."

Patricia considered this new information. "So, why was …? Oh, my God."

It was just starting to sink in for me. "It gets worse. I just saw on the news that Margo's husband was found dead in Hermosa Beach. Shot in the head."

Patricia responded, "That seems kind of crazy, though, when you think about it. Why would Margo kill the hitman she hired to kill her husband when he was probably the least likely to be caught if he's on the FBI's most wanted list. They only get on there if the police are having trouble finding them. It seems like she would only have killed him if she was afraid of being implicated by him. Something is missing here."

Something struck me odd about her comment. I brushed the thought aside and attributed it to my exhaustion. "I agree. I don't have a clue."

She patted my arm. "To be honest, this Margo didn't need to involve you in this. I hate to say it, but it seems like she set you up."

I guess deep inside, it occurred to me, but I hadn't allowed the thought to take control. "I know you're right, Patricia. I've been trying to come up with another explanation, but I haven't been able to."

I spent the rest of the day trying to develop a scenario that didn't implicate Margo, but I failed.

Chapter 13

When I awoke on Tuesday in Patricia's guest room, I was disoriented but rested. I went down and snuck under the yellow tape and into my apartment. The place was a mess with fingerprint powder all over everything, drawers pulled open, and to-go coffee cups scattered on the counters and coffee table. I turned on the TV as I got ready for work, expecting to see Margo's arrest on the news but saw nothing. I became obsessed at work, checking the internet every hour or two to see if there was an update.

Toward the end of the day, Tea stopped by my workstation, "Are you all right, Hon? You seem really preoccupied today. Did everything go all right on your trip back to the big boss' hometown?"

I smiled for the first time since I got to the office. "The trip was great. I really enjoyed it. But since I got back, nothing has gone right. I haven't had a second to think about Jason." I shifted gears, needing to tell her about the business at home before she saw it on the internet or heard it on the news "You remember last year when the internet and the press were all over me because my upstairs neighbor killed her roommate, but they thought I was involved anyway?"

She nodded, "Uh-huh."

I took a deep breath. I wasn't all that sure I wanted to share, but I figured it would get out anyway. "I found a dead body in my apartment."

She stared at me like I was an alien. "Wow. You're starting to scare me with this death thing. Did you know this one?"

I was surprised by how little empathy she had for me, but she was young. "I didn't know him but had seen him once. It's a long story."

She seemed to realize that she wasn't being as supportive as she could be. "I'm sorry, Miranda. I know it's not your fault that dead people seem to follow you around. It can't be easy for you."

Tea grabbed her bag, ready to head out the door. I figured I'd go out with her since I was utterly distracted and never would catch up from my days off. "Hey, I'll walk out with you," I said as I shut and locked the customer service door behind me.

She laughed, "Well, look at you, leaving at five. Is that how it's going to be now that you've snagged the boss?"

I punched her on the arm. "Very funny."

She giggled as she got in her car and yelled out the window on her way out of the parking lot, "Have a great evening."

I waved and headed to my Rover, wishing I were as carefree as a twenty-something. As I drove home, I realized what I needed to do. I needed to call Margo, even though the detective had warned me not to. I just wanted to gauge her reaction to the news that the man she had met with had turned up dead in my apartment and to offer my condolences on the untimely death of her husband.

It would have been ideal to get that reaction in person, but I wasn't up for a six-hour drive when I wasn't even sure she would be home or available. I pulled up in front of my house and was surprised to see the crime scene tape removed from my front door. I went inside and punched her number into my phone, holding my breath until she answered.

"Margo Prentice."

I exhaled and starting talking faster than I had intended. "Margo, it's Miranda. How are you? I heard that someone killed your husband. Are you okay? I almost drove down there, but I figured you'd have your hands full. I—"

She interrupted. "Whoa, girl. At least give me a chance to respond. I'm doing okay. I've been talking to the police almost non-stop since they found him. What a horrible thing. Why would someone shoot Malcolm and hide his body at the beach? I don't understand what's going on with the world today."

I wasn't sure how to broach the next subject, so I jumped right in. "There's been a lot happening here too. I found a body in my apartment when I came back from a weekend trip with my boyfriend."

She gasped. "Oh my God, Miranda. Are you all right? Did you know the person? Are you a suspect? I mean, it's your apartment, so I'd have to guess you are."

I hesitated, but I was in too deep now not to spill my guts. "Well, actually, you know him or knew him. It was the guy you met with when you were staying with me."

She gasped. "Oh, my God. Tony's dead? How did I miss that? It must have been all over the news. I guess I've been a little distracted with Malcolm's disappearance and his, God bless his soul, untimely death. At least Malcolm was able to avoid that heartache. Tony Sansone has been his best friend since childhood."

This turn of events was stranger than fiction, and I was struggling to process it. "So you were meeting with Tony, to—"

She completed my sentence, "Convince Malcolm to give me a divorce." There was a long silence. She was putting two and two together about my call. "You thought I killed Tony, didn't you?"

I still wasn't convinced that she hadn't, but I figured I'd play along. "Well, it was looking pretty bad. You meet with a hitman, and suddenly your husband's body turns up just days after the meeting. Then the hitman winds up dead near where you met him. It does look a little suspicious."

"Hitman? What are you talking about? He's Malcolm's closest friend. Where'd you ever get the idea he's a hitman?"

"The police told me."

Margo chuckled, which I couldn't help but feel was somewhat inappropriate under the circumstances. "That's just crazy. They have to have him confused with someone else. As for me killing him, well, I can't say that I wouldn't be flattered under different circumstances, but I'm not quite as ruthless as I used to be."

I hesitated to say this, but I wasn't sure Margo and I would ever speak again. "I have to say you don't sound too broken up about all of this."

She responded with an undertone of humor in her voice. "Miranda, it was no secret Malcolm and I had our differences. Why he adored me so, I'll never understand. There's a particular personality of man who craves you, even more, when he knows you want nothing to do with him. Take it from me. These men are worth their weight in gold during a divorce. As for Tony, I only met him a couple of times and honestly didn't know him very well."

Since she had opened up this topic, I was intrigued. "You *were* planning on divorcing him, right?"

"Oh, yes, and the negotiation was going pretty well. But, admittedly not as well as it turns out. Now that Malcolm's dead, I get everything. Kinda sad, isn't it?"

Even with her blunt nature, the callousness of the statement surprised me. "So, aren't you going to be the prime suspect?"

She seemed more bored than concerned. "I suppose so, but I'll have a rock-solid alibi. He also had more enemies than you can count on two hands, so they won't ever be able to pin this on me."

I could never tell when this woman was serious or if she ever was. "So, you're saying you didn't hire Tony to kill Malcolm and then kill Tony when you thought he might spill the beans to the police?"

Margo was probably one of the only people I had ever met who wouldn't be offended by that question. "Oh, God, no! I went to your place to meet with him as a desperate measure before spending a fortune on legal fees. I figured Tony could convince him to do the right thing in the divorce."

I knew I was reaching, but if I thought of these things, indeed, Wanda would too. "And you're sure that was your intention and Tony misunderstood and killed him? After all, that's evidently what he's good at."

I heard a doorbell ring in the background. "Hey Miranda, I've gotta run. Let's get together soon, okay?"

I said, "Okay," and she said a rushed, "Goodbye," and she was gone.

I had no idea what to make of that conversation. Margo was either telling the truth or she was an excellent liar. I wished I had had her right in front of me, but there was nothing in her voice that told me she was lying.

After cleaning my apartment, I collapsed on the couch still confused and exhausted by events of the last couple of days. I figured I'd have to tell Wanda at some point that I had called Margo, but not if I could avoid it. I spent the next couple of hours on my laptop, aimlessly reading the regional news. It was nearly 10:15 when a new story flashed across my screen.

"Long Beach heiress charged with her husband's murder."

#

111

My stress level was growing as I came to terms with the implications of Margo's arrest. I needed to get a different perspective.

I called Jason. He answered on the first ring. "Hey, darlin', what's up?"

My heart jumped unexpectedly when he called me 'darlin.' "Oh, you made my heart gush there."

He whispered, "There's plenty more where that came from." He realized how rare it was for me to call him, especially at eleven o'clock at night. "Hey, is everything okay? You're usually in bed way before now."

I hoped he'd be on board with my plan. "Well, my life's been in a bit of turmoil since I found that dead body in the apartment after you dropped me off."

He cleared his throat. "I'm sure it has. I do wish that you'd told me about it before I heard it on the news."

He was right. I wasn't quite used to having a significant other yet. "Yeah, I'm sorry about that." I didn't want to dwell there, knowing I had hurt his feelings. "Do you think you could get Diane to fill in for me? I really need to get home and spend some time with my family. There are some things I need to put into perspective."

He sounded worried. "Yeah, sure, I'll see if she's available. Are you sure you're okay? This doesn't have anything to do with you and me, does it?"

It touched my heart that he cared. "Absolutely not. You and I are fine. I had a great weekend."

I could tell he was smiling. "I did too. Who knew you loved Lucille Ball that much?"

I got serious. "I just need to get home to see my mom. The last I heard, her cancer was in remission, but I've been a terrible daughter lately. Also, my sister Sabine is always able to provide insight into my issues. The bottom line, I want to take a little time for myself while I still have a reasonable anxiety level. My therapist suggested that I tend to let things spiral out of control before I ask for help, so I'm trying to change that."

He spoke in soothing tones. "Take as much time as you need. If Diane can't come in, I'll have Pho fill in. He'll hate it, but he'll do it for you."

I laughed, "Yes, I can already see the expression on his face when you tell him. He tries to be tough, but he's a real pushover."

We were wrapping up. "Let me know, Sweet Girl, if you need anything. You know I'm here for you, right? I wish I could do more to help."

I felt like I wasn't being a very good girlfriend right now, but I had to go with my gut on this one. "Yes, I do, and I really appreciate it." I should have added something like Honey or Sweetie. It would take time to get used to these little endearments.

He seemed to understand. "I just want you to do what you need to do. Don't worry about the company or me; we'll be fine. How long do you think you'll need?"

I hadn't really thought about it. "I think, at most, the rest of the week." I was feeling optimistic about going home and getting a new perspective. "Thanks, Sweetheart. I appreciate it. You're the best." There, I'd done it and it felt right.

He responded, "Seriously, though, Baby doll, take care of yourself and let me know if there's anything else I can do. I'll miss you."

I smiled at how concerned he sounded, but Baby doll? I cringed a little. "I'll miss you too. I'll keep you posted on how it's going. Talk to you later."

We hung up.

Chapter 14

My plane landed at Louis Armstrong New Orleans International Airport just before noon on Wednesday morning. I texted my mom that I had arrived but she was already waiting for me outside the baggage claim area.

Mom jumped out of the car and ran to meet me as I emerged from the airport exit. We hugged for what felt like ten minutes. It was lucky that she ran to me because I barely would have recognized her with her short hair with bangs hanging almost into her eyes. She was pushing sixty but looked at most, forty. Her eyes were on fire with excitement and life. This was the mom I had always longed for during my troubled teen years.

I held her at arm's length. "Just who are you, and what have you done with my mom?" I giggled.

She gushed, "Oh, Miranda, I'm so happy to be alive and to have family to spend my life with. I decided I needed a new look to remind myself and others that I'm not the same miserable woman I used to be."

We talked all the way to the house, like best friends, with none of the guilt she used to heap on me every time I came to visit. I had noticed changes in my mom on my last couple of visits since she was diagnosed with breast cancer, but she had completed a transformation since I last visited. The outfit she wore today was filled with bright colors and fitted to accentuate her curves rather than hide them.

When we pulled into the driveway at the house in Meraux, I couldn't believe my eyes; milling around in the small front yard were my stepdad Tom, my sister Sabine, her fiancé Mark, and my brother Michael. They held a sign, spelling out: "Welcome home, Miranda!"

I jumped out of the car and hugged each one of them. As usual, it had been too long since I'd been home.

After our hugs and hellos, I addressed the group. "I figured rather than handling my life like I usually do, where you hear about me on the news before you hear what's going on from me, I just thought I'd change it up."

They all stared at me with anticipation. I suddenly felt self-conscious and exposed. "Let's go in the house."

We all filed into the kitchen, which was the natural communication area, even though the living room was far bigger. Mom and Tom sat on their stools at the island. Michael stood by the kitchen counter, and Sabine and Mark sat at the kitchen table. I joined them at the table.

I wasn't quite sure where to start since I hadn't spoken to them in a while. I spoke briefly to Mom on the phone the Sunday before I went back to meet Jason's family, so I figured that was an excellent place to start.

"I'm not sure how much each of you knows, so if I'm repeating something you already know, bear with me. Wait, you all know that I'm living in Santa Clara now and everything that happened leading to that, right?"

Michael said, "I'd like to hear that part of the story because everything we know about it is from the news, but we can talk about that later."

I nodded to Michael, acknowledging that we needed to catch up. "Okay, we'll talk about that later." I once again spoke to the whole group. "Last weekend, I went to Jamestown, New York, with my boyfriend Jason to meet his family. And before you ask, yes, we're becoming serious."

My mother beamed. "We can't wait to meet him."

I smiled at her. "He wanted to come this time, but I thought that might be too much. Besides, if he and I both took the week off, I'm not sure the company would still be there when we got back."

I continued, describing everything that had happened from when I got home to my apartment, found the body, called the police, talked to Margo about it all, and got her explanation.

Michael asked, "Who's Margo?"

I took a moment to explain.

My mom gasped. "Miranda, how do you get into these messes? No wonder they call you the Queen of Murder."

I corrected her, "Princess of Death." I couldn't believe that I apparently had accepted the title. "Believe me; I have no idea how I get into these messes but they just keep on coming. So, knowing that Margo was on the police's radar, I expected her to be arrested for murdering the man I found in my apartment. So, yesterday, the police arrested her for murder. Not for his death but for the death of her estranged husband."

Listening to what I was saying, it was hard to believe. "So, we have two dead men, a friend of mine arrested, and the whole thing ties back to me since one of the two dead men was found in my apartment. Thank God, I have a rock-solid alibi, or I would probably be arrested for that one." I almost had to laugh. It was so absurd.

Mark, ever the lawyer, piped in. "These days, I'm not even sure your alibi would do you any good if they had DNA evidence or suspected that you used a hitman to kill the hitman."

Sabine glared at him and spoke for the first time since I arrived. "Perhaps, we should try to look at this more positively. Miranda has reached out to the ones who love her before everything gets out of control. That's a great first step. She clearly realizes that she shouldn't try to take everything on alone like she's tended to in the past."

I wanted to say, "I'm standing right here, right?" But I knew she had a point to make.

Sabine continued, looking directly at me. "Miranda, we are here to support you in any way you need us. Your mom and I have put behind our differences and make quite a formidable team. In fact, she and I raised more than $2500 recently for a breast cancer fundraiser."

My mom hugged Sabine. "By the way, if I haven't said it before, thank you so much for everything you did. I'm afraid you raised a lot more than I did."

Sabine laughed, "Well, some rich people owed me favors, so why not cash them in?" She then turned to Michael. "Mark and I met with Michael yesterday to discuss how he could help you right now. He's got some army buddies in your vicinity who could be instrumental if you need protection of any sort."

I was impressed by how my family had mobilized on my behalf. I responded, "Wow! I really appreciate everything you guys are doing, but right now, I need you to think as if you aren't my family. I know that I'm too close to this situation, and there might be some obvious clues that I'm missing. And before the cops decide that I'm a prime suspect, I was hoping that you guys could provide some alternatives to feed to Detective Marshall."

Mom interrupted. "But you came to us because we're your family? What did I miss here?"

"I didn't mean it that way. I mean that I'd like you to be objective for me."

Mark had been quiet to this point but had been formulating some questions. "So, Miranda, who out there has access to your apartment? Who else has a key?"

This was precisely why I was here. I hadn't been able to formulate the most straightforward and obvious questions. I thought for a second. "Well, my landlady has a key, of course. I gave Patricia one since she lives upstairs. I'm pretty sure I never gave Sarah upstairs one before she moved out. Otherwise, I have no way of knowing who might have one if the landlady didn't change the locks whenever she rented it. It was student housing for many years, so the apartment probably had dozens of tenants."

Mark inquired, as any good attorney would do, "And you trust this Patricia?"

I nodded. "With my life."

Mark responded, "God, I hate to say it, Miranda, but you said the same thing about Heather."

Sabine glared at him.

I responded curtly, "Thanks for pointing that out, Mark." Sometimes, he could be a real jerk.

Mark continued, "Would it have been possible for Margo to have stolen a key or had one made while she was visiting you?"

"The detectives already asked me that and the answer is that it's possible but not likely. We went to bed late after drinking a lot of wine and I doubt she woke up in the middle of the night to look a twenty-four-hour hardware store."

I thought for a minute, deciding to move on and not hold a grudge. "I do have a spare key in a cup on the kitchen counter."

"So virtually anyone who visited you may have known about the extra key?"

"It was just mixed in with a bunch of keys in a cup. There was no reason for Margo to even look in there."

He continued on his *lawyerly* questioning. "Can you provide a list of everyone who has been in your apartment over the past six months?"

I hesitated. "Sure, I guess. I'm not sure what that will get us, but the list is very short. I'm not a real social butterfly now any more than when I was growing up here." I started counting on my fingers, "Here's a list of everyone who's been in my apartment since Sarah upstairs moved out—Margo, Patricia and her parents, Charles and Toni White. Of course, there was John Blake, who abducted Patricia and me. He's dead now, so I'm not sure he counts. Oh, and Jason. I don't suppose he's a suspect but check me if I'm wrong."

He took some notes in a notebook he must have brought with him for this interrogation. "Just how much do you know about Jason?"

I was getting annoyed. "Gee, we've known each other for several years and have been dating on and off for about a year. I don't think he's setting me up. I met his family in upstate New York last weekend. They were all very nice."

Mark chewed on the end of his pen. "He's not a likely suspect, but we need everyone. Someone got into your apartment and killed a man there or killed him elsewhere and carried him to your apartment. Why you? Who would want to pin a murder on you? I know you don't have a history of making a lot of friends, but your enemies seem to multiply."

There were times when I wished somebody could temper Mark's tendency to be brutally honest.

"That's what we're thinking. That he was killed someplace else and dumped in my bathtub. No blood spatter. No mess."

"Who's we?" Mark asked.

"The police and me."

"You're involved in the investigation?"

"No. Just a figure of speech. So, okay, Mark, I get it. I'll never win a popularity contest, but I've gotten a lot better at making friends than I used to be, and I can't think of one enemy

I've made since moving to Santa Clara." That might have been a slight exaggeration, but Mark was fully aware of my tendency to stretch the truth a bit.

Sabine interrupted, "Calm down, *Mon Chere*, just let us help you. That's why you came home, no?" Her French accent was fading with the years, but it made me feel warm inside when she spoke to me in her native language.

Mark waited to make sure Sabine was done, then continued. "Was John Blake alone in your apartment at any time?"

I searched my memory. "Well, yes, he was. I wasn't entirely dressed for company when he showed up at my door, so I left him out there while I changed. Then I lost consciousness and was abducted, pretty much in that order, I think. It's kind of a haze."

He pushed on. "So he could have stolen a key, had copies made and distributed them around to all of his friends, hypothetically."

I pondered his question. "I guess so, there's no evidence to support that."

Mark had already moved on to the next suspect. "You said that Patricia's father's name was Charles White? Is he the up-and-coming gubernatorial candidate in Colorado?

I nodded. "I was surprised, as Patricia had only recently mentioned it, but she never talks much about her parents. They seem very protective of her, but he's also very ambitious and doesn't want anything to sideline his candidacy—"

Mark interrupted. "The word is that he's on a fast track to the presidency which makes sense since he's intelligent, moderate in his political views, and has no black marks against him that anyone knows of. He makes a good appearance on television. He's not a life-long politician, which, these days, is what the public seems to be looking for."

I said, "I would have to put him low on the list of suspects since he needs to keep his record clean; besides what motive could he possibly have?"

Mark continued chewing on his pen. "Well, we do know that he's very protective of Patricia. What if this Tony Sansone could be tied somehow to John Blake and his partner? What are they being called now, the Surfing Brothers? Since they were the prime suspects in your and Patricia's abduction, if Charles somehow found out that Tony Sansone was behind it, could he have killed him?"

I laughed. "You definitely have a vivid imagination. And besides, it's the Surf Brothers."

He smiled. "I suppose you're right. I'm just not ready to cross him off the list of suspects right now."

I agreed. "I'm not ready to cross anyone off the list quite yet, but there's no obvious candidate either. Patricia has a key to the apartment. She stayed with me for a couple of days before she moved upstairs. Patricia is my best friend in the world, but she also has a record of falling for the wrong men, like Larry, the father of her child and convicted killer of our teammate, Tara. I don't even want to consider this, but what if she was, somehow, mixed up with this Tony Sansone character? Had she killed him, my apartment would be the perfect place to leave the body. She had access and opportunity. If we can come up with a motive, she'd be the most solid suspect. Again, if we can tie Sansone to John Blake, we might come up with the missing motive."

Mark scribbled some notes. "Hey, Miranda, Sansone was fully clothed in the bathtub, right?"

I responded, "Yeah."

He continued, "Seems to me that he would have to have been killed by someone pretty strong and carried to your bathtub after the fact. Doesn't sound like a woman to me."

121

The rest of the family listened while we evaluated suspects. I wondered what they thought about all this. "Michael, being that you have no background at all in this case, who sounds like the best suspect to you?"

He smiled at my recognition that his opinion mattered. "Based on what I've heard, I'd have to go with Margo. She's the only one, at least at this point, that you can tie to Sansone. She's a suspect in her husband's murder, and she may have been involved in the deaths of several of her other ex-husbands. If I were the DA, I'd go with her. With Tony Sansone dead, it'll be even more difficult to tie any of the other suspects to him without some other solid evidence. But, also, based on your comments, I'd have to agree, it's not something I picture a woman doing."

Tom spoke up for the first time. "I don't know why, but I'm leaning toward Charles White. When it comes to politicians, who knows what's going on behind the scenes, and if he had presidential aspirations, he may consider his actions justified based on his greater goal of leading the country."

My mom laughed. "Leave it to Tom to pick the politician. He's never gotten over losing that election for Parish Council. He believes all politicians are crooked, and all elections are rigged." She poked him in the side and then kissed him. I loved seeing my mom so happy.

Sabine had a thoughtful look on her face, so I wanted to make sure we heard her. "Sabine, what do you think? You've got a pretty good head for this stuff."

She smiled. "*Merci mon amour*, I know I haven't met Patricia, and I know you two have become very close. But when I think back about her lack of judgment when she hooked up with that psycho-killer and how poorly she treated you during that time; it's hard for me to completely rule her out. You even said that you thought she still had a soft spot for John Blake, even after he tormented her in Denver, followed her to California, abducted her, and left you two tied up in a deserted warehouse. What if she'd been working with Blake and Sansone killed him, and she found out about it, so she killed him? Perhaps she hired someone to help her?"

I had a hard time imagining the Patricia I knew now being involved in this, but I had to admit if I thought back to our Extreme Team days, there wasn't much I wouldn't put past her. I responded to Sabine, "My gut and my heart says 'No,' but my head agrees that Patricia is probably capable of just about anything." I looked at the group to see if anyone had anything else. "Is there anything or anyone that we might have missed?"

Mark responded, "Well, the toughest suspects to identify are the ones we don't even know about yet. It's always possible that there's someone else that's not on the list."

I agreed. "I guess we'll have to rely on Detective Marshall and the rest of the Santa Clara Police Department or the FBI to come up with those. They have access to a lot more sophisticated databases than we do. But thanks to everyone for your input; it gives me lots to think about."

I addressed Mark individually, "Mark, I know that you're busy here, but I may need you, depending on what happens from here. I can't imagine I would be a serious suspect with my rock-solid alibi, but stranger things have happened. If Patricia is implicated, I imagine that her parents already have a defense attorney lined up."

Eventually, we migrated to other topics, such as Mom's health, when Mark and Sabine were getting married, whether Michael was going to propose to his latest girlfriend, who he had been dating for several years.

My mom served dinner around six, and it felt like old times. I was so thankful to have family and wondered why I resisted coming home. My latest therapist had been working on the topic of family for more than a year, and it was probably her input that helped me decide to come home this time.

After dinner, Sabine took my hand and led me to the back yard where we could have some alone time. I missed her so much. Although we had different mothers, we shared the same father and she had always been the perfect mix of sister and mentor. "So *mon gamin,* why have we not seen you more after you promised you'd be a part of this family again."

I felt twelve again as Sabine had a way of making me feel. "I am not a brat! I'm a woman who has to work for a living too. My days of just watching the money roll in are over but I can't complain. I love my job, even though it doesn't leave me much time for anything else. And my work is like a family, too. I have some great friends there, not to mention Jason." I reddened a little at the mention of his name.

She took my hand. "I can tell that you like him very much. But do you love him?"

I stared up at the moon. "I think I do, but we are taking it slow and he seems fine with that."

She smiled. "I'm very pleased that you've found somebody special."

We hugged. "I'm going to bring him home soon. I'd love to get your opinion."

She nodded. "And I'd love to give it." Sabine shifted gears. "You're going to be here a few days, right?"

I responded, "Yes. I told Jason not to expect me for the rest of the week. I'll go back on Saturday or Sunday."

She held me at arm's length. "Well, why don't you stay with me at least one overnight, okay?"

I pulled her close again. "Yes, I'd love to. How about tomorrow night?"

We hugged before we ventured back to the house. She smiled. "Yes, tomorrow night would be perfect."

I was glad tomorrow worked because I knew my mom would want me to stay here tonight. Since high school, she had left my room untouched, which was a combination of comforting and kind of creepy.

After Sabine and I went back inside the house, the gathering was breaking up. Mark had an early day, and Michael had a date with his girlfriend. I never knew how he could burn the candle so effectively at both ends and still function. Sabine and I made plans for me to head to her house tomorrow evening.

Mom and Tom were seated in their traditional spots at the kitchen counter, whispering to one another. It did my heart good to see how much in love they were after my parents' disastrous marriage. After a cup of decaf and a goodnight hug with Mom and Tom, I headed upstairs to relive my past in my childhood bedroom once again.

I stretched out on my old single bed, the one I slept in since I was a toddler. Until I left home. Home hadn't always felt like the most welcoming place to me, but it was starting to more and more.

Chapter 15

I slept until nearly ten and took a luxurious shower, testing the hot water heater's capacity. I slipped down the stairs in jean shorts and a Bon Jovi t-shirt. As if they hadn't moved since I went to bed, Mom and Tom were seated on their counter stools.

My mom gushed, "It's so much fun to have you home! What would you like for breakfast?"

There were already waffles and bacon on the counter, which was fine with me as long as there was coffee.

Tom smiled, "That's a nice change. Usually, I work my fingers to the bone; you have coffee and slip out the door before we have time to catch up."

I still hadn't quite gotten used to Tom having an opinion about anything because he had deferred to my mom for so long, but I was starting to like it. "Well, Tom, I'm here and not going anywhere. And now that Mark is with Sabine, I don't even have anyone to slip off with," I said, referencing my visit of several years ago. "I'll be happy if nothing on this trip turns out as that one did. Being arrested for murder was not the high point of my life, even if I was eventually acquitted."

Mom took the opportunity to change the subject. "Let's not talk about the past. What about this Jason fellow? It's been a long time since you've been with anyone. Is it serious? I'd love to see you happy, sweetheart."

I smiled, feeling so much more comfortable discussing the topic of my love life with my mom than I used to. "He's a nice guy. We have a lot in common. He treats me well and we enjoy spending time together."

Mom seemed so much more grounded these days. "That's all you can ask in a new relationship. I'm happy you're putting yourself back out there. It seemed like you had given up for a while."

I confessed, "You're right. I had. It didn't seem worth it, meeting the same kind of men I couldn't stand. Ironically, it wasn't until I lost my company, my house, and my money that I finally was able to find someone who wanted to be with me for me, not what I could add to their portfolio."

We had a great breakfast, talking about whatever came into our heads. I let my mom know I would be staying with Sabine overnight, and she responded, "That's so nice that you two can still do sisterly things. I want you to have as much fun as you can while you're here."

I briefly stared at her in disbelief, because two years ago, this would have turned into a major fight, that I wasn't spending enough time with my mom and Tom, and how could I spend so much time with *that woman,* which was how my mom had referred to Sabine most of the time. How things had changed gave me hope that humanity was finally on the right track, and my family was healing. I walked over, hugged her, and said into her shoulder, "Thanks, Mom."

She asked, "What for?" And then she winked.

I smiled. "I think you know."

I had pleaded with her to give Sabine another chance even though I was never entirely sure what their problem was. Possibly, they were too much alike.

We finally let go of our embrace. My mom sounded unsure when she asked, "So, Miranda, it's okay if you don't want to talk about it, but I'd like to hear what happened to your business and how you ended up in Santa Clara. I've gotten bits and pieces from our phone conversations, and Mark has shared a few details, but I'd really like to hear it from you."

I hadn't seen my mom in person since the government shut my business down, and I had relocated to Santa Clara. We had talked a lot on the phone, but she wasn't one to pry about details unless I was ready to speak about it. I finally felt healed enough to spill my guts.

I exhaled loudly, clearing my lungs and my mind. "Just a little background, the government, namely the Centers for Medicare and Medicaid, had been asking for information from me about the company and our provider contracts for more than a year, dating back to when I was out here to help Sabine with her shrimp case. Heather and I provided them with everything they asked for. Well, as far as I knew at the time. I put all my trust and faith in Heather, and she completely let me down."

My mom gasped. "Really? I know you thought the world of her."

I chuckled. "Well, yes, I did, until it turned out that she was using me, stole money from me, and disappeared from the face of the earth. But either way, somehow, it came to the federal government's attention that I was making money through commissions paid by providers out of Medicare funds. That is illegal. I didn't know it at the time, and when I started the company, ninety-nine percent of the surgery provided by my network was cosmetic, usually breast enlargement. But when Medicare began paying for reconstructive surgery following a mastectomy, that's when I inadvertently got in trouble."

It felt good to be able to talk about it without getting choked up. That had taken a while. "Bottom line, I could have ended up losing everything and spending many years in prison. So when they offered me a deal that I could afford to pay with a guarantee of no jail time, I jumped on it. To this day, Mark believes that he would have gotten me a better deal, but I was just happy that it was over. I was relieved to be done with the company, believe it or not. I didn't feel like I worked hard enough to make the kind of money I was making. I know that sounds odd, but it's true."

Both Mom and Tom were glued to their seats. Tom said, "So, how did you end up in Santa Clara?"

I continued, "During the peak of my First Extreme All-Girl Sports Team days when we were competing in the street luge finals in San Francisco, I met Jason. He was playing at the bar in my hotel. We hit it off immediately, and he told me he worked for a small power systems manufacturing company, and to call him if I ever needed a job. We both thought it was a joke at the time, considering that I was worth millions and living in Malibu, but God has a way of laughing when you make plans.

"So when it all fell apart, I gave him a call, and the rest is history. I actually love what I do. I'm respected in the company, work hard, and sleep well at night. I'm not sure I'll work there forever, but it's working right now. My dream is to run a catering company. My co-worker, Tea, and I have been talking about that for a while, and maybe, someday, we'll make it happen."

I smiled broadly, glad that I'd finished my presentation. "Bottom line, I'm happy, self-sufficient, and looking forward to the future. What more could a girl ask for?"

Judging from the looks on their faces, I thought they might both have questions, but if they did, they kept them to themselves.

My mom said, "As long as you are happy, we are. Now, if you could just figure out how to keep yourself away from murder, we'll all be happier. I don't know how it is that you seem to attract death."

I thought for a minute but didn't have an answer. "Just lucky, I guess." I crossed my eyes.

They laughed. I knew they worried about me, which made me feel good.

We moved back to other less controversial topics. By mid-afternoon, our tongues were tired, and it was nearly time to get ready to go to Sabine's. I wasn't sure how I would maintain my half of the conversation once I got over there, but I suspected that a couple of bottles of wine might help.

By the time I walked over to Sabine's house, which was just a couple of blocks away, my head was spinning with the with everything we talked about all afternoon. It felt good, though, to have shared my experiences and cleared the air about how I got to where I was today. I think they may have speculated that perhaps I had knowingly defrauded the government, which couldn't have been further from the truth.

I didn't bother to knock when I got to Sabine's, and she was vacuuming the living room when I found her. She jumped a mile when she turned to see me standing there. "*Oh mon Dieu,* you scared me to death!"

She dropped the portable Dyson and ran over to me, and we shared a heavenly hug. After all was said and done, Sabine was my favorite person in the world. We didn't talk nearly as much as my mom and I did, but she was far more in tune with me and how I was faring in the world.

She held me at arm's length. "*Tu m'as manque,*" she scolded.

I smiled at her attempt to test my French recall. "I missed you too, my sweet sister."

She kissed me on both cheeks. "*Je t'aime, ma belle!*"

I was excited to see a bottle of *Chateau Pape Clement* Red on the coffee table, open and breathing. Despite my preference for California Cabernets, she preferred the French version. I was impressed, knowing this particular vintage ran in the $300 range for a bottle.

I laughed. "I remember when I could afford a bottle of that."

She 'tsked' me. "Now, we both know what kind of wine you can afford doesn't mean anything. I just wanted to serve my favorite and only sister the best."

I felt warm and safe whenever I was one on one with Sabine. I knew she cared about me as much as I cared about her. I said, "I'm so happy we could have some time together. You were uncharacteristically quiet last night at Mom's."

She touched my arm. "I knew I'd get you alone to get the real story. Besides, Mark had to do that lawyer thing he does to make himself look important." She looked me straight in the eye. "Now, *ma belle*, I want the whole truth and nothing but the truth. First, how are you *really* doing with everything you lost? And don't give me the company line or the public version you've made up to make everyone think you are okay."

Sabine had a way of squeezing the plain and often ugly truth out of me. Sometimes I didn't even know I was lying to myself until she interrogated me. I hoped this wasn't one of those times. I met her gaze. "You know, Sabine, I was proud of what I had put together and the money and things I had accumulated, but I was a stranger in a strange land. I didn't relate to my neighbors or my potential suitors. I'm a simple southern gal, and I was never meant to be rich. The fact was that I spent so much time feeling guilty about my success; I didn't have time to enjoy it."

She held my gaze as if she were penetrating my brain, searching for the smallest lie. Then she smiled. "You're are still my girl after all these years. I sometimes feel the same way. Yes, I like the nice things that my life affords me, but I sometimes feel guilty about it too. So, you're really okay?"

I met her smile with mine. "Yes, I'm fine. Yes, there are times I'd love to be out on my deck overlooking the ocean. But the further I get from that time, the more I realize that I can feel just as relaxed sitting on the front porch of my apartment."

Relief showed on her face. "I believe you. But what about this craziness that seems to have followed you to Northern California? I felt so bad for you when I followed that group of nuts, hounding you on the internet. People need to get a life; then, they wouldn't have so much time to worry about yours."

I laughed. "I know. Right? I have to admit I took it personally for a while, but I've put it all in perspective. I'm still awaiting the onslaught when they discover that another body has been found in my vicinity. Maybe the fact that it was someone on the FBI most wanted list, they'll cut me some slack. I've been on the road quite a bit since I discovered the body, so the press could be camped out in my front yard right now for all I know."

Sabine shifted gears, "So tell me about your job. That sounds like quite a change from anything you've done before."

I was proud of my capabilities, and this was the time to let them shine. "Actually, having my own company taught me a lot about how to run things efficiently and how not to. The fact that I could run a multi-million-dollar business with just two people was a tribute to how efficient we operated. Ion Systems, my present employer, is the complete opposite. Their procedures are outdated, their methods are suspect, and their senior management is not very accepting of change of any sort, especially when it involves spending money."

Sabine beamed. "I know who I'm going to use as a management consultant if I ever need one. I'm impressed. I hope they are paying you well because I'm sure they have no idea what your true value is."

I winked. "I have a feeling Jason knows my value, but there's also a lot he doesn't know about me."

Sabine looked at me quizzically. "So, you really are okay, aren't you? I feel a new energy in you that has been missing for years since you moved out west. If I didn't know any better, I'd say you are in love."

I smiled confidently. "Actually, it's even better than that. I might be in love, and I might not be, but I've come to realize that it's not a man that's going to fulfill my life. It's all in here in my head and my heart. I never felt that way in Malibu. I always felt like I had to impress people, to justify living among the rich and arrogant. Now, I couldn't care less about that."

She hugged me again. "That's the Miranda I love with all my heart. I'm so glad you came to visit. I was so worried about you, and now I realize that was totally unnecessary. You are the woman I always knew you would become. You make me so proud."

We ate a perfect dinner featuring shrimp scampi, salad, broccoli, and chocolate mousse. As usual, Sabine never broke a sweat serving and cleaning up after the wonderful meal. Her linen sundress didn't have a stain on it even after washing the dishes. I could never pull that off.

We spent the rest of the evening drinking wine and reminiscing until we went to bed, happy and exhausted.

Chapter 16

When I got back to my apartment on Sunday evening, I felt rested, grounded, and the best I had felt since moving to the Bay area. I wished I could bottle this feeling and remember it every time I thought of traveling home. I got so mired in the day to day; it always seemed too complicated, expensive, or tiring to go back to New Orleans. This trip proved that none of that was true.

A dozen roses on my front porch with a sweet card addressed to 'Darlin' from Jason was the icing on the cake. I guessed that was his new name for me. It was sweet but kind of made me feel like I was in a movie, not a relationship. I needed to talk to my therapist about this. I made a mental note.

After traveling most of the day, there was nothing I looked forward to more than getting cleaned up and having a glass of wine.

I arranged the gorgeous flowers on the kitchen counter. The aroma of fresh roses was heavenly. It had been a long time since I received flowers from a man, especially with no occasion or expectations attached. I swooned at Jason's thoughtfulness despite my mixed emotions about my new nickname.

I dragged my suitcase into my bedroom, hesitating briefly to make sure there were no dead bodies in the bathtub.

I slipped out of my clothes, went into the bathroom, and started running my shower. I was still a little freaked out about using the bathtub. When I was about to step under the water, I caught the full-length mirror on the back of the door out of the corner of my eye. I stopped in my tracks. Written in blood-red lipstick, it read,

Leave the murders alone or die.

My heart started pounding at the combination of the message and the fact that someone had entered my apartment to write it. I held onto the wall and slowed my breathing as I could feel my heartbeat racing, my ears ringing and my vision blurring. Know what would probably come next, I sat on the toilet, leaning back, closing my eyes, and letting the wave of dizziness take over.

\#

After a few moments, I tested my sea legs and found that I could walk with a little assistance from the sink. I glanced up at the mirror, hoping I had dreamed the message, but no such luck. It was still there. I grabbed my phone but only got Wanda's voice mail so I left a brief message.

My mind raced with what to do next. I wrapped a towel around myself and ran into the living room. I grabbed a kitchen chair and wedged it under the front doorknob.

Giving up on the idea of making myself vulnerable by being in the tub, whether showering or bathing, I opted for a quick sponge bath and then dressed in jeans and t-shirt.

I listed in my head the actions I needed to take. First and foremost, I needed to talk to Wanda then get my locks changed. I wasn't sure if that were something the landlady would take care of or if I needed to call a locksmith. I thought I remembered some wording in the lease, but I couldn't remember right now. Not knowing if I was in immediate danger, I debated calling Patricia to see if I could spend the night with her. I'd call her after I spoke to Wanda.

With Patricia's and my captors dead, I had thought I could rest easy. However, whatever trail I was now on was definitely making someone nervous. That meant I was on the right track, even though I wasn't even sure what track that was. The message was clear. "Leave the murders alone." But what murders? There had been four murders. John Blake, David Miller, Tony Sansone, and Malcolm Wilson. Which ones was I being threatened about, and which ones were related?

My phone buzzed. It was Wanda. "Marquette, are you okay?"

"Detective, I've had another break-in. This time they wrote a threatening message on my bathroom mirror while I was away for the weekend.

She responded immediately. "I'll be right over."

While I waited, I realized I needed to call Mark to see what he made of this on top of everything we had discussed relating to Tony's death and who had access to my apartment. Instead, I headed to the kitchen and pulled an open bottle of wine from the fridge and poured a glass, taking it to the living where I reclined on the couch while I waited for Wanda to arrive.

My therapist had suggested that I get more in tune with my feelings because I tended to ignore or avoid them much of the time. I looked within and determined that my overwhelming feeling was anger. I came home feeling great, and whoever had violated my space, and my life had taken away that feeling. It wasn't fair. I hadn't asked to be put in the middle of this mess. I was helping out my friends, Patricia and Margo. It was no wonder my friendships rarely lasted.

I took some deep breaths, attempted to feel more grounded. I transported myself to the beach, my favorite place in the world. In my mind, I watched the seagulls hover over the shallow water, looking for clams and hermit crabs. I listened to waves breaking over the shore again and again.

I was feeling a little calmer by the time the doorbell rang.

There was Wanda at my front door. "Hey, what's up with you and your bathroom?"

I said, "God, I don't know. Maybe whoever it is knows that's the one room where I'm guaranteed to go. It's all so crazy."

She headed toward the bathroom, and I followed. "I'm just going to take some samples from this mirror." She looked at me. "Do you have someplace to stay tonight?"

I yawned, "I was just going to stay here. It's probably too late to call Patricia upstairs."

She shook her head. "Nope. Not happening. There is too much going on here and too many people with access to this apartment. You need to get the locks changed, but until that happens, you're coming home with me."

I looked at her like she had two heads. "What? No. I couldn't possibly put you out like that."

She insisted. "Miranda, you're practically like family; I've seen you so much in the past year. Just throw a sweatshirt on, grab a few things for work tomorrow, and you'll be all set. I'll get a locksmith over here tomorrow."

I said, "Okay," and once again retrieved my still-packed suitcase from my trip.

#

The alarm woke me at 6:30. I normally set it for 7, but I wanted a little extra time to get my bearings this morning. When I came out to the kitchen, she had made pancakes, bacon, coffee, and poured orange juice.

She looked like she had slept twelve hours. "Good morning, Miranda. I made breakfast, help yourself."

I grabbed the coffee she handed me. "Thanks so much, Wanda. I literally don't know what I would do without you."

We spent the next half hour talking about our backgrounds, which were remarkably similar, considering how different we were. Both of our dads had left the household when we were fourteen, and neither of us had fully recovered. That explained a lot.

As I drove to work, I realized my plan to call Mark would have to wait until the workday was over. Mondays were always busy with all the orders that came in over the weekend. Had they mechanized that part of the process, the system could have processed them with no human intervention, but there was no point in wishing for changes that would probably never happen.

I arrived about fifteen minutes early and had already processed ten orders by the time Tea arrived. She was dragging, which was typical of her on Mondays. She and Mike hadn't figured out yet that they weren't in high school anymore, and they had partied big time over the weekend.

She groaned as she came through the door. "Thank God you're back, Miranda. That Diane is *so* boring. She never laughs. I can't even get her to talk to me. The harder I try, the worse it is. Please don't ever leave."

"You got it. I'm not going anywhere. And if I ever do, I'm taking you with me." I thought for a minute. "Hey Tea, I've got a wild idea that keeps coming back to me. Have you ever thought about going into business for yourself?"

She looked at me with questioning eyes. "Sure, plenty of times, but I also come to the same conclusion. I have no idea what I would do. I mean I guess I could do people's taxes or something, but I'd be afraid I'd make a mistake. I'm probably safer here."

I continued, "No, I mean something really wild. How about a catering business? How hard could that be?"

She laughed. "Um, I think it could be pretty hard."

I smiled. "Oh, I don't know. You cook some food and serve it. I'm French, it's in my blood."

"But I don't know how to cook. Maybe you could teach me then I can help you and keep the books and stuff."

I leaned back in my chair and stared at the ceiling. "Oh, it'll happen even if you have to learn how to cook. I'm not staying here forever, even if Jason wants me to. He'd better make sure he appreciates me, or he's going to be in a world of hurt." I laughed. It was good to be back and to have a distraction from the events of last night.

My desk phone rang. It was Jason. "Hey, Darlin', how was your trip?"

I hesitated and said, "The trip itself was fine, *Jason.*"

He laughed and said, "Okay. How was your trip, Miranda?"

I smiled even though he couldn't see me. "Much better. You won't believe what happened when I got home."

"Yes?"

Tea hovered nearby. I said, "The roses are beautiful. Thank you so much."

He seemed to catch that I wasn't free to talk. "Um, Tea's there. Right?"

I realized I was supposed to be working and needed to sound busy. Besides Tea was hovering, listening to every word. "Hey, Jason, I'm going to have to talk to you later, or I'll never get these orders processed."

"Um, do you want to come over later, after work? I'll cook dinner."

It sounded like fun, but I had to deal with my issue at home. "I'm sorry, but can I take a rain check? I've got to get my locks changed and do a few other things around the house. How about tomorrow?"

He seemed satisfied. "Okay, tomorrow it is. See ya." He hung up.

Tea called over from her workspace, "Hey, could you pass over the orders you've already processed? We need to get some work done around here."

It was so nice to be in love, or infatuation, or whatever it was. But nothing was ever simple.

The rest of the day went routinely. As soon as I got home, I called Wanda. She answered briskly. I almost hung up. "Marshall here."

I replied tentatively, "Um, Wanda, this is Miranda."

Her voice softened immediately. "Miranda, how are you?"

I hadn't really thought about what I was going to say. "I wanted to thank you for last night. That was so far above and beyond. I just can't thank you enough."

She hesitated. "I'm just here to serve the community. Any of us would have done the same thing."

I didn't want to embarrass her, and I knew I already had. "Well, I doubt that, but thank you again."

She acknowledged me, "Okay, you're probably right, Miranda, but don't tell anyone that I'm not the hard ass I pretend to be. And just let me know if anything else happens, okay?"

I smiled at being given brief access to her softer side. "Okay, Wanda. Thanks again."

She nearly hung up, but then seemed to remember something. "Hey, Miranda, are you home right now?"

I answered, "Yes."

She jumped on the chance. "Stay put. I've got a couple of questions for you."

I could hear her letting her captain know she was leaving. "On my way."

She only took five minutes to get to my apartment and was all business when she arrived, very much back in detective mode. We both sat on the couch.

The detective seemed to have something serious on her mind. "So, after we spoke, you didn't call your friend Margo, did you?" She asked it very casually, but I knew it was anything but an off the cuff question. Having the opportunity to ask me in person was probably why she rushed down here when I called.

I wanted to lie because she had asked me not to, but I knew I had to come clean. "Well, yes, I did."

She pinched her lips and glared at me. "Marquette, I told you that for your own good. You know that she's been arrested for her husband's murder, right?"

I nodded. "I know. I think her local police arrested her right after we got off the phone."

She pressed on. "So you know that one of the first things we will do is to check her phone records for recent calls, and yours will be the first number they find." I nodded but was missing her point. "And she visited with Tony while she was visiting you. It wouldn't be hard for them to put together that you two were colluding in some way, that you introduced her to Tony, or that you had used him in the past. No matter what, having multiple phone calls to or from you is not a good thing."

I knew she was right, but it was too late now. "So, do you want to know what she said on the phone?"

"Absolutely. Exactly what she said."

I tried my best to recollect our call. "Well, Margo told me she didn't kill either Malcolm or Tony. Malcolm and Tony were friends from childhood, and Margo asked Tony to convince Malcolm to give her a divorce."

She took out her notepad. "Did she pay Tony to *convince* him?"

I thought about that night. "She didn't tell me she paid him, but she left with a briefcase and didn't come back with it." My gut told me Margo was telling the truth. "She flat out told me she didn't have Malcolm killed and didn't kill Tony. There was nothing in her voice inflection that told me that she was lying. She is a professional ex-wife. She marries for money. Divorce and alimony are her best friends."

She pointed her finger at me. "But what if she decided she wanted it all instead of half? And she took advantage of the fact that you knew her but didn't know her well, to put you in the wrong place at the wrong time. Now, her meeting was at your place, and Tony's body was found here. Once she gets off Malcolm's murder charge due to lack of evidence, who do you think they're going to come running to for answers?"

I shrunk back and said meekly, "Me?"

She jumped up. "Right, but we're not gonna let that happen, are we, Miranda?"

I stood up too because her pacing was making me a little nervous. "No, we aren't going to let that happen." I wished I felt as confident as I sounded. How did I get myself into these messes?

She scanned the ceiling for ideas. "So, if Margo was in custody, who snuck into your apartment and wrote that on your mirror?

I chewed my thumbnail. "Maybe Margo has an accomplice."

"Gee, thirty seconds ago, you thought Margo was innocent."

"Yeah, I did. She was very convincing on the phone, but I think there is more to Margo than it appears. I know she exaggerates, but I don't think she'd lie about something like this. I'm the kind of person who always thinks the best of a person until they prove otherwise. Maybe she's proving otherwise now.

The proof in the pudding will be if she tries to use me as a scapegoat."

She was sitting again, writing on the pad. "We have to assume she's going to use you. At least that's what I would assume if I were you."

I sat and faced her directly. "Hey, Wanda, thanks for being here for me."

She looked me in the eye. "I have to admit that I misjudged you. When it turned out that you had nothing to do with your upstairs neighbor's death, and then when you came directly to me with the information about your abduction, I started to trust you. So, don't let me down. I understand why you called her, but you did go against my orders when you called Margo just before she got arrested. So, you're still not batting a thousand."

I felt the heat of a blush. "It was an interesting call. If she does go to court, we got some good insight into what she's going to use as a defense. And I know you aren't prosecuting her murder case involving her husband, but if you can prove that she killed Tony Sansone, I could see a promotion in your future."

She laughed. "I hope so!" Then she got serious again. "I think that you were a good cop and I like your instincts. Working with me, you can continue to use your experience and training without all the mundane hours and paperwork you had to deal with when you were an actual cop. Besides, I know you know how it is. I don't have many friends. They don't come easily in this line of work."

I high fived her. "Okay, we're officially a team."

She looked me in the eye again. "And friends."

I smiled. "And friends."

Chapter 17

I slept better than I had in a while, getting my locks changed and feeling like I had a real ally in the police department. I still had an underlying feeling of uneasiness as I headed into work on Tuesday.

I reminded myself to touch base with Patricia this afternoon. We hadn't had much time together since I went home with Jason and then went back to New Orleans. I also never called Mark last night, and I still needed to.

Tea and I had an uneventful day. It seemed like she and Mike had been fighting again, which always made her sullen and quiet. I wished she would reconsider her choice of men, but it looked like she'd have to decide that independently. I had done everything I could.

I timed my ride home from work perfectly. Patricia was just parking her car as I pulled my motorcycle in between her car and another.

She jumped out of her car while I was removing my helmet. She laughed. "Aren't you a sight for sore eyes, helmet hair and all."

I whipped my ponytail around playfully. "After I did everything I could do to work my magic, even this darn ponytail?"

We hugged. She whispered, "You always look good, Miranda. I'm just jealous that I could never get away with half the outfits that you can pull off."

I mock-punched her in the arm. "You're a model for God's sake. With your coloring, you look good in almost anything. Some days what I wouldn't give for your complexion and hair."

I could tell by her blank expression that she wanted to get the topic off her beauty. "Hey, I'm gonna go upstairs and change, then I'll be down so that we can catch up." Her voice trailed off as she headed up her outside stairs.

I took a quick shower and put on shorts and a t-shirt.

I was opening a bottle of wine when she strolled in looking like a million dollars, dressed in a pink t-shirt, white shorts, and flip flops. I handed her a full glass. "So, how is your job going? Are you still loving it?"

Patricia took an uncharacteristically long swig of wine. "Well," she started, "it's interesting."

"Judging from that first swallow of wine, it looks like there might be trouble in paradise."

She collapsed on the couch. "I guess it's just typical work stuff. This guy, Geoff, who's on my team, hasn't been subtle about the fact that he wanted my job, deserves my job, and will not stop harassing me until he has my job. Sadly, he's kind of cute, but I will take him down if I have to. For the time being, I'm trying to get to know him so that I can find out his vulnerabilities. I figure if he thinks I'm taking an interest in him, maybe he'll straighten himself out as an employee. If not, I'll cut him loose like a rabid dog."

"Wow, this management thing really suits you," I said after taking my first sip.

Patricia closed her eyes and put her head back. "Well, there's one thing I can tell you about Karma, it's eat or be eaten. They pretend to have a totally open and understanding work environment. Still, there's always someone ready to take advantage of an opportunity someone provides them unwittingly by offending the wrong senior manager. I figure the best thing I can do right now is to get my job done and talk as little as I can when it comes to people at my own level. But as far as my subordinates go, they had better play it straight, or we're going to have a big problem."

I was suddenly thankful to be working in a relatively small company. Ion Manufacturing had its fair share of office politics, but it sounded nothing like Karma. I felt for her because there was nothing I hated worse than that. "Have you talked to Susan about it? She seemed pretty cool from what you told me."

She sighed. "Well, kind of. I made a little bit of a joke about the cut-throat nature of the staff, and she said, 'Welcome to Karma!'"

I didn't know if there was anything I could say to help. I tried, though. "Well, maybe it was just one of those days. We all have them. There are days that Tea is irritable from the moment she comes in to when she finally drags herself out the door. Those days drag as much for me as I'm sure they do for her. But then, a few days later, she's on top of the world."

She managed to force a smile on her face. "I know you're right, Miranda; let's declare work to be off-limits for the rest of the night."

I high fived her. "Deal!" I searched my memory for what had happened in my life since we last spoke. "Oh, you wouldn't believe the interesting time I had with Detective Marshall last night. I guess this will only make sense when I tell you why she was here."

She sat up on the edge of the couch. "Yeah, why was she here?"

I figured I might as well just say it now. "Well, when I came back from my trip, there was a message in lipstick on my bathroom mirror."

She gasped. "What was it?"

"The words are etched in my brain. 'Leave the murders alone or die'."

She didn't say anything for a few minutes and then said, nearly in a whisper, "This is a replay of what happened to me in Denver."

I knew what she was thinking. "The guy responsible for that is dead."

She drummed her fingernails on the arm of the couch. "At least that's what we've been told."

I laughed with a touch of sarcasm. "I'm not ready to go with a conspiracy theory quite yet."

Patricia stuck her tongue out at me. "Okay, Miranda, but don't say I didn't warn you."

"So what do you think it means? Why is someone warning me about multiple murders? Do you think they mean all four murders: The Surf Brothers, Tony, and Margo's husband? Are those murders related in some way? Wanda seemed to believe they were related and that Margo is the common denominator. And that well may be true, but I'm not ready to buy it yet."

She sat, thinking for a while. "Who else could it be?"

I couldn't be quite as blunt as my family had been over the weekend since Patricia was technically one of the suspects with a key to my apartment. I tried a more subtle approach. "Hey, have you given anyone the key to my apartment?"

I had a feeling of impending doom as the question sank in. I was reminded of some very difficult conversations she and I had in Thun, Switzerland, a couple of years ago. I counted backward from ten, waiting for the explosion.

Patricia's mouth twisted with disgust as she perceived what I had asked her. "You think I'm somehow involved in this, don't you, Miranda? All this drinking wine and beating around the bush. Why don't you just ask me? Ask me if I killed someone. Ask if I hid it from you. Ask if I'm trying to pin the murders on you." She got louder with each statement.

It had been so long since I'd been the recipient of her anger, I felt like I wanted to crawl in a hole. The fact was, sure, she was on the list of suspects. She had unlimited access to my apartment when I wasn't around. But my goal was to eliminate her as a suspect, not to accuse her of anything. But I guess it didn't come out that way.

I tried my best to retreat. "I'm not accusing you of anything. But you do have a key. I didn't know if there might have been someone else that got hold of the key somehow."

She folded her arms, her glass of wine still in one hand as tears ran down her face. I was happy she hadn't stormed out as she would have two years ago. Therapy was helping her too. I suddenly felt like the worst friend in the world.

We sat like that for a few minutes before she spoke quietly. "I didn't want you to think it was lost on me that I'm probably one of the few people with a key to your apartment, and now all these things are happening. I sit upstairs, waiting for the police to knock on my door and arrest me."

I really felt for her. There was nothing I hated worse than being falsely accused. "I'm so sorry. I just had to ask. It's so weird that someone seems to have free access to my apartment and just comes and goes at will."

I poured each of us another glass of wine, and we sat at the kitchen table. Patricia thought for a minute. "I don't know. Is there anyone else you can think of that it could be?"

I was going to mention the conversation my family had but since she and her parents represented half the people who had visited my apartment, I thought better of it. So instead, I said, "Everything points to Margo, even though I don't want to believe she would do anything like this"

Patricia nodded but didn't comment further.

I figured it was time to change the subject. "So when is your dad announcing his candidacy for governor? That has to seem surreal to you."

She took a swallow of wine. "It really is strange, and it's changed my parents in ways they don't even realize. They are so concerned about the press, and what everyone thinks, it's hard to remember what our lives used to be like. I don't expect to see them much between now and the election. I plan on getting Nate and putting him in daycare full time within a week."

I smiled, knowing how much she was missing him. "That's so great! It seems like everything is coming together."

She nodded. "It really is. This Karma job has been a Godsend. Yes, there are things I don't like about it, but all in all, it's pretty great."

We talked for the next couple of hours before we went off to bed, our friendship still intact.

#

The news was on when my clock radio woke me up. Since we were in California, I was surprised that Charles White's candidacy for the Colorado governor was being reported. They also noted that he was most likely being groomed for the presidency, considering how meager the field of Republican candidates had been in the last few elections.

I was relieved that nothing was amiss in the apartment when I got home from work on Wednesday. I was the only one with a key to my new locks at this point, and I planned on keeping it that way for as long as I could. My lease required me to provide one to the landlady, but what she didn't know wouldn't hurt her at this point.

I put my feet up and turned on the TV, which was rare for me. I wasn't surprised to find out that they had released Margo on bail. The time frame tied into the lipstick incident. I decided it was time to take matters into my own hands. I punched Jason's number on my cell phone.

He was cheerful as he nearly always was these days when I called. "Hi, Sweetheart. I was just missing you."

I was a pretty terrible girlfriend, rarely doing anything spontaneous or fun, especially now that my focus was primarily on the murders. He seemed to take it in stride, though. "I miss you too." I hadn't thought about what I was going to say, which was never a good idea. "But do you mind if I take tomorrow off? I need to go to Long Beach."

He got serious. "Margo? Has she been released?"

I was surprised that he was that up on my current events. "Wow! You really do pay attention! Yes, she's out on bail, and I need to talk to her face to face. That's the only way I'm ever going to know if she's lying. And I want to surprise her, so she doesn't have time to make up a story. Do you think Pho can cover for me?"

He didn't sound worried about work. "I'm sure he can. If not, I'll enter the orders myself. The fact is that I'm not all that busy, but if you breathe a word of that to anyone, especially Bob, I'll deny it to the death!"

I just remembered the call I'd promised myself I'd make to Mark. This moment seemed like as good a time as any. "Thanks, Honey. I'll keep you posted by text, or I'll give you a call when I know when I'm coming back."

I hung up and dialed Mark. "Miranda, is everything okay?" I guessed I finally made his phone contact list. He usually had no idea it was me when I called him.

I smiled at his concern. "Yes, I'm fine. I wondered if you had any additional insights since I left about who might be responsible for these deaths. And before you answer, I have another clue."

That piqued his interest. "Really. Do tell."

I continued without comment. "When I got home after my visit, there was a message on my bathroom mirror in lipstick: 'Leave the murders alone or die.'"

"Wow, they said 'murders?' That's interesting. That means they are tied together, or at least more than one of them is. That could mean Malcolm and Tony. I guess it could mean John and David, which you would already have to figure, were tied together. Or any combination of those, even all of them. Although the simplest explanation and the most likely are Malcolm and Tony, and Margo is responsible. But isn't she in custody? How could she have been in your apartment?"

I agreed. "I'm not sure when they released her on bail or even if she has someone she's working with up here. If she knew Tony, there's a chance she has other friends in Santa Clara's underbelly." I laughed, "Until all this, I didn't even know Santa Clara had an underbelly. I thought all the bad stuff happened in Oakland."

Mark chuckled. "So, what's your plan?"

I figured this was a good time to bounce this off of him. "I'm thinking of going to Long Beach and visiting Margo. I need to talk to her face to face, to gauge her reaction to questions, to get a gut feel for if she is lying. You know, see if she looks me in the eye, angers inappropriately, laughs at the wrong time, that sort of thing."

He sounded worried. "Well, in theory, not a bad idea. But what if Margo is the killer? What's to stop her from adding you to the notches on her belt? If you get killed while testing your theories about Margo and I knew about the visit in advance, Sabine will have my head. And I can forget about her ever marrying me."

I couldn't control my sarcasm, especially knowing that Mark had had a big crush on me in high school. "Seriously, that's the only reason you would feel bad that I was dead? Because Sabine wouldn't marry you? You've got to be kidding me."

He backtracked. "Well, you know what I mean. I didn't think I had to state the obvious that I'm also worried about you."

I let him off the hook. "Okay. I know Sabine can be tough, so I get it. But thanks for caring. I can't think of any other way to determine if Margo is a real suspect or is just mired in circumstantial evidence. I'm going to ride down there tomorrow. I'll let you know what I find out."

I hung up and headed upstairs to Patricia's. I knocked on her door, but she didn't immediately respond. I looked through the curtained window in her door and saw a suitcase standing near the door. Within a few seconds, she appeared. "Miranda. Sorry, I'm leaving in a few minutes. I'm going back to Denver for a couple of days."

Her eyes weren't exactly meeting mine, so I wasn't sure if she was telling the truth. "Oh, that seems kind of last minute. Is Karma okay with that?"

She smiled reassuringly. "Yes, I called Susan, and she was fine. I need to talk to my parents and pick up Nate. Things are going to get crazy with this election, and I want him out of the firing line. There is also something I didn't tell you the other night."

I was hopeful that this would be meaningful to the case. "Oh?"

She pulled her suitcase to the door, indicating that she was on her way out. "I want to find out who my birth parents were."

That completely took me by surprise. "Wow, I didn't see that coming. I had no idea. With you being orphaned, I assumed you knew."

She hurried around her apartment, putting last minute things in her purse. "No, they were presumed dead. They were never found. The whole thing gets more and more suspicious the older I get. As a kid, I accepted it. Now, I'm not so sure."

I scratched my head. "How do your parents feel about that?"

She started down the stairs after she locked the door. "Sorry, Miranda, I have to catch a plane. I don't really know, but I'm going to talk to them about it first. It's really important to me."

I followed her. "I understand. It's just that you never mentioned it before."

She loaded her suitcase in the trunk of her car. "Hey, can you look after my apartment while I'm gone?" She jumped in the car.

I didn't have a chance to let her know I would be gone tomorrow, but she'd already pulled away.

Chapter 18

On Thursday morning, I woke early, excited about the prospects of determining if my friend, Margo, was telling me the truth or using me as a scapegoat for murder. The eight-hour motorcycle ride down the familiar California Highways, especially the coastal 101, made me feel happy and encouraged about my day. I absolutely loved to ride, plus I hoped that she could prove her innocence so that I could report back to Detective Marshall.

I was accustomed to working for the defense when Mark was the attorney of record. So shifting to providing support for Wanda and the prosecution was a change for me.

My destination was 20 37th Place in Long Beach. According to the internet, Malcolm Wilson bought it for $7.25 Million, and Margo and her late husband were listed as the owners. It was a gated home called Casa Oceana. It had three bedrooms and five baths and was nearly 7,700 square feet on a 1.28-acre lot directly on the ocean.

The property boasted a heated pool, spa, and plenty of fountains and patios for entertaining. Originally built in 1928, I would have loved to have more time to find out who designed and built it. I wondered if Margo knew.

I left at 5 a.m., hoping to arrive by early afternoon. LA traffic would dictate whether I arrived at one or some later time, or at all. That was what I hated about living in LA. My personality demanded a certain level of control over my life, and not being able to control traffic didn't play well into my needs. That was the beauty of lane splitting. California was the only state that allowed motorcyclists to ride between lanes on multi-lane highways. So, assuming I was able to get to the 405, I was home free from there.

The temperature was a perfect 69 as I rode over La Honda Road to CA 1. I would never forget street luge racing on this same stretch of road in my previous life when I had my goals set on a reality TV show and a winning Extreme team. I've had to reset my dreams a couple of times since then, but I was still moving forward.

My stress level fell as I passed through some of my favorite towns as I rode south. Santa Cruz, Carmel, Big Sur, San Simeon, and Oxnard. I loved the smell of miles and miles of strawberries that dominated the fields in Oxnard as I approached my old stomping ground of Malibu with a lump in my throat.

I was almost tempted to stop by my old house, knock on the door and inquire who was living there, but they'd probably have me arrested, knowing the paranoia of most people living on Malibu Colony Road.

So I continued on past Malibu Beach and the rest of the beach towns until I reached Long Beach. I couldn't get the Beach Boys' "Surfin' U.S.A". out of my mind the further I rode. It made me long for simpler times when my biggest worry was which parent would pick me up at school after detention.

I pulled my motorcycle up to the gatehouse at Casa Oceana at 12:34. The press camped outside Margo's gate. I knew her security wasn't particularly tight when I told the guard on duty my name, and he immediately opened the gate and let me in without calling her or asking me for ID.

I was surprised by how welcoming the house was once I passed through the gate. The front door was as accessible as any house on a typical suburban street. I parked my bike in the driveway, removed my helmet, changed from my boots into running shoes, and stashed my gloves and boots in my saddlebags, hanging my helmet from the handlebars.

I felt a bit uneasy as I approached the front door, knowing that a part of me suspected that Margo was trying to frame me for the death of Tony Sansone. I was working on my best innocent-until-proven-guilty' attitude, at least for now.

I couldn't have been more surprised when Margo, wearing a bright yellow chiffon top and floral printed pedal pushers, burst through the front door. She gently set down the Yorkie she was carrying, which couldn't have been more than eight pounds, ran to me, and threw her arms around me.

"This proves once and for all that there is a God. I have been praying night and day for a savior."

I blushed, feeling guilty about the real reason I was here, but hugged her back. "I've been so worried about you. The news is so sketchy and downright inaccurate these days, so I figured I'd better see you for myself."

We walked arm in arm through her front door and into her spectacular ocean-front mansion. They had decorated the classic house with wood beams and Italian tile inside and out. I had been in plenty of beautiful homes when I lived in Malibu and dated several LA businessmen, but this house was in a whole different class. Everywhere I turned, from the professional kitchen to the courtyards, there were spectacular surprises. My mouth hung open as she gave me a tour, each room, and outdoor space more gorgeous than the last.

As we returned to the Great Room she said, "You should have seen it when I got back from my arraignment. The place was trashed from when the police searched it. We just managed to get it cleaned up a little while ago."

"We?"

"The help. They've got the rest of the day off. Bonus for working above and beyond."

"Did the cops find anything?"

"What could they find? There was nothing to find."

We sat in the Great Room, just off the kitchen side by side on a white Moroccan leather sectional. Margo beamed with pride. "So, what do you think?"

I could barely form words. "It's well, unbelievable. I'm so glad I don't live in my Malibu house any longer, or I'd be so jealous!" I wasn't sure why that made sense since I was now living in an apartment in Santa Clara, but somehow, she got it.

She smiled, "It's been a lot of hard work getting lots of rich men to fall in love with me. That can be exhausting, you know."

Despite her present challenges, she hadn't changed a bit since the first time we met. I took her hand. "So tell me every last detail about what happened after they arrested you. What did they charge you with? Does your lawyer think they have a case?"

She scoffed. "It's all a misunderstanding. I would never have met with Tony had he and Malcolm not been friends. And Tony wouldn't have killed Malcolm for all the money in the world. Like I told you, they were friends. They went way back. I didn't know Tony well and I needed a favor, so I thought paying him would be a polite thing to do. All I asked was for Tony to help him come to his senses."

I looked her straight in the eye. "Margo, do you have proof that's all you asked Tony to do?"

She didn't flinch. "Of course I do. Why would you even ask me such a thing. I recorded our whole conversation on my phone; I couldn't have been more clear. It was in my pocket, so the quality could be better, but it's not bad. Here, I'll play it for you." She dug the phone out of the pocket of her peddle-pushers.

She hit play.

Sound of her getting in the car.

Margo: As I said on the phone, I need your help

Tony: What kind of help?

Margo: You and Malcolm have been friends for a long time, right?

Tony: Right, so what's that got to do with anything?

Margo: I need you to help him listen to reason.

Tony: What kind of reason?

Margo: He doesn't believe that I don't love him anymore. I need a divorce. He is killing me.

Tony: How so?

Margo: I hate my life. I'm afraid I'll do something drastic, and I don't want to do that. I just want him out of my life.

Tony: Have you asked for a divorce?

Margo: Yes, the court served papers six months ago, and he just ignores them.

Tony: So you just want me to talk to him?

Margo: Yes, friend to friend. He'll listen to you.

Tony: So what's in the briefcase?

Margo: $50,000 for your trouble.

Tony: Whoa, you don't have to do that.

Margo: I insist. If you don't want it, donate it to charity.

Tony: You're sure?

Margo: Absolutely.

Tony: Okay, then I'll do it. I'll be in touch regarding the timing. Don't tell anyone we spoke, got it?

Margo: Yes, Thanks.

Tony: Don't mention it. Maybe when you have some real business, you'll think of me.

Margo: Thanks.

Sound of her getting out of the car.

I stared at her phone. "That's pretty conclusive. So did he ever get to carry out your request?"

Margo responded, "I honestly don't know. The timing is so crazy. I'm not sure exactly when Tony was killed, and since

Malcolm and I were separated, I had no idea of the timing of his daily comings and goings. I did ask his assistant whether Tony had set up a time to talk to Malcolm, but Malcolm kept his personal calendar. His assistant only kept his business calendar."

I grabbed her hand, hoping my question wouldn't offend her. "Margo, do you have *any* idea who killed Malcolm?"

She held my unwavering gaze. "I have no idea. Malcolm had his share of enemies. He was a powerful man. There are plenty of people who would love to see Malcolm dead, people he stepped on, on his way up. He was also smart. Any time he felt threatened by someone, even if it were the result of his own actions, he wrote down their name and relationship to him and forwarded it to the Long Beach Police. He had a longstanding relationship with Lieutenant Willie Ames. I don't know the full story, but evidently, Malcolm saved his life, so he felt that he owed Malcolm."

My head was spinning. I hadn't expected either Margo or Malcolm to be this organized or well-documented. I couldn't help but ask, "Do you know where the list is? Do you know who's on it? Have you ever seen it?"

Margo shook her head. "No, no, and no. Malcolm was very protective of me and thought if I had access to the list, it would only put me in danger. However, I meet with our attorney tomorrow, who is going to review several issues regarding Malcolm's estate, and I'm hoping he can provide some insight or even, perhaps, the list."

I thought further about the list. "So you said that Malcolm would send the name to this Willie Ames at the Long Beach Police Department. Did he also let the person in question know that he was forwarding their name to the police?"

Margo nodded, "Yes, that was the beauty of the list. It not only gave the police department a running list of suspects if someone killed Malcolm, but it also provided a deterrent to those on the list since their name was already in the hands of the police."

Something was amiss. "So, was *your* name on the list?"

Margo laughed. "Oh, God, no. At least I hope not."

It had to be said, "Then what led them to arrest you?"

I was afraid she would take offense to my question, but we were on the same wavelength. "That's exactly what I plan on asking Lieutenant Ames when we meet this afternoon."

I grabbed her hands. "You're meeting with Lieutenant Ames? Do you mind if I tag along?"

She hesitated. "Well, it's fine with me. I'm not sure if the lieutenant would feel the same way. He agreed to meet with me because he feels like he owes Malcolm, and since I'm his widow, he owes me."

I was confident I could make it work. "And I'm working with the Santa Clara Police Department to solve the murder of Malcolm's good friend, Tony Sansone. It's the least he could do for Malcolm to assist in helping to wrap up the murder of one of his best friends, right?"

Margo nodded. "Well, I see your logic. If Lieutenant Ames does, then you're home free. It's worth a try. You've got nothing to lose. You can ride with me, and we can discuss our strategy on the way."

She led me to the twelve-car garage in which there were eight cars, two motorcycles, and a motorhome. She showed me to a white Mercedes Benz SUV, which she pulled smoothly out of the garage to 37th Place, then to Ocean Boulevard, which we followed to Chestnut Avenue and, finally, to a ten-story glass and stone building on West Broadway. The twelve-minute drive didn't give us much time to strategize, but I figured the lieutenant was probably going to be calling the shots anyway.

The waiting room of the Long Beach Police Department was modern and neat, appointed with marble and tile, clearly not the pedestrian architecture of many police buildings built today in strip malls. There were two receptionists behind bullet-proof glass. Within less than a minute, a graying black man, probably in his early sixties, came through a metal door from the rear of the building. He motioned both of us to join him.

He shook Margo's hand and smiled. "It's so nice to see you again, Margo. I just wish it were under better circumstances. And who's your friend?"

I offered him my hand, and he shook it graciously. "I'm Miranda Marquette, a friend of Margo's. I'm working in conjunction with the Santa Clara Police Department to solve the murder of Tony Sansone, who, as you probably know, was a good friend of Malcolm's. So, when Margo told me she was meeting with you, I begged her to let me tag along. I hope it's all right."

He smiled. "May I ask who you are working with in Santa Clara? I did my time up in the Bay Area also, and I still have some good friends back there."

I crossed my fingers for a glint of recognition. "I'm working with Detective Wanda Marshall."

He burst out in laughter. "Pinky? Oh my. I haven't thought about her for years. You make sure you tell her 'Buster says Hi.'"

The three of us walked back to a small office on the first floor near a series of generic interrogation rooms. Behind his desk was a bookcase with five shelves, all filled with pictures of his family.

He called to someone in his outer office and asked them to bring coffee. Then he focused on the purpose of the meeting. "Margo, I wanted to express my sincere condolences about

Malcolm. He was a good man, and his death is a great loss. He was such a modest man. I'm sure he never explained how he saved my life."

She shook her head. "No, he didn't. I'm curious."

I thought that description sure didn't match the one Margo gave of her husband.

He sat back in his chair. "Well, here's the story. I was a patrolman back then, thirty years ago. We were responding to a burglary in a home on Ocean Boulevard. My partner was sick that day, so I was alone. There was supposed to be back-up, but they got held up. I was sitting in my patrol car across from the house, not wanting to go in alone, debating whether I wanted to wait for back up to arrive.

"Suddenly, a perp came from out of nowhere and had a gun to my head. He seemed to be all messed up on crack or something, and I couldn't talk any sense into him, and he's just yelling and screaming at me, saying he's going to kill me. He said he had no choice because he didn't want to go to jail. I'd heard it all before a million times. So, anyway, he says he's going to shoot me on three and starts counting backward: Three, two, bang. I figured I was dead, but the guy dropped to the ground, and who was standing in his doorway with a pistol? Malcolm."

I was always amazed at how thin the line was between life and death. I said, "That's an amazing story. So, you became friends after that?"

He shrugged. "Well, kind of. Malcolm was an unusual man. He was ambitious and made several enemies along the way. I had always promised him that I'd protect him because he had saved my life. So, we made a deal. In exchange for him saving my life, he would provide me with anyone he felt had a motive to kill him. He would then let those on the list know that he had provided their name to me. He figured it would act as a deterrent. And it worked pretty well for thirty-plus years." He wiped a tear from his eye. "Until now. I let him down. I couldn't protect him."

We were interrupted when a young, uniformed officer knocked and entered with a tray full of coffees. We each took one. It wasn't Starbucks but it wasn't bad for police station coffee.

The three of us sat in silence for a few minutes. Then Margo asked, "Would it be possible to provide us with the list?"

Willie shook his head. "I'm afraid I can't do that. I was sworn to secrecy except when testifying in a court of law."

Margo asked the question I was waiting for. "Was I on the list?"

He struggled with his response, wanting to keep his deal with Malcolm intact. "Let me put it this way. He told everyone when he added them to this list."

Margo thought to herself but spoke aloud, "Then I wasn't on the list. At least he never told me I was."

Willie was ever loyal to Malcolm but said quietly, "No, Margo, you weren't on the list."

She asked equally as quietly, "Why was I arrested then?"

He looked grim as he leaned across his desk. "Let me tell you something in confidence. I personally would never have had you arrested, but I don't call all the shots around here."

Chapter 19

My mind raced as I rode the same route back to the north. I planned to ride until it got dark, then to reevaluate my situation. I wasn't a big fan of riding on two wheels in the dark. There was too much left to chance. Too many riders had been killed or seriously injured running over a tractor-trailer tire or a deer carcass.

I stopped at the Fireside Inn on Moonstone Beach in Cambria. I had ridden by it many times. It always looked inviting with the Adirondack chairs on the patios outside of every ocean-front room, each room with a gas fireplace. The reduced mid-week rate was also a very welcome sight.

I laid on the bed, reflecting on my trip to Long Beach.

My visit with Margo had been a surprise on so many levels. On a personal level, I felt that I had misjudged her. While she acted bold and loud, that was to cover up the quiet and thoughtful person she was inside. We talked for a couple of hours after visiting the police station, and I left with a much clearer understanding of the Margo I hadn't known.

Like Patricia, her parents died when she was very young. Still, she hadn't been as lucky as Patricia had been, to be adopted as an infant, and was shuffled from foster home to foster home, facing all sorts of physical and sexual abuse from the age of ten. She worked her way through college and traveled the world after she graduated, taking odd jobs to replenish her bank account before moving on.

At the age of twenty-three, she emigrated to the island of Montserrat in the Caribbean, which is a British Overseas Territory. In an unbelievable rags-to-riches story, she met and married a prince who was a member of one of those tiny European countries no one ever heard of and became royalty. They lived on the island for fifteen years until several previously dormant volcanos erupted, killing her husband and half the population. She then fled to Miami and started her life once again.

She'd been married several times since then. All very tragic stories. She seemed to attract the wrong men, which could be traced to her background. One thing was consistent, though, they all had money. She learned early in life that money was something she didn't want to live without.

When I asked her why she never told me this before, she took my hand. "Miranda, on the flight to Switzerland, you were an acquaintance. Although I loved your company, in my mind, the odds of ever seeing you again were less than zero. Now that we've reconnected and you literally know more about me than any other person on earth, I'm never letting you go."

I was touched by how she had opened up to me. I knew from experience how hard that was. I took the opportunity to tell her the story of my life. I told her about my storybook childhood in the Meraux, south of New Orleans, the heart-wrenching divorce of my parents, and my escape to North Carolina after high school with a man twice my age.

I told her of my nearly decade-long career as an undercover cop, resulting in a life-changing ambush and a gunshot wound to the face, and a year of plastic surgeries. I described the rise and fall of my internet empire and my present happy and satisfying life, with a new boyfriend and a job I loved.

I could tell by the tears in Margo's eyes that she had never had someone open up to her as I just had. Our lives were so different, and yet, she and I weren't that different. We hugged for a long time before I walked out of her door to jump on my

165

motorcycle. Nothing about this trip had turned out as I expected. But I had gained another friend, and you couldn't put a price on that.

#

I awoke with the sun reflecting off the ocean through my slightly drawn curtains. Judging from the sheets that had barely been disturbed, I had slept soundly all night, which was rare for me. I was excited to get on the road, remembering the connection between Willie Ames and Wanda Marshall. Something in his timeline didn't make sense, since he said it had been thirty years since Malcolm has saved his life while working as a patrolman in Long Beach. He couldn't have worked in Northern California before that with Wanda, because she would have been ten years old at the time. Perhaps he had taken a break from LA at some point in his career. I couldn't blame him for that.

I had left Jason a voicemail on his work line sometime in the night. I let him know that I wouldn't be in today, so I was in line for a nice long weekend. I probably needed to stop taking time off, or I wasn't going to have a job or a boyfriend. That was something I would ponder later.

Just up the beach, I pulled my bike into the Oceanpoint Ranch for breakfast at The Canteen. The fact that they brewed their own Starbucks Coffee was reason enough for the stop, but the cinnamon French Toast and thick-cut bacon were sufficient to make me think about coming back again despite the three-hour ride. Sandy, my tattooed thirty-something waitress, was a wealth of information about the celebrities who had stayed there over the years.

#

Just before noon, I pulled into the Santa Clara Police Department parking lot. I had no reason to go back to the apartment, besides, I was dying to hear about Wanda's

166

connection to Willie Ames and what this Pinky and Buster relationship was all about.

Wanda was venturing out the front door just as I dismounted. She didn't see me immediately, but I flagged her down before she got in her car. "Hey, stranger, heading to lunch?" She smiled widely. "Miranda, just the woman I wanted to see. What trouble have you been stirring up in Long Beach?"

I took a chance that she would take the fact that I had gone to see Margo without telling her first with a sense of humor. "I don't know, Pinky, why don't you tell me?"

She winced slightly at the nickname then looked around and motioned to me. "Get in the car. Let's get some pizza."

We took the two-minute drive to Round Table Pizza on The Alameda, the same place my previous upstairs neighbor, Sarah, and I had gone after she gave Wanda her statement last year. Wanda ordered a large pepperoni, and we waited for it at a nearby booth.

I half-whispered to Wanda, "So what's the big secret?"

She smiled. "It's nothing really. Willie was working up here on assignment, on a mob case. So we ended up spending quite a bit of time together on stakeouts. More often than not, we were bored to tears. Normally, we were on eight-hour stints, but this one time, we ended up having to do a full twenty-four hours. All we had to drink was coffee in an old thermos, and all we had to eat were some stale Twinkies. Anyway, we started playing games, anything to help each other to stay awake. So we started making up stories pretending we were different people. My name was Pinky Twinky, and his name was Buster Longo." She broke into uncontrollable laughter. Every time she tried to speak, she'd laugh even harder until tears were rolling down her cheeks.

After a few minutes, I couldn't help myself. I started laughing too. I hadn't even been there, and, quite frankly, Wanda's description wasn't all that funny, but her reaction had me laughing completely out of control. Other tables of people started staring at us, which made it worse. When they called out Wanda's name for us to pick up our pizza, we got even worse.

Five minutes later, with our stomach's hurting, we tried to stuff down our pizza to keep our mouths full and our composure and dignity intact. After a few bites, I finally felt like I could talk without spontaneously giggling again. "So did Willie email you?"

Wanda looked around, usually holding off on police business until she was safely back in the department. "Yes. He sent me a list of suspects. We can go over it in my office. I can tell you this. It's eye-opening."

I whined, "I can't believe you can tell me that but not share any details. You are torturing me."

She tweaked my cheek. "Stop whining, Miranda, it's unbecoming."

I smiled. "Come on, Wanda, you're not that old. You sound like my mother."

She smiled back. "I'm old for my age. I had to raise nine brothers and sisters."

My mouth dropped open. "You are the oldest of ten kids?"

Wanda nodded. "I don't regret it. I think it helps me to feel more like a kid now since I kind of missed out on my real childhood." Wanda wasn't one to spend much time talking about herself. "So, was coming to see me, your way of telling me you went to Long Beach after I strictly forbade you to speak to Margo about this case?"

I wondered when she was going to get to that. "I had to see her with my own eyes to see if she was lying."

She drummed her inch-long fingernails on the table. "And was she?"

I thought long and hard about my conversation with Margo. "She is a lot of things, an orphan, a princess, an heiress, and a survivor, but she is not a liar."

Wanda looked me in the eye. "You know what I wish, Miranda?"

I had an uneasy feeling. "No."

Her face hardened. "I wish you had thought enough of me to have told me that you were going to see Margo, or better yet, I wish you had brought me with you. I thought we had a breakthrough the last time we were together. Now, I'm not so sure."

In a way, I knew she was right, but I couldn't acquiesce. "Wanda, I hear you, but I also need to work independently if you want me to help you. I needed to gain Margo's trust. And, honestly, bringing a cop along probably wouldn't have helped me accomplish that. Besides, as soon as I got anything substantive, I immediately brought you into the picture. I know it's not perfect, but it's pretty darn good."

She leaned back in the booth. "Okay, well, you did get me the list of suspects and a good laugh. So that does count for something." We got up from the table after polishing off most of the large pizza. She hugged me. "Sorry I got mad. I'm not used to working with a partner."

I chuckled. "It's pretty obvious that you don't give Detective Connelly much more responsibility than filing paper."

We walked toward her car. "We don't exactly hit it off."

I figured that was enough said on that topic. We rode in silence back to the police station. I wasn't sure what her plan would be when we got back, so I let her take the lead.

She motioned for me to follow her. "So, you want to see the suspect list or what?"

"Well, um, of course," sounding like the perfect Valley Girl. She locked her office door behind me. "You can't be too careful."

I had no idea about the internal politics of the Santa Clara Police Department, and I was probably better off. I stood behind the detective's chair, focusing on her screen. On the screen was a list of names and relationships to Malcolm Wilson. There were approximately fifteen names. I read through the first few, and they didn't ring a bell. As I scrolled through the list, a couple of the names sounded vaguely familiar, and I thought they might be regional political figures. But then I stopped in my tracks and gasped when I read the last two names: John Blake, David Miller, both listed as former business associates.

Wanda read the list several times. "Wow, he had some high-powered enemies. I recognize all but two of them, but I'll bet they all have ties to organized crime. I wonder if your friend, Margo, knew what she was messing with."

I kind of shook my head then asked, "And what else do you know about John Blake and David Miller?"

Wanda went through some notes on her desk. "They have been medium-time thugs for a while, between them, wanted in seven states, pretty much cruising below the radar. The word on the street was, they were getting a reputation as up and comers. They even had a street name: The Surf Brothers. Well, you saw them, so you can guess why."

I laughed. "Yeah, you mentioned that before." I tried to piece it all together. "I know how I feel. But for you, does this make Margo more or less of a suspect?"

I moved from behind Wanda's chair and sat in a chair in front of her desk. My feeling of well-being from earlier this morning while riding up the coast had all but vanished. "Why would these two guys tied in with Malcolm Wilson have abducted Patricia and me? I used to be a cop, so I don't believe in coincidences, and I'm sure you don't either."

The detective closed her eyes, trying to will something that made sense into her consciousness. She spoke slowly, "Talk about coincidences. When you met Margo on the way to Switzerland two years ago, who did you also spend time with while you were there?"

I nearly lurched out of my chair. "Patricia!" I paced around her office. "So, what does that mean?"

"I have no idea. Maybe nothing. It just seems like you have all been running in very similar circles for some time now." She looked at the ceiling with her hands behind her head, laying back in her reclining desk chair. "So what did this Malcolm Wilson do for a living?"

I winked. "You mean you haven't looked him up online? He was big into real estate investments."

"Great work, partner."

I got up and shook her hand. "At your service—partner." I walked out to my motorcycle, more confused than when I arrived.

Before I climbed on, I called Jason. He answered on the first ring. "Hey, Sweetheart, tell me you're home. I miss you like mad."

"Wow, I'm going away more often."

He begged, "Please don't. Work is a nightmare, and my personal life isn't so great either."

I looked at my watch. It was nearly four. "Hey, come over to the apartment when you get off work. We can have some dinner and talk."

I could hear a smile come to his face. "You've got yourself a deal, Darlin'. I'll see you then."

I jumped on my motorcycle and headed for home.

Chapter 20

I barely had time to shower and get spruced up before Jason was scheduled to arrive. It felt like forever since I'd seen him, and I was excited that he had missed me as much as I had missed him. Maybe we did have a future together. I hoped I wouldn't jinx the relationship by seeming too anxious.

When the knock came on my door, I was ready to throw my arms around him. The only problem was, it wasn't him. It was Patricia. I realized, looking at my watch, that it was still at least fifteen minutes before Jason could get here after work, and that was if he left right at five.

Tears streamed down her cheeks. She collapsed into my open arms. "Oh, Miranda. Why did I ever think my parents could treat me as an adult?"

I took her hand and led her to the couch. "So, I take it they weren't open to your finding out who your birth parents were."

I texted Jason. Um, gonna have to take a raincheck on your lips. Patricia's having a meltdown. Sorry ☹

She jumped up from the couch and paced my apartment floor. "Not *open* doesn't half describe it. They went ballistic, threatening to take away my inheritance. They even threatened to take custody of Nate. I couldn't understand their reaction. You would think they'd *want* me to know where I come from!" Even though it wasn't particularly cold in here, she was shivering. I got her a sweatshirt. "I stormed out of the house and went for a long walk. I didn't even know where I was going; I was so angry. It was like that time when your mother told you that Sabine was your sister, not your cousin, and you walked ten miles in flip flops."

173

I hadn't remembered telling her that story, but she was exactly right.

She continued pacing. "Anyway, I don't even know where I was, but it started getting dark, so I called a taxi and took it to the airport. I went to the Southwest desk and told them I lost my boarding pass, and they printed me another. So here I am. No suitcase, no blow dryer, no toothbrush, well you get the picture. All I had was my purse and the clothes on my back."

I stood up and hugged her again. "I'm so sorry. I know how much this meant to you. Maybe they'll think about it and have a change of heart."

She snorted. "Nope, not happening. I've seen this look in my dad's eyes before. He's not changing his mind. This was the same look he had when I told him I didn't want him to run for governor." She suddenly stopped talking, realizing she hadn't told me that.

I couldn't let it go. "I didn't know. Why's that?"

Her face turned red. "Oh, never mind. No-one understands."

I pushed. "Come on, Patricia, you've told me everything up to now."

She sat next to me on the couch. "It's not safe. There are too many crazies out there. And governor is one thing, but he wants to be president. First of all, just being a member of the governor's family puts us at risk. What about Nate? He'd need protection twenty-four hours a day. And if Dad became president, we'd never be able to go anywhere or do anything without clearing it with bodyguards. I don't want that kind of life for my son."

After a few minutes, I asked, "So, what do we do now?"

Patricia shrugged.

I pulled her chin up. "Well, I know what I'm doing. I'm going to help you find out who your birth parents are. Honestly,

I'm pretty sure your if your parents had known the birth parents, they probably would have said something, but I don't think that's always the case. Maybe the mother's background has information they really don't want you to know about. But there are ways to search for your birth parents. I'm surprised you've never looked them up on the internet."

She brightened, "Really? So, where would we start?"

I grabbed my laptop. "Right here."

I brought up Adopted.com, which is one of several resources for adoptees and parents who are trying to connect with their birth children. I helped her to set up a profile and to enter her vital statistics, such as birthdate, where she was born, and other critical information.

I handed her my laptop, and she completed the information within a minute or two. She had a broad smile on her face, which was a huge improvement from when she arrived. "Now what?"

I stared at the screen. "Now, we wait."

I was interested in her fears regarding her dad's political aspirations. They seemed a bit over the top to me. "So, what's this about you not wanting your father to run for office? How long have you felt that way?"

Her face went cold. "Since the moment he brought it up. Why can't he just be happy with what he has? He's got all the money anyone could ever need, a beautiful wife and daughter if I do say so myself. My mom doesn't say anything, but I know that she hates it too. Sure, she smiles and makes public appearances and stands by his side, but she's a very private person."

I faced her on the couch, moving my laptop to the kitchen table. "Have you told your dad exactly how you feel?"

She seethed. "Of course I have. It's all we've talked about for months. He just ignores my concerns and pats me on the head like a child. I would have thought after the threatening messages we received at the house before I moved, and then being abducted here after I moved to California, would have gotten his attention. Still, he doesn't see a connection."

I studied her face. "And you believe there is a connection between those events and his candidacy?"

She frowned at me like I was stupid. "Of course. Nothing like this ever happened to our family until he decided to seek public office."

I hadn't really thought about the connection. I figured as a rich, prominent family in Denver, they would always have had the potential to be the target of some crazy. "I guess you're right. So, I guess you'll never know for sure, but are you saying that John was never personally interested in you, that he was just using you to get to your father?"

She thought for a minute. "I don't know, Miranda. I haven't had a lot of time to think about that, especially since he was murdered. I guess the truth went with him to the grave." She wiped a tear from her eye, which told me more than her words.

I had a feeling I'd never know the real story.

#

We talked until late into the night, and Patricia slept on my couch after we shared a couple of bottles of wine.

Sometime before I got out of the shower the next morning, she went upstairs to her apartment. She remained a mystery to me. I loved her dearly, but she had a long way to go until her parents treated her as an adult. If I were her therapist, I would tell her that she enabled them, and she was comfortable in her role as a child and enabler. But as her friend, I would continue to do everything in my power to help her gain her independence from her overbearing and domineering father.

My cell phone vibrated. I pulled it out of my pocket in anticipation of a call from Jason, but it was the Santa Clara Police Department. I responded, "Wanda, we really have to stop meeting like this."

Detective Marshall was not in a playful mood. "Miranda, we need to get together. I have some evidence we need to talk about. Can you come down to the station?"

As I was already dressed in jeans and a t-shirt, I was ready to go. "On my way." I hung up, exchanged my slippers for my boots, grabbed my helmet and headed to the police station.

I was surprised when Wanda met me in the parking lot. "Let's take a drive."

I gave her a questioning look.

She whispered, "I'm afraid I'm being watched. Too many weird coincidences are going on around here lately."

I chuckled. "So what makes you think your cruiser isn't bugged?"

She nodded. "Don't think I haven't thought of that. We're going to ride quietly to the park and take a walk."

I was worried that Wanda was getting paranoid, but that didn't mean someone wasn't out to get her, so who was I to question her sanity?

We rode for a couple of blocks to Fremont Park, one of the parks on Jane, my upstairs neighbor's running route, where we searched for her body when she disappeared last year. I knew there were a couple of tables adjacent to the playground, so we sat there to talk.

She looked like she was ready to explode by the time she felt she could finally talk safely. "We've been doing a lot of forensics and ballistics on Tony Sansone's weapons. As you can imagine, most of his firearms were bored out so that the bullets were not traceable to any particular weapon. However, we have

177

been able to trace back so many unidentified bullets to gangland-style killings over the years; it was almost a no-brainer to trace them back to one of Tony's weapons now that we have them in our possession. This information will likely wrap up countless open cases, but there are two open murders tied to these weapons that I thought you'd find interesting—the Surf Brothers."

It took a minute for that to sink in. "The man who met with Margo killed the guys who abducted Patricia and me? How could that possibly be?" I spun the ring on my finger, a new nervous habit I had developed. "Hey, Tony Sansone was killed, did you find any records of who ordered the killings? I know some hired guns keep meticulous records and are very proud of their accomplishments."

Wanda shook her head. "Not that we've found yet. We're still looking." She looked around suspiciously.

I had finally had enough. "Okay, what is up with all of this? You won't talk to me in your office. You're acting like somebody may have followed us."

She spoke quietly with intensity. "We just had a meeting with our chief, who said that there's suspicion of surveillance in our station, our vehicles, and elsewhere. It's only been discovered, and they're doing their best to eradicate it, but until they do, we need to be extra vigilant." She wiped her forehead with her sleeve.

I nearly laughed, but she was so serious, I thought she might hit me. "Okay, just let me know what I need to do."

She sat straight as a board. "Just act normal."

She was a cop through and through and couldn't help herself. "Okay, so Tony Sansone killed John Blake and David Miller. That is surprising to me. I've been away from the criminal element for a while, but for someone with Tony Sansone's stature to be knocking off two-bit punks seems out of whack.

There's honor among thieves, but there is also a hierarchy that we are seldom privy to. It's just like where convicts have their own sort of laws that they enforce in prison. You know what I'm talking about."

She nodded. "Yes, don't be a child molester and end up in a maximum-security prison."

I smiled. "Okay, this is slightly different, but if there's going to be an inside killing of someone in the lower echelon, it's usually done by someone on the same level. In this case, it should have been a low- to mid-level hitman. Not a Tony Sansone. Something doesn't add up." The timing of their security issue seemed coincidental too. "Do you think there's a tie to this case and your surveillance issue? It seems very convenient."

She seemed a little more relaxed for the first time since we'd been at the park. "I don't know, but it's driving me crazy. You might be able to tell."

I laughed. "Um yeah. Just a touch."

She stood up. "Let's get out of here." But instead of heading back to the parking lot, she headed across the park. "It seems like a shame to waste such a gorgeous day, especially since I can't get any work done in my office."

There was a food truck selling tacos and burritos on the other side of the park. We each bought a couple of burritos and sat down at a picnic table nearby.

She waited until she'd taken a couple of bites. "So, whatever happened to your police career? It seems like you have good instincts, you love investigation, you generally keep your cool. I'd love to have a partner like you."

Police generally weren't very sympathetic about my story, so I hesitated. "Do you promise you won't judge me?"

She nodded. "Promise."

It had been a while since I'd told anyone about my past. "I'm originally from New Orleans but went to North Carolina right after I graduated high school. I was impetuous and innocent as hell, but I thought I knew it all. I took up with a man twice my age and grew up fast.

"He was a cop, and encouraged, well, strongly encouraged me to enter the police academy. I graduated at the top of my class, and within a couple of years of graduation, I was an undercover detective."

I wiped the burrito sauce running down my face. "Most of my co-workers were great, but there were one or two who didn't believe that a woman should be a cop, much less work vice. Whether it was a horrible mistake or done on purpose, I was left hanging in a drug deal, literally holding the bag. I ended up getting shot in the face. I had ten surgeries over twelve months, got a nice settlement from the force, and moved on."

She looked closely at my face. "You look beautiful. You must have had excellent surgeons."

I blushed. "They were the best. I would go back to Charlotte again if I ever needed plastic surgery."

Wanda looked down at her hands. "That must have been horrible. I can't even imagine." She reached across the table and touched my hand. "Thanks for sharing that with me. It means a lot."

After we ate, we strolled slowly across the park to her cruiser.

Once I settled in the passenger seat, I rubbed my belly, "I am so full! Why did you make me eat so much?"

She mock glared at me. "I made you eat too much? I usually don't eat during the day. I'm afraid it'll slow me down. So, this is on you, my friend."

It was nice to have a friend, as unlikely as it had been when we first met over a dead body in the cemetery just a few blocks from here.

#

Jason and I went to dinner and a movie after I went home and spruced up. We then drove up into the canyons east of San Jose and parked, sitting on the hood of his car, staring up at the stars for hours. For the first time I could remember, I felt safe and sound and peaceful.

Chapter 21

I was awakened to the sound of loud knocking. I glanced at the alarm clock as I stumbled to the door. It was just past 7:30. Who was knocking at this God-forsaken hour on a Sunday morning?

I opened the door. There was a squad car parked on the street, but no-one at my door. They knocked again, but it was upstairs at Patricia's door. I gasped. I rushed inside after I heard, "Patricia White, you are under arrest for the murder of Tony Sansone. You have the right to remain silent ..."

I was stunned. I just had lunch with Detective Marshall yesterday, and she didn't mention anything about Patricia even being a suspect in Tony Sansone's murder. I understood that I was a civilian and wouldn't be privy to that information, but I was still angry. I dialed her direct number.

She recognized my number, "Miranda!"

I jumped down her throat. "Don't *Miranda* me! How could you? I thought we were friends."

She didn't seem to have a clue. "Could you possibly narrow it down?"

I hoped she wasn't playing me, or I could get a hundred times angrier. "There are two beat cops outside arresting Patricia for Tony Sansone's murder. It seems like we were just talking about Sansone yesterday, and you never breathed a word that you were close to an arrest."

There was silence at the other end of the phone. "Those bastar—," She cut herself short. "Let me call you back." She hung up.

I was still seething as I watched them load Patricia in the back seat of the squad car in handcuffs. I knew that feeling all too well: humiliation, confusion, anger, and helplessness. I paced the apartment like a panther, knocking innocent papers off the countertop, kicking kitchen chairs from under the table, and tossing dirty clothes in the general direction of the washing machine. I dropped onto the couch, only immediately to jump up and make a pot of coffee.

Luckily before I caused too much damage to my apartment, Wanda called back. Before I could continue my rant, she took over the conversation. "Miranda, I'm so sorry. With our internal communication issues here at the station, we got our signals crossed. The Sansone murder is such an important case; we have two teams working on it, and, well let me put it this way, one group didn't know what the other was doing. At least that's the official story. I'll tell you what really happened sometime over a beer."

I was still frustrated and angry. "So, where does that leave our investigation?" I tried my best to sound cold and flat.

She didn't let me get away with it. "Come on, Miranda, you have to work with me here. I didn't even know she was a suspect. I was working on the ballistics and forensic angle, as I told you yesterday. With the privacy breach, the team could not get back together this morning, and the other half of the team took the action they thought was appropriate based on the evidence they had."

I knew I was reaching, but what was the point of having a friend in the police department if you couldn't take advantage. "And what evidence was that?"

She sighed. "You know I can't tell you that."

I lightened up a touch. "Yeah, I know. But you can't blame a girl for trying." I searched for my car keys. "I'm coming down there."

She cautioned me. "You know there's not much you can do. They'll be booking her and all that goes with it. That'll take a couple of hours. You might be better off working for her on the outside, calling her parents, seeing about legal counsel. I can make sure she's taken care of in here." She laughed at the irony. "Now that I know she's here, you can rest assured I will be giving the other team hell for acting without my knowledge. I'm not happy about that, but I'll deal with it."

I nodded, even though I knew she couldn't see me. "Okay, Wanda, you're probably right. I can do more for her from my apartment than I ever could sitting in the police department lobby or even your office."

She was ready to go. "Okay, I'll give you a call when I know anything."

I smiled. "Thanks, Wanda. Sorry, I got a bit hot under the collar there for a minute."

She laughed. "I get it. I felt the same way. Talk to you soon." She hung up.

I thought about what my next move should be and decided to call Patricia's parents. I figured her one phone call would be to them, but I wasn't sure how quickly the police would allow that to happen, so I dialed their number.

Her mother answered, "Toni White."

I sounded nervous. "Mrs. White, this is Miranda Marquette." I felt kind of stupid using my full name, but I had no idea how many Mirandas they knew."

"Miranda, is everything all right?" I guessed she realized I wasn't making a social call.

I didn't know what to say, so I just blurted it out. "Patricia's been arrested."

She responded, "Oh dear," and covered the phone. I could hear her yell in the background, "Charles, Patricia's been arrested."

Then I heard some garbled conversation between them, and finally, Charles grabbed the phone. He sounded very serious, rushed, and businesslike. "Miranda, thank you for calling. Can you tell me why Patricia has been arrested?"

I was taken aback that he didn't sound concerned or that he felt for her. "The police arrested her for the murder of Tony Sansone."

It sounded like he swore, but I wasn't quite able to hear. "When did this happen? Does the press know?"

My blood ran cold with his lack of emotion. "This morning. Just a few minutes ago, so I doubt anyone else knows yet. I heard the police at Patricia's door, and I woke up. I briefly thought they were knocking on my door, but then I realized it was hers. I feel so bad for her. I know she's the last person who would murder anyone. So if there's anything you need from me, just let me know."

He responded, "I don't think that will be necessary, Miranda. I'll take care of it from my end. Our attorney will be in touch with Patricia as soon as possible to work on her defense. Of course, her mother and I will travel to see her during and after her incarceration, if possible."

I stifled a gasp at my perception that they had no intention of visiting. The feeling that I was going to throw up made me want to get off the phone immediately. "Okay, thank you. Goodbye."

I grabbed my stomach and ran to the bathroom. The nausea subsided and a drink of water helped soothe my stomach.

I felt horrible, both physically and mentally, as I flopped on the couch. My head was pounding, my ears were ringing, and I was sweating profusely. I was on the verge of a panic attack. I shut my eyes and did the visualization exercises my therapist taught me. At least I didn't feel so dizzy, like I could pass out.

One thing was for sure, Charles White was not the man I wanted for president. I imagined since he was running for Colorado governor—conservative right to life and law and order candidate— that his daughter being arrested for murder wasn't the best news he had gotten this week. However, as a parent, most parents, under those circumstances, would have shifted into protective parental mode. My perception was that he was in candidate damage-control mode. Not cool at all.

I wished I could bring Mark in as Patricia's attorney, but I knew her parents would never allow it. Maybe having an in with the prosecution wasn't the worst position to be in to help Patricia. I was pretty sure she hadn't killed Tony Sansone. He was one of the most famous and most difficult to catch hitmen in the country, and she didn't even own a gun. The thing that bothered me about her case was the Surf Brothers. She admitted having a soft spot for John, even though he treated her terribly and basically chased her out of town. There was more to that story than she was telling me.

I laid down on the couch, feeling somewhat better than I had after my phone call with Mr. White. Just as I was getting comfortable, a knock came at my door. I had never lived in a place with so much foot traffic. I slogged to the door anticipating anything from an Amway salesman to a serial killer.

I was pleasantly surprised when the man of my life was standing there, looking scrumptious carrying two little white bags.

He grinned as he held the bags up. "Coffee and bagels."

I threw my weary arms around him. We kissed and kissed and kissed. This was just what I needed after a morning I'd had so far. We had such an easy conversational style that we ate and talked and laughed all morning, never missing a beat. Then, we watched old movies on TV all afternoon wrapped in each other's arms.

We had the perfect relationship. He never pressured me to stay overnight mostly because his lifestyle didn't allow it. He had a couple of dogs, chickens, and several barn animals that he needed to tend to. The truth was, no matter what our relationship was, I preferred to sleep alone. I was a very light sleeper, and someone on the other side of the bed moving, snoring, breathing, touching, or infringing on my side of the bed, didn't work for me. Some people loved it, lived for it, and couldn't wait to get married so they could do it every night for the next fifty years. I avoided it at all costs.

After a very eventful day, I kissed Jason goodnight one last time as he went out the front door. Minutes later, I fell peacefully asleep, alone in my bed, dreading that tomorrow was Monday.

Chapter 22

It was very unusual for me to wake before the sun came up—today, I did. The fact that I was not only awake but wide awake, I took as a sign. I had promised myself I wouldn't take any time off this week, but I couldn't face working today. I remembered that Margo had told me that she seldom slept past five, so I took the opportunity to call her.

She picked up after the first ring. "Hi, Miranda, are you part of the night owl group now too?"

"I guess I am. I had no plans on waking up any time before seven, but here I am, and I have a wild idea. Can you meet me at the Portabella in Carmel around noon? It's about halfway, give or take. I'd love to see you again. You have a real Zen effect on me, which I could use right now."

"Are you all right, Miranda? I'll come all the way up there if you need me." Her voice showed far more concern than Mr. White had for his own daughter.

I smiled, "That's so nice of you, Margo, but you know how I love to ride. It's just that I don't think I can handle twelve hours round trip today."

Margo continued, "Oh, believe me, I know. This pretty little butt of mine has done more hours on the back of a motorcycle than I'd like to admit."

"I learn something new about you every time we talk, Margo. You are, by far, the most fascinating person I know."

She giggled. "Well, I'll take that as a compliment, but you haven't been around nearly as long as I have. By the time you're my age, you'll probably know plenty of people more fascinating than I am."

I thought carefully about everyone I had known. "I sincerely doubt that, but good try."

We hung up after a few minutes, and I spent the next hour straightening, cleaning, vacuuming, washing dishes, and then showering, blow drying my hair and getting dressed. Then I left a message on Jason's voicemail to let him know I wouldn't be in. The good news was that he knew I wouldn't take time off if I couldn't afford to and I was pretty much caught up with my orders. I crossed my fingers that I wouldn't be sorry tomorrow for missing the Monday orders.

The weather was perfect for a California Route One trip to Carmel-by-the-Sea. I had been to Portabella a couple of times on my way through town, and the local fresh seafood was spectacular. From the outside, it looked like a gingerbread house that should have been nestled deep in the woods in Germany, not carefully placed amid a seaside haven. From the first time I stepped in the place, the owner treated me like he had known me forever. And since then he'd been consistently friendly and welcoming.

I sat at one of the outdoor patio tables while I waited for Margo. I didn't have long to wait. She arrived in sunglasses and a green and white striped summer dress with white gladiator sandals strapped up her legs. She looked a lot cooler than I felt in my riding leathers. You would never know she was out on bail for first-degree murder.

My intuition told me they wouldn't take her past the preliminary hearing. And not because she was rich or had a great attorney. It was because she didn't do it. She wasn't on Malcolm's list. What was the point of his list if his killer wasn't on it?

Besides, she had such a calm and relaxed way about her; it was impossible to believe that she was guilty of any crime, much less murder.

We hugged, and she sat next to me at the round table. She explained, "We don't want the whole world to hear what we are talking about, I'd imagine." She smiled and put a finger to her lips.

Upon her arrival, the thirty-something waiter immediately came to our table for our drink order. Thankfully, wine instead of a cocktail was also Margo's drink of choice. I usually didn't drink at all when on two wheels, but I figured we'd be here a couple of hours, so I allowed myself to have one glass.

She perused the menu. "I think I'll have the mussels. It's actually an excuse to have the homemade fries that come with them. How about you?"

I closed my menu. "The prawns."

We could have had a wonderful time talking small talk all afternoon. Because of Margo's unusual background, she looked at the world differently than anyone else I knew, and it was both refreshing and surprising every time we talked.

Finally, we got to the topic at hand. Her reaction was precious. "So what is it with this Patricia friend of yours? In my world, I would have tossed her off a boat somewhere in the Caribbean when no-one was looking, years ago. She is way too much work."

I couldn't help but laugh. A part of me had to agree, but Patricia did have her saving graces. I stuck up for her. "I know she's not perfect, but none of us are."

Margo was enjoying herself completely. "Let's look at the scorecard here. Okay, first of all, this is a woman pushing forty, and this is literally the first time she has lived on her own without her parents. And *they* have her child because they don't believe she can handle taking care of him." She thought back. "Oh, wait a minute, let's talk about why she has a child in the first place. After a member of your Extreme team is killed by the eventual father of her child, she takes up with him as his rebound girl and gets pregnant before he gets convicted and goes to prison."

She pretends to counts on her fingers. "Okay, how many points does she have so far? Um, I can't count that low. Zero! Let's face it; she'd be negative if we allowed that."

I rolled my eyes, knowing it was true.

It was kind of amusing listening to it with Margo's dramatic flair. "So, then she takes up with a local guy who just happens to be a two-bit thug who then basically runs her out of town, but then follows her, picks up a partner, and kidnaps both her and you. Coincidentally, these criminals end up dead, and now Patricia is arrested for the murder of their likely killer. Now, do I have this straight?"

I tried to reel her in. "Well, I was hoping that you could see something in the situation that I didn't. And you do, but it's not quite what I was hoping for. Am I that blinded by my friendship with Patricia?"

She looked me in the eye. "In a word, yes. When we flew to Switzerland together, and you talked about Patricia, you seemed to me to have a far more accurate view of her than you do now. I know you probably don't want to hear that, but that's how I see it."

I was a sucker for a happy ending. "But I do always hope for the good in people to come out in the end."

She laughed. "I love Hallmark movies too."

I looked at my feet. "But ..."

She put her finger under my chin and lifted it. "I love that about you, Miranda. I really do. And you were going to say,

191

'But, you never know.' Right? You're kind of hopeless in that way, but it's very endearing."

I had to go at her from every angle. "So from everything I've told you about the situation, you're saying you think Patricia is guilty of killing Tony Sansone?"

She leaned back in her chair and breathed out a heavy sigh. "What I'm saying is that Patricia has poor judgment, is tremendously immature, is a marginal parent, and not that great a daughter. However, do I think that she masterminded the death of one of the most sinister paid killers of the twenty-first century? Don't look at me like that; I did my research. Malcolm's best friend was a very scary guy. And I absolutely don't think Patricia was capable."

We both sat quietly, thinking for a few minutes. "Doesn't it strike you a little bit odd that Sansone killed the guys that abducted Patricia and you? Looking back, though, what was your perception of that job?"

I hadn't thought about it much. "Well, they tied us in a very unprofessional way using rope instead of cuffs or zip-ties, like it was their first time. They left us alone in a deserted warehouse with no-one watching us, no security cameras that I am aware of, and no alarms or security systems that detected our escape. They didn't even thoroughly search the building once we had gotten free. And once we did escape, they practically walked right into the arms of the police by coming back to my apartment the next day. None of it made any sense."

"What? They were arrested at your apartment?"

"Not at. They were caught on our street heading toward the house. The police intercepted them there. Pretty stupid of them, I'd say."

Margo bit her lip. "Do you think they staged it?"

That seemed a little far-fetched. "I don't know. The Surf Brothers were certainly arrested for real and then killed for real. It's a strange case. It seems equally strange that the police pegged Patricia for the murder. I have to get to Wanda, my police detective friend, to see what evidence they have on her." She wasn't willing to let it go. "People do everything for a reason. They abducted Patricia for a reason. We just need to figure out why. Once we do that, I have a feeling we will know why someone hired Tony to kill them. And once we know who that someone was, we'll know who killed Tony. I can tell you with almost a hundred percent certainty, as much as I don't particularly care for the woman, Patricia didn't do it."

I had an idea. "Hey, you should meet Patricia. Everything you know about her is only based on my perceptions. Besides, that would give me a reason to hang out with you again."

She hesitated. "Well, let's see how my situation progresses. I'd love to have the case dropped at the preliminary hearing, but I'm the kind of suspect they love to hate."

We stood up and hugged our good-byes. I whispered, "Who could possibly hate you?"

She turned down the street to get her car, and I stopped by my bike. She turned around and said, "Oh, you'd be surprised, my pretty. You'd be surprised."

Chapter 23

First thing Tuesday morning, I called Susan, Patricia's boss. I gave her very little information but wanted to let her know she wouldn't be at work today or possibly the rest of the week. An arraignment and bail hearing could take just a day or two, or weeks depending on the court, but I was optimistic.

She said she'd seen it on the news and was very nice about it. She assured me that Patricia's job was not in jeopardy and that Karma prided themselves in having understanding in very diverse personal situations. Susan said before she got off the phone, "I'm sure you know Patricia better than I do, but I don't believe that she would kill a fly; in fact, I've seen her catch a spider in the office and carry it outside. She has a respect for life that very few even come close to. When this travesty is straightened out, she'll be right back here where she belongs. She's a Godsend."

I agreed. "I know. She used to work for me too. I never had to worry about any details. She took care of everything."

She asked, "Well, can you keep me abreast of what's going on? The news is so unreliable these days."

I laughed. "You can say that again. I will let you know as soon as I know anything, but I'd be surprised if she's not arraigned and free sometime this week."

She said, "Thank you, Miranda. You're a good friend."

I smiled. "I try to be. Good-bye."

She said, "Good-bye," and hung up.

I looked at my watch and gasped. "Oh my gosh," and rushed out the door. I grabbed my car keys and locked the door on the way out. It was nearly ten of eight, and I'd barely make it to work on time if I sped. The motorcycle wasn't an option today. I didn't even have time to put on my boots.

I raced Tea to the door for the second time in a week. I had to stop doing this to myself. I groaned when I saw my workspace with my inbox piled high with new orders and post-it notes all over my computer screen. Sometimes, taking time off was completely unrewarding, although I was thankful I had gone to meet Jason's family, and getting my family's perspective was critical to my state of mind.

Tea was in a super-talkative mood after her weekend. I assumed she and Mike were back on track. I couldn't keep up. She pulled her chair next to mine. "I can't believe they arrested your friend Patricia for murder. Does this mean we should be expecting the Miranda-hating internet trolls to re-assert themselves any time now?"

I glanced at her, taken by surprise at the comment. "Wow, I've been so busy I haven't had time to think about the Princess of Death movement. I wonder if I should move to a hotel for the next few weeks. Or," I winked, "maybe I should stay with Jason."

She punched my arm, "Like you don't already have enough unfair advantages. That's all we need. I can see it now. 'Jason, Honey, did you remember to make my lunch? Let's go outside at noon and eat at the company picnic table. Okay, Sweetheart, see you then.'" She made a gagging gesture.

I couldn't deny that she was right even though we weren't living together. "Well, he is sweet."

She sighed. "I hardly remember Mike and me that way. In fact, we were never that way. But now that we've been together for years, I can't even imagine it. We're like an old married couple. You know, it's like, "Hey, did you take out the garbage.?" "Uh, No. Can't you do it?" "I did it last week." "Okay, but you're not getting any for a month."

She rolled her eyes, then remembered why she had come over to my desk. "So what's the story with Patricia? Did she do it? Did she kill one of the most famous mob killers of the last twenty years? They shouldn't put her in jail. They should be paying her a bounty." She picked up her phone. "Hey, look at this. It started on Facebook this morning. It's the 'Free Patricia' Campaign. It already has 3,000 likes."

I grabbed her phone. "Let me see that." I looked to confirm that she wasn't pulling my leg. "Why did everyone choose to hate me when I went to jail for something I didn't do, and still to this day, they think I'm a killer?"

She scrolled to another Facebook account on her phone. "Um, I think it might be these pics of you." She handed it to me.

There were multiple pictures of me during my adolescent Goth days covered in everything black: lipstick, studded leather collar, hair, fingernails and toenails, a leather halter top, and a leather skirt, topped off with safety pins in my cheeks. Okay, I looked pretty scary. I had to agree.

"I'd even want to throw me in jail looking like that." Thank God I'd resisted the body tattoos that I had considered.

She went back to the Free Patricia site. "Look at the cute pics of her and her mom modeling. They are what America is all about."

She turned her phone toward me and I stared at the pictures of Patricia and her mom. They were a perfect match, almost like twins with their pale complexions and straight, black hair, even the same eyes, the same shape of their mouth. And where Patricia didn't look like her mom, she looked like Charles: his high cheekbones, the shape of his earlobes. Something wasn't right. They really looked like they could be her birth parents—but she was an orphan, right?

Since Charles White was a public figure, there were plenty of pictures of him on-line, pictures of him at all ages. I opened up photos of him in college, of him as a teen, as a child. There was an expression that he had on his face at virtually every age; it was the same quirky half-grin that Patricia had. Oh, my God! I would bet my life that he was her father, her biological father. So, why would someone fake an adoption?

Tea soon went back to her desk, and we were mired in our work after that. I didn't have time to think about anything but orders, parts, manufacturing, warehousing, and shipping. I couldn't complain, though, I was never bored, and I was good at what I did. The day flew by.

I called Wanda on the way home. "Hey, it's Tuesday, and you guys arrested Patricia on Sunday, when is the arraignment? Doesn't it have to happen within seventy-two hours?"

She laughed. "Hi to you too. Yes, that's normally true. However, because Charles White wanted to use his counsel, he asked to delay it until Thursday."

I seethed. "This son of a—whatever's daughter is sitting in jail, and he extends her stay further to use his lawyer to advise her to plead innocent?"

The detective commented, "Well, I've seen it happen for plenty of reasons. But, I agree, if my daughter were in jail, I'd want to do everything I could to get her out as soon as possible."

I couldn't contain myself. "I spoke to both of her parents. I was the one who let them know she'd been arrested. I can tell you his first reaction was he seemed to be worried about his candidacy, not how he could do what was best for his daughter. Facebook, for God's sake, is more concerned about Patricia than he is. They've already got 3,000 Likes on the Free Patricia page."

"That's just great, Miranda."

Her voice suggested she was less than happy with that news. I decided this wasn't the best time for us to speak. "Um, I'm going to call Patricia's work with an update on her arraignment date, if that's okay with you," I said more sarcastically than I probably intended.

I heard her say, "Miranda ..." as I hung up.

Deep inside, I knew none of this was her fault, but she was acting too police-like for my agenda right now, so I had no patience for her.

I called Susan at Karma to let her know that it would be at least Friday before Patricia returned.

"As I told you yesterday, we're here for her. Please let her know if you get a chance to speak with her."

I smiled and hoped it translated over the phone. "Thanks so much, Susan. I look forward to meeting you one of these days."

She sounded very friendly too. "Can't wait to meet you either. Patricia speaks so highly of you. I almost feel like I know you. I'll talk to you soon, and if Patricia's schedule changes, just let me know. We can't wait to get her back. Thanks," she said and hung up.

For some reason, I was reminded that I wanted Margo to meet with Patricia. Still, it didn't seem like this week was a possibility for her, so I decided to see if I could meet with Patricia alone sometime before the arraignment, which only left this evening or tomorrow sometime.

I called Wanda back, hoping for a more satisfying conversation. "Marshall." I know she knew it was me, but she was continuing her business-like treatment from earlier.

I groveled. "Okay, Wanda. I'm sorry about earlier. I'm angry at Patricia's father, and I shouldn't take it out on you."

She wasn't quite ready to bury the hatchet. "It's fine, Miranda. At the end of the day, we are on opposite sides of this case, and there's nothing we can do about that. Maybe we should stay more professional until this is resolved. Otherwise, we will have conflict, and we both have the potential to be put in a compromising position when it comes to sharing confidential information with each other."

I could see her point. "That doesn't stop us from sharing our points of view with each other. I think we are both intelligent enough to differentiate the lies from the truth." I hesitated, thinking this might not be the right time, but continued. "I read the California law, and I know you only have to allow family or her attorney to visit. But since she has no family here, is there any way you can make an exception and let me visit with Patricia, just for a few minutes?"

There was a hesitation on the other end of the phone. I couldn't tell if she was considering my request, talking to a co-worker with her hand over the phone, or answering a text.

Finally, she spoke as if she had been putting the right words together. "Miranda, you drive me crazy. And you make me so mad sometimes. But I do think it would be helpful to provide each other's perspectives during this case, and possibly others. I think we are both professional enough to handle the conflict of interest. That said, yes, you can visit her. Can you be here in an hour?"

I jumped from the couch. "Really? I love you! Well, okay, I like you a lot."

She laughed. "Awkward! I'll see you in a few minutes."

"Thanks, Wanda. You're the best. I'm just going to change out of my work clothes and I'll be there."

Chapter 24

I couldn't imagine staying in a holding cell not knowing how long I'd be there while they figured out whether they would charge me with a crime, let me out on bail, or throw away the key. I remembered what being in jail was like, even though it had been several years ago. I remembered the smells, the fears, the unknowns, the sounds, the inability to sleep, and the voices at night. I never even had to share a cell, and I still panicked with every sound I heard.

Wanda met me in the lobby and had, very kindly, set Patricia up in a lounge area, much like a living room, with several couches and love seats, instead of a cold interrogation room or conference room. I thanked her with my eyes as she and an officer watching Patricia left her and me to reconnect. I was sure we were being monitored, but that was what they did; I couldn't blame them for that. I didn't see any two-way mirrors.

I was happy to see she was wearing one of the outfits I had dropped off on Saturday after they arrested her and how un-prisoner-like she looked. Everything was up in the air, so I wanted to make sure she at least had something familiar and clean to wear. I couldn't even fathom the mess her father had created because he couldn't get his attorney here fast enough for the arraignment and bail hearing.

She got up from the couch, looking small and meek. She buried her head into my shoulder as we hugged and she whispered into my shoulder, "Thank you for coming."

I whispered back, "I wish I could have come sooner. Everything is taking longer than I expected or I wouldn't have gone away on Monday. I've been working on your case, though. I met with Margo."

Patricia looked confused. "How can Margo help my case?"

I responded, "Her husband was friends with Tony Sansone." I suddenly realized that it was likely the police were listening, and recording, everything we were saying. And while it probably wasn't anything I wouldn't tell Wanda, I wanted to control who had the information."

I picked up my iPhone and started typing in the Comments application and handing the phone to Patricia, awaiting her response.

I typed. She met with Tony Sansone a few days before he was killed, in a limo outside our apartments.

She responded. Well, maybe SHE killed him. I've never even heard of the guy.

I typed. That was the body in my bathtub! It looks like Tony Sansone killed John Blake and David Miller.

Her already alabaster face went completely white. Why?

I typed. I have no idea. I thought Margo might know. Tony had a connection to her husband. They had been friends for many years.

She responded. Who is this Tony Sansone?

I typed. I told you before. He was a hitman, a paid killer. On the FBI's most-wanted list.

She glared at me like I arrested her and typed. This is crazy. Why and HOW would I kill a professional killer?

I typed. I'm going to do my best between now and your preliminary hearing to figure out why they brought you in. It makes as little sense to me as it does to you. I'm happy to hear it from you, though.

She frowned at me. You better not have thought that I actually did this!

I typed. Sorry, I used to be a cop, so I had to hear it from you. You can bet I'll be talking to Wanda about this.

She typed. OK, can we just talk now? It's about what happens now.

My fingers were getting tired too. I said, "Okay, here's what I know. Your arraignment and bail hearing will be on Thursday. That was the earliest your dad's attorney can get here." I couldn't help but get that dig in.

She grabbed my hand. "Do not tell me that I've stayed in this place a second longer because my dad's attorney couldn't get here any faster."

I had wanted to put a prettier face on it, but that would have been a disservice to her. "The court was ready to do the arraignment Monday morning."

I thought her head was going to explode. I know that mine would have under the same circumstances. But instead of screaming, she said, barely above a whisper, "I knew my dad should not have run for office. It's changed him and not for the better. There was a time when if I even whispered, 'Daddy I need your help,' he would have been at my side in an instant."

I felt so sorry for her and I couldn't help showing it. "So, what's it been like here?"

She leaned back on the couch and exhaled loudly. "It's been incredibly boring. Evidently, it's a slow time for criminals in Santa Clara, so there are no other women in holding cells right now. They don't mix the holding cell people with the actual prisoners, thank God. So, I've had my own cell. They let me borrow a few books. I was petrified the first night, but they've been decent to me. I think they feel sorry for me, to be honest."

I tried to remember everything I was going to tell her. "Oh, I called Susan, your boss. She was very nice and said not to worry; they weren't going anywhere."

She smiled.

The officer who had been with Patricia before I joined her, knocked on the door. "Five minutes."

I wanted to ask, "Is it really that critically important, whether it's five or ten minutes?" But I figured I might need these people at some point. I was glad, though, that we had had this time together. Patricia was faring far better than I ever would have predicted. I wanted more than five minutes but knew that we were going to have to wrap up.

I took her hand. "I'm going to be at the arraignment for moral support. They really are a piece of cake, though. You'll just plead innocent, the judge will come up with some reasonable bail, and we'll all move on."

"You make it sound so easy. Thank you, Miranda."

We hugged, and the officer came back for her. Wanda was with the officer. We went in opposite directions after we left the meeting room, Wanda and I to the right toward her office, and the officer and Patricia back to the holding cell for another day. That was a crime.

Wanda sat at her desk, and I sat on a chair opposite her.

I stared at her while she looked at her computer screen.

She finally looked away and met my stare. "What?"

I searched more carefully for words than I would have at one time. "How involved have you been with this case?"

She typed on her keyboard while she talked. "As I told you before, Miranda, I have been involved in the forensic and ballistic side."

I continued, "And has there been any evidence in the forensic and ballistic side that would have led *you* to arrest Patricia for killing Tony Sansone?"

She continued to type. "No, but I'm not working that side of the case. I'm working on recent murders that Tony may have been involved in, with the thought being there might have been some retaliation from someone related to those murders."

I pursed my lips and put my index finger to my mouth. "Oh, okay. Now we are getting somewhere. So, you believe that since Tony killed the Surf Brothers, it's possible Patricia was avenging those murders?"

She nodded. "That's a part of it, yes." She didn't tell me what the other part of it was. She was going to make me go on a fishing expedition.

"So, was there some other evidence that tied Patricia to the Tony Sansone killing—a weapon, some fingerprints, DNA, evidence that they had even ever been at the same place at the same time?"

Wanda stared straight ahead. "I can't comment on that right now. It's confidential and a matter of National Security."

I glared at her. "You know when you said this was a bad idea earlier. You were right." I stood and walked out. I climbed into my Rover and pounded on the steering wheel. I drove home too fast, angry, and frustrated.

Chapter 25

Between last week, when Wanda and I had gone to the park, and now, she had drunk the Kool-Aid. National Security, my butt. Something was wrong, very wrong.

I tossed and turned all night with nightmares about evil forces taking over the country. I wasn't sure if my imagination was spurred by my encounter with Wanda or my phone conversation with Charles White. Either way, it wasn't good.

I barely made it through my workday on Wednesday, distracted, and feeling helpless about Patricia. I would be so relieved once they released her on bail. Oh my God, what if they didn't allow bail? Now I had something else to worry about and lose sleep over.

When I got home, I called Mark; he was always good at giving me a different perspective and getting me back on the right track. He answered on the first ring. "Miranda, what's up?" He knew I'd make fun of him if he didn't recognize my number. He was learning.

"Hey, I'm not sure if you heard that they arrested Patricia for Tony Sansone's murder."

He responded, "Well, I guess she was on a small list of suspects. However, she doesn't really fit my cold-blooded killer mold. I'm still leaning toward Margo."

I protested, "I don't know about that, Mark. I've had a couple of eye-opening visits with Margo since we were together. There's a lot more to her than a smart-mouthed rich woman. I'd love for you to meet her some time. Anyway, Patricia is about my last suspect on earth too. I had been working closely with Detective Wanda Marshall of the Santa Clara Police Department

J. T. Kunkel

until yesterday, and suddenly, she went all 'National Security' on me. It was weird."

Mark pondered some other questions, "So, when was Patricia arrested?"

I barely could remember at this point. "Um, Sunday."

He ticked off the days. "So she's out on bail?"

I expressed my concern. "No, that's one of the reasons I'm calling you. Charles White wanted to hold off on the arraignment until his fancy attorney was available, so she's still sitting in a holding cell at the Santa Clara Police Department. The city's been ready to roll since Monday."

Mark was outraged. "I've never heard of a parent trying to keep their child in jail *longer* than the law allowed, especially a well-connected one."

I felt justified for my concern. "Thanks, Mark, I was starting to feel like I was going crazy. At least they've been treating her well in jail, but she's not a strong person. I visited her last night. She seems depressed and pretty confused, not at all like a guilty murderer to me."

I was so happy to have Mark in the family.

"So, is there anything you need me to do?" he said.

"Not at this point. Just be there to let me bounce things off you. Thanks. I'll keep you posted. Bye." I hung up.

I decided to call Jason because I forgot to let him know I was going to the arraignment tomorrow morning. It was the least I could do for Patricia. It went right to voicemail. "Hey, Honey, I forgot to mention that I won't be in the office in the morning because I'll be at Patricia's arraignment. With any luck, I'll be in by late morning or early afternoon. I'm all caught up on orders because I was a zombie today and data-entered like there was no tomorrow. You can thank me when you see me. See you, hopefully tomorrow."

I went into the bathroom and ran some bathwater. I needed a stress reliever, and that was the best one I could think of that didn't involve alcohol. I wanted to keep a clear head to be on top of my game for Patricia tomorrow morning, even though the arraignment should be a slam dunk. As I soaked in the tub, I ran through all the possible suspects who could have killed Tony Sansone and placed his dead body in the bathtub I was lying in right now. I put that part of the thought immediately out of my head. I guessed because Patricia had a key, it could have been anyone who ever visited her in her apartment or anyone I ever had in mine. We had pretty much analyzed that list to death when I went to visit my family.

Wait a minute, how about our landlady? She had complete access to both of our apartments at all times of the day and night. I actually knew very little about the woman, except that the building had been in her family for many years and that she had grown tired of renting to students.

I couldn't remember her last name as I laid back in the tub with my eyes closed. I tried to picture the name on the lease and kept coming up blank. It was kind of a funny last name and fit her to a tee. Red. Red hair. Dyed obviously, but red.

Yes, Sally Maureen Reddy. I was going to look her up on the internet after I finished my bath. Who knew, she could be an ex-cop or an ax murderess. I also had no idea how or where she stored her apartment keys. Anyone she had frequent contact with could have had access to our apartment keys and thereby our apartments.

I wondered how many students had lived in this apartment, and if Sally consistently changed the locks between tenants. If not, there could have been decades of students with access to my apartment.

My bathwater was starting to get tepid, and my curiosity was getting the better of me. I got out of the tub, toweled off, and dressed then found my phone, and opened my browser, typing in Sally Maureen Reddy. I got the usual variety of people with similar first or last names, having nothing to do with my landlady. There were high school and college students, homemakers, and political figures, but then something caught my eye. It was a newspaper photograph circa 1960 of a woman in her thirties with fifteen girls, age eighteen to twenty-two or so, with a headline. *'Famed Madam, Sally Maureen Sansone, arrested in San Jose on prostitution charges.'*

I nearly dropped my phone. Sally Maureen Sansone. Could this be Tony's mother, or was that her maiden name? Were they somehow related, and if so, did he have access to my apartment? I needed to contact her and get some questions answered. I could call her to let her know I had changed the locks to pretend I needed to arrange to get her a set of keys. It was all such a wild coincidence; I had to at least eliminate her as a suspect before the arraignment.

I ran to the filing cabinet and dug out my lease. Sally had printed her phone number on the bottom below her signature. I dialed and crossed my fingers. She didn't seem like she was in her eighties, which she would have to be if I did my math right.

"Hello?"

I talked faster than I should have. Even *I* thought I sounded nervous. "Mrs. Reddy, this is Miranda Marquette, your tenant in the first-floor apartment on El Camino Real."

She didn't respond right away but I could hear her breathing so she was there. "Mrs. Reddy?"

"Yes, Miss Marquette. I would understand if you want to move from the apartment," she said in a fragile voice.

"No, no. I don't want to move. Um-you see, I had the locks changed because of—that incident. And I wondered whether I ought to mail a new key to you."

"You could do that or leave one in the mailbox for me to pick up at some time."

I thought about that and decided against that. "I'll mail it. I know that you once had the name Sansone and wondered if—"

"I don't know how you know that but it's not something I want to talk about. Thank you for calling." She disconnected before I could say anything else.

That surprised me. I didn't know whether it would be appropriate to send condolences or to just drop the whole matter. Poor woman.

I decided to crawl off to bed, confused as ever.

Chapter 26

Another night of tossing and turning as worry about facing Patricia's arraignment and bail hearing left me exhausted on Thursday morning. I had gotten used to attending arraignments as a supporting member of the defense team; this time it seemed a little more intimidating, not feeling like I had a strong ally on either the defense or the prosecution. I thought I had a partner in Wanda until this week when she suddenly got weird.

The gallery filed into the Robert F. Peckham United States Courthouse and Federal Building on South 1st Street in San Jose. It was an attractive white building that looked like it held a Japanese fan. I was surprised that it wasn't in Santa Clara, but the locals joked that no one knew where Santa Clara stopped and San Jose began, so as a transplant, it was even more confusing.

I was only slightly surprised to see Sally Maureen sitting in the back row as I sought out my seat, finding a space in the third row. I didn't have the energy to approach her, but her presence answered my questions about her past and her link to Tony Sansone.

I should have known, the killing of a well-known and fearsome criminal such as Tony Sansone would bring out all sorts of spectators, but the fact that they had to turn people away for a preliminary hearing was surprising, even to me. The press was well represented outside, and I was happy to have gotten past unnoticed. That would never have happened a year or two ago. I guess I had fallen off the radar. I wasn't sure if I should be happy or sad about that. I had spent so much time trying to get publicity, it seemed counter-productive for it to go away. It was so much more fun when I was able to manipulate it for my own purposes.

But today wasn't about me; it was about Patricia. She was seated in the front with a very attorney-looking fellow. They were sitting in silence. Patricia, even though I could only see her from the back, looked stiff as a board which looked like intense fear to me, which I couldn't understand since she was likely about to be set free. Maybe she wasn't enjoying the company of her father's very political attorney.

I looked around the gallery and recognized several members of the press, but there was no-one I knew personally. Her parents weren't even there, which I found sad, since she could use all the support she could get.

The bailiff stood and introduced the judge. "Ladies and gentlemen, please stand and acknowledge the honorable Judge Richard Robinson, magistrate."

After the bailiff led us in the Pledge of Allegiance, the fifty-something judge, with graying temples and a kind face, sat and motioned us to sit down. He then directed his statements to Patricia. "Patricia Ann White, you have been charged with the murder of Anthony Sansone, in the first degree. How do you plead?"

She glanced over at her attorney. He spoke to the judge. "Your honor, may I approach the bench?"

The judge motioned him up.

They talked for a few minutes, and then he motioned the District Attorney to the bench also. The judge announced to the gallery. "We are going to my chambers and will be back in a few minutes. Feel free to talk amongst yourselves."

I was confused and worried. How hard was it to plead innocent? My mind wandered as I waited for the three to return.

I wished I could go and sit with Patricia for a while to see how she was doing. I was worried about her.

Finally, they filed back into the courtroom to a hushed silence.

The judge spoke to the court. "Due to circumstances that have been provided by the defense and acknowledged by the prosecution, the charge in the case of Tony Sansone has been reduced to first-degree manslaughter."

Then he spoke directly to Patricia. "Do you understand these charges?"

She spoke barely above a whisper, "Yes."

I didn't like how this was going, and I felt like the whole world was moving in slow motion.

The judge continued. "How do you plead to this charge?"

She looked at her lawyer, who pointed her to the judge. "Guilty."

The courtroom exploded with chatter. Our landlady stood, with tears in her eyes, swept an angry gaze over the room, and stormed out. The members of the press raced outside so they could set up for comments when the gallery filed out later. I had already made eye contact with several of them who had recognized me from our prior encounters. I searched for another exit, finding none.

The judge pounded his gavel. "Order. This court is still in session."

People immediately quieted.

The judge was eager to finish the proceedings and addressed the defense and prosecution tables, "Counsel, we will book a sentencing hearing as soon as possible, and in the meantime, Miss White will be remanded to the Federal Correction Institution in Dublin, California. This court is adjourned."

The bailiff said, "All, rise."

The judge rose and slipped out the rear door. My knees were weak as I struggled to stand. Walking was out of the question, so I sat down again, while the others filed from the courtroom. I figured they wouldn't let me stay in here indefinitely, but it might buy me some time while I regained my sea legs and avoided the press. This court appearance was one of those 'what just happened' moments that come few times in a lifetime. The good ones are fantastic, the bad ones, like this one, monumentally horrifying. I had only a few minutes to come to terms with my best friend going to prison for a murder that I had no doubt she didn't commit.

My iPhone vibrated in my pocket, and Facebook directed me to a press conference called by Charles White. He stood on a podium, with his wife Toni at his side, in front of the Capitol Building in Denver, sounding and looking extremely presidential. My gag reflex was fully in place.

"My fellow Americans. It is with a heavy heart that I come to you today to let you know that our," he put his arm around Toni, "adopted daughter Patricia pleaded guilty to the first-degree manslaughter of a criminal who has been on the FBI's most-wanted list for over a decade. While we certainly do not condone Patricia's actions, we support her in every way. We will help her to rehabilitate her way back to society as she serves her prison sentence."

He paused briefly, looking concerned and fatherly, then continued, "Earlier this year, Patricia, completely against Toni and my wishes, relocated to California, which we know has been suffering from increased lawlessness due to the influx of millions of illegal immigrants. Clearly, against her will, she was sucked into the ugly underbelly of a state where illicit drugs and murder for hire have become a way of life."

J. T. Kunkel

I had to put him on hold while I tried to comprehend how Charles White, through his daughter's plea bargain, could put the whole state of California on trial. It was, in a way, brilliant, but also frightening and polarizing.

He was finishing up. "So, let me just assure you of this. I will continue to stand for law and order, the right of all citizens to bear arms, and the right of all babies to be born, and until those rights are guaranteed in this nation, I will not rest."

The highly partisan crowd cheered. There were no questions allowed from the press in the audience, and the event was over as quickly as it had begun. As I reviewed it in my mind, I realized that this was Charles White's attempt to do two things. One, to distance himself from Patricia by referring to her as his adopted daughter. And two, to try and make lemonade out of lemons when, in fact, his daughter going to prison for murder could derail his campaign completely, not only for governor but for president. So, his whole future depended on how the public reacted to this speech.

Knowing I couldn't stay in the courtroom forever, I decided to venture out of the building, hoping the press had completed their post-trial interviews and was packing up to go home. For the most part, that was true. However, Lyanne Melendez from ABC 7 was perched on the steps just outside the building with a lone cameraman as I came out the door. Lyanne had always been a fair journalist, so I didn't mind that she had stayed behind.

She smiled when she saw me exit the building. "Miranda, do you have a minute?" She motioned for me to sit next to her, which I did.

She had a couple of questions scribbled on a small note pad. "As people may remember, Miranda Marquette knows more than her share about death and dying, and I just learned you are also a friend of Patricia Ann White. Is that correct?"

I smiled. "Yes, Patricia is a good friend."

She smiled back and continued, "And I'm sure you know, Patricia is the daughter of Charles White, candidate for Governor of Colorado and, many think, a presidential hopeful for the future. How do you think her admission of guilt in this case will affect his chances?"

I wasn't quite sure what to say publicly about how I felt but decided I had nothing to lose. "I believe that Patricia was coerced into agreeing to this plea by someone who convinced her that there was enough evidence to convict her of killing Tony Sansone, which is preposterous because she didn't kill him."

She didn't seem to be taking me seriously. "And how can you possibly know that?"

I tried my best to appear as confident as I felt. "I met with Patricia earlier this week, and she was nothing but confused about why they had arrested her in the first place. She didn't even know who Tony Sansone was. I would bet my life on her innocence."

Since this clearly was mostly my opinion and I didn't have much to back it up, she was ready to let me go. "Well, it's always interesting talking with you, Miranda, and I hope that our paths cross soon."

The camera light went off.

I was about to leave when Lyanne grabbed my hand. "Miranda, personally, this case really worries me. I don't believe that she did it either deep down in my gut. I've heard stories where the FBI wanted someone so badly that they took them down and framed a civilian to take the fall. This smells an awful lot like that."

I was surprised that this woman, who jabbed with me on camera for so many years, was confiding in me. Or was this a test of some sort to get me to spill my guts? I thought about her question, though. "But why Patricia? She seems like the least likely candidate for the FBI to hang something like this on, unless ..."

She hung on my every word. "Unless?"

I chose my words carefully. "Unless they have something to hang on Charles White."

She had a questioning look on her face. "Like what? Can you elaborate?"

"Not really. Just something I was thinking about."

She looked at me, puzzled. "So, can I quote you?

I stood to go. "Absolutely not, Lyanne."

She stood up too. "Okay, Miranda. I understand, I suppose."

I appealed to her sense of fairness. "Patricia is my best friend, and I will do anything I can to help her. I don't believe that this is over, despite her guilty plea."

She nodded.

I continued, "I think that you and I could be friends under different circumstances. We both want the same thing. We just set out to get it in different ways." I thought for a minute. "Do you think we could have a cup of coffee sometime? It'd be nice to chat person to person, get your perspective on things. From your point of view, not the network, not what you're told to say, but what you really think."

She smiled a genuine smile. "I'd love that, Miranda. You're probably right. I'll bet that you and I aren't that different. Give me your cell phone number, and I'll text you. I'm pretty busy, but early morning works best for me, especially on weekends. I'll make sure that I make time for you."

I stuck out my hand. "You've got a deal. I can't wait." I waved as I headed to my car.

I was too stressed to go to work, and I really didn't want to call Jason and explain why. I thought of a trick I had learned, call him on his office phone when I knew he had a meeting scheduled and leave a voicemail, then I wouldn't have to actually speak to him. I knew that he met with Bob every Thursday at noon, so I'd call him at 12:15 and leave some sort of message detailing why I wouldn't be returning to the office today.

Chapter 27

When I got back to the apartment, I started formulating a plan. I needed to find out first if I could speak with Patricia before they hauled her off to the Federal Penitentiary for processing. I knew that weeks might go by once they transferred her before she would be allowed to have visitors. Even though Wanda wasn't my favorite person right now, I wondered if she could help me with that.

I had to call Mark to see if he ever heard about the FBI killing people on their most wanted list and prosecuting private citizens for their actions. Knowing what I knew about the government, it wasn't out of the realm of possibility; I just had never heard of it before.

Margo was the third person on my list to call. She was a wealth of knowledge and was also in the midst of a murder trial. I wondered if any of her experiences could be of help with Patricia's situation.

But first I was calling Patricia's parents, namely Toni. I had no desire to speak with Charles again as long as I lived, and I figured a mother's perspective would be much more helpful in a situation like this. Unfortunately, I only had their landline. Who even had a landline anymore? So it would really depend on who answered. I figured this had to be a private line since they would never have freely answered a phone that the general public could have access to.

I took my chances, feeling like a high schooler calling for a first date. Charles answered, sounding harried. I kept a positive thought. "Mr. White, hi, this is Miranda Marquette, is Toni available?"

You would have thought I had just launched a missile to start World Was III. He spit out his words, "No, you can't speak to Mrs. White. In fact, do not call us again. Haven't you done enough to ruin Patricia and our lives? Just leave us alone." I started to respond before I realized he had hung up. "What have I done—" but it was too late. I stood, holding my phone, my hand shaking, and my heart racing.

I sat on the couch, trying to get my bearings. Ever since Patricia's guilty plea, something had been eating at me, like I was missing something right in front of me, but every time I tried to focus on it, it eluded my vision.

Once I regrouped, I realized I hadn't yet called Wanda about visiting Patricia. I hit her number. She was curt and businesslike. I wondered if she knew who it was. "Marshall."

I hoped she was just busy. "Wanda, it's Miranda."

I waited for what seemed like an hour for her response. She whispered. *"Miranda, meet me at the park where we went that day and make sure you aren't followed."* She hung up.

This situation was getting more and more bizarre every second. I grabbed my helmet, pulled my boots on, jumped on my motorcycle, and headed toward the park.

When I got there, Wanda was leaning against her car, smoking a cigarette. As far as I knew, she didn't even smoke.

I said as I pulled off my helmet, "What's this?"

She took a final puff and ground it into the blacktop. "It's something I do when I get stressed. I quit a couple of years ago, for the most part."

I tried to get a feel for where she was at. She had been all over the place for the last several days. I walked closer to her. "So, what's up, Detective?"

An uncharacteristic tear ran down her face. "I've been a detective for twenty years, and I believe I do a good job. I have never pursued an individual that my gut told me was innocent."

I was so taken aback by her display of emotion, I wanted to hug her, but I figured that would have been so outside of her comfort zone, I stood my ground. I said quietly, "And you don't believe Patricia killed Tony Sansone?"

She snorted, "God, no. There's not a snowball's chance in Hell that she killed Tony Sansone. Every cop on the force wants to take down a local criminal on the FBI's most wanted list, especially a guy like this who's been on it for twenty years. Someone like Patricia, no offense, doesn't just kill a guy like that, willy-nilly. This was done by a professional, most likely financed by someone with a lot of money. I didn't even think this case would survive the preliminary hearing. So when she pleaded guilty, I freaked out. There are forces much bigger than us working here."

I could understand that, but I was surprised she was so emotional. "So, what's going on with you personally? Stuff like this has to have happened before."

She thought long and hard before responding. "It took me a long time to rise up in the good 'ole boys network as a woman, and especially as a woman of color. Well, suddenly, I feel like the odd woman out again while the white men stand together in solidarity. I can't even tell you if my perceptions are real or imagined, but that's how I feel, and I haven't felt this way in a decade. And this Patricia White case is bringing it all to the surface. Do you think I'm crazy?"

I shook my head. "No! I thought I was the crazy one. Then I spoke off the record with Lyanne Melendez, and she was feeling the same way."

A look of panic overtook her face. "The newswoman?"

I smiled. "It's fine. We weren't on camera. We even agreed to have coffee soon. Maybe Lyanne's not as much of a shark as she seems." I finally remembered why I called Wanda in the first place. "So, is there any chance I can see Patricia before you ship her off to prison?"

She perked up as if she just remembered something. "Hey, that's another weird thing. Dublin is a minimum-security facility. That's where they send people who cheat on their taxes or steal from their grandmother. This is not where they send a woman who killed an FBI Most Wanted hitman."

I thought about it. "Well, that's good. Right?"

She scowled. "None of it is good. I was going to quit the force earlier today."

I stared at her in disbelief. "With everything you've accomplished?"

She stood fast. "Yes. And it's not just this. It's everything. The world is going to hell."

I asked, "So why didn't you quit?"

She looked me dead in the eye. "Because you and I are going to find out what is really going on here. I can do both of us more good from the inside than from the outside."

I grabbed her arms at the biceps, which surprised both of us. "I had a dream last night that had been swirling around in my head. It involved me and a group of highly competent and successful women joining together to help other women in need." I let her arms go, having gotten her attention. "Think about it. During the last couple of weeks, I've befriended you, Margo Prentice, and Lyanne Melendez. Think of what kind of powerful force the four of us could be together."

Wanda chewed on her upper lip. "I don't know, Miranda. I'm kind of a lone wolf."

221

The more I thought about it, the more I like the idea. "We all are. That's what makes it great. We are all amazing on our own but put us together as a group and imagine what we can accomplish!"

Her face softened. "Well, hey, maybe it would work. I hate always having to do it all."

"I know what you mean. I spend so much time living in my head; I can barely think outside of it."

A look of concern came over her face. "Isn't Margo in the middle of a murder trial herself? I'm not sure this would be the best time for her, and quite honestly, the best time for us to be associating with her."

I rolled my eyes. "Spoken like a true cop." I thought for a second. "Maybe you should call your friend, Blinky or Stinky, whatever it was."

She hit my arm. "Buster. It was Buster."

"Right." I laughed.

She grinned. It was nice to see her in better spirits. "What do you think about you and I getting together with Patricia before she's shipped off to vacationland. Maybe together we can get this figured out once and for all before she's forced to spend the next five to ten years behind bars. Do you think your boss would allow that?"

She thought for a minute. "Yes, we were all so surprised, including the judge, that she pleaded guilty, I don't think anyone would object to us doing some final due diligence before she is shipped out, even if that means holding her a couple of extra days. If he doesn't jump on the idea, I'm pretty sure I can convince him."

I wasn't sure if she'd be on the same page. I chewed on my thumbnail. "You were easy because this was your case, and you have a built-in sense of fairness because you're a cop, but what if you and I get together with Margo and Lyanne to get a broader perspective, and then we can play who meets with Patricia by ear?"

Wanda thought for a minute. "You just aren't going to drop this thing, are you?" She sat thinking for a minute. "Well I'll give you this, Lyanne is a professional interviewer. She might be able to question Patricia in ways that we can't to get her to share more information. And we could convince her to join us by promising her an exclusive if this all works out. If we get Patricia off, she, and she alone, can have the story. I bet she'd jump on that. I'm still not convinced that Margo adds value to be honest. You're going to have to sell me on her."

I started pacing around the parking lot. I felt like we were getting close. "Okay, here's what I think Margo offers. She's had to struggle through life from day one and has figured it out. She was an orphan who married into royalty in her early twenties. Within a very short period of time, she was struck with tragedy when a live volcano destroyed the kingdom and killed her husband, the prince. She then emigrated to the U.S. and married a successful businessman who died an untimely death. Then a couple of divorces and now her latest one died. She's the one who should be called The Princess of Death. She's had to dust herself off time and time again. She's a survivor. I believe that her life experiences will have taught her exactly the right questions to ask Patricia to elicit the truth. It's just my gut feeling from knowing her a relatively short period of time. I have come to know her and to trust her."

Wanda looked at me for a long time. "Okay, Miranda, I'm going to trust you on this one and keep an open mind." Wanda started toward her car. "Okay, I've got my marching orders. I'm going to make sure we keep Patricia around for a couple more days, and I'll get the captain on board just making sure that we're taking care of all the details. This is a high-profile case, and he's not going to want to look bad. In an unusual case like this, a little extra scrutiny never hurt anyone. I've got this." She jumped in her car and drove off.

I wondered briefly who this woman was, but I wasn't arguing. I grabbed my helmet and sped back to the apartment to make some calls. The good news was, if neither Lyanne nor Margo decided to join us, Wanda and I could handle it, but the more heads we had, the better.

Chapter 28

I knew I had to call Margo first. Lyanne was a much newer friend and much less of a loss. I believed that Margo was the missing link to solving the mystery of Patricia's guilty plea, even if she didn't know it yet. I punched in her number.

She answered on the first ring. "Miranda, I didn't expect to hear from you so soon."

I wasn't going to beat around the bush because she deserved the truth. "Margo, I need you. Now."

She laughed. "Miranda, this is so sudden. But I have to tell you, I prefer men."

I nearly choked on my own laughter. "Thanks, Margo, I mean, gosh, I find you attractive and all that, but I don't swing that way either. What I really mean is that Patricia needs you, and not *that* way." I figured I would dispense with all that nonsense before she started it again.

She asked, "Whatever for, dear, I understand her father is even richer than I am. As a matter of fact, I have found out while going through Malcolm's financial records that he was a big contributor to Charles White's political campaign. There were a couple of calls on Mal's phone showing calls from Colorado. I have to say, I plan to do a little more digging here. I'd still like to find out who the hell killed him. Divorce is one thing, but honestly ..."

I heard what she said but didn't figure that had any relevancy to what I had to say. "Okay, bottom line, Patricia pleaded guilty to first-degree manslaughter in the death of Tony Sansone and is headed to Federal Prison in Dublin, California, unless we do something and do it quickly."

She responded like it was my fault. "Well, why didn't you tell me?"

I struggled to hold it together, wondering if Margo was on her second or third glass of wine. "They arrested her last Saturday for the murder of Tony Sansone. Figuring she would plead innocent and be freed on bail, I wasn't particularly worried. But Charles White sent his attorney in, and everything went to Hell. Quite honestly, the court and the police are so concerned about due process, they're allowing me and Detective Marshall to put together an ad hoc group to interview Patricia to make sure that everything is on the up and up."

That was pretty close to the truth and sounded way more appealing than "You're accused of killing your husband and we want to pick your brain." I needed to remember this story for Lyanne either way.

Margo finally came around. "I would love to join the expedition for the truth."

I raised my right first and whispered, "*Yes!*" Then I realized I still had to put together the details. I supposed that Lyanne's schedule would be the hardest to coordinate with. "Can you keep your calendar reasonably empty over the next several days and I'll be in touch."

She responded, "Absolutely, Miranda. Thanks for thinking of me. And I'll keep searching on my end."

"Thanks for being someone I wanted to think of. I'll talk to you soon."

I was thrilled to have Margo, and I would have been disappointed if Lyanne couldn't round out our foursome, but something told me I could count on her. There was something about the fact that she was the last woman standing when I left the courtroom this morning. I knew that she had a passion for what she did. She wasn't just along for the ride. She wasn't just a reporter. She wanted to get the story right, but she also deeply cared about people. I had seen reporters over the years who, after they completed their interview, packed up their gear, and walked away. I had seen Lyanne, in the past, stick around and get to know people or lend a hand if they needed help. I really admired her for that.

I checked the time—nearly five. I had no idea what Lyanne's life was like, whether she got home for dinner every night, if she was married, had kids, or spent every night editing interviews until midnight. It helped not knowing when I dialed her cell phone. She answered after three rings, and there was some traffic noise in the background. "You've got Lyanne Melendez, what can I do for you?"

I was just momentarily taken aback by her phone answering style. "Lyanne, this is Miranda Marquette. How are you?"

I wasn't sure if she was driving or walking but she sounded a bit preoccupied. "Tomás, stop putting straws in Anna's ear." That answered my question. She had kids. I assumed she was married. I wasn't sure if that helped or hurt my argument to join our group.

"I'm sorry, Miranda, I'm on parent duty today. My husband and I trade-off."

Another reason to admire her. "How adorable. I love it. Is there maybe a better time to catch a few minutes with you?"

"Actually, this is probably the best time, believe it or not. At least there are no adults to interrupt."

But there were kids. I wasn't sure but plunged ahead. "Okay, here goes. I've got a proposal for you. I will get you an exclusive national interview with Patricia White if you help me and two other women determine if Patricia was served with due process during her plea and bail hearing. The court and the police

227

department want to make sure she understood her plea before they send her to prison."

She sounded skeptical. "Really? I've never heard of that."

I confessed. "Well, I had a little something to do with it as well as my friend, Wanda Marshall, a detective at the Santa Clara Police Department, but we agreed you'd be perfect for this. The fact is, it makes no sense that Patricia White pleaded guilty. Before she's put behind bars, we just want to find out why, and rather than interviewing her separately, it only made sense to get several subject matter experts together."

She thought for a minute. "Well, I'm flattered that you thought of me. I'm not sure that I'm really a subject matter expert, but if I can finagle an exclusive interview with the daughter of Charles White, I'll go for it. When would this be?"

I nearly jumped for joy but tried to stay contained. "Well, it has to be soon. Would Saturday around noon work for you? I'll have to coordinate with the others, and you probably have the heaviest schedule."

She hesitated, probably checking her calendar. "I think I can make that work."

I had so much to do to get this coordinated. "Okay, I'll get with the other two, and confirm with you as soon as I can. And Lyanne, thank you so much! I'm so glad that you are the person I thought you were."

She sounded very sincere. "Well, thanks, Miranda."

"I'll talk to you later. Thanks again."

My mind was racing. So much to do and so little time. I had to call Wanda first to see if and when we could arrange to meet with Patricia. Everything hinged on that. I punched in her direct dial.

"Detective Marshall."

I laughed, "I guess you don't have your caller ID on."

Miranda, I was just about to call you. How are your calls going?"

I was excited, but not ready to spill my guts. "Good, did you speak to your captain?"

She was talking fast. "Yes, and we need to move before he changes his mind. This meeting is so unorthodox; he's starting to get cold feet. The district attorney is pushing to get her out of here, so we can't hold her much longer."

I crossed my fingers. "How about Saturday at noon?"

She continued, "He said he didn't want to see her here on Monday, so that should be perfect."

I needed to call the other two, especially Margo since I hadn't thrown a time out for her yet. At least Lyanne had a tentative time to work with. "Okay, I'll let you know when it's all nailed down. See ya." I thought of something before I hung up. "Hey, wait a minute. Can Patricia refuse this meeting?"

She thought for a minute. "Well, technically, no, but she can refuse to answer any of our questions. That's where we'll count on you and your relationship with her."

I swallowed hard. "Okay, great. Thanks."

I hit Margo's number. "Okay, Miranda, where are we?" She surprised me with her readiness after her blasé attitude on the first call.

I didn't want to waste any time. "Saturday at noon."

She responded immediately. "I'll come up tomorrow get us a suite at the Hyatt for us."

I giggled like a schoolgirl. "I'd *love* that. Let's meet at my apartment at seven and go over from there."

She sounded hurried. "Okay, I'm working on questions. I'd hate to be the slacker in the group. I'll see you tomorrow."

"You, a slacker? Not likely. See ya."

229

J. T. Kunkel

I always felt good inside after talking to Margo. It was so funny how a chance meeting of a quirky woman on an airplane to Switzerland had turned into such a good friendship.

I called Lyanne back. "Lyanne, back at ya."

Apparently, she too could be a little quirky. "Lyanne, Miranda. We are confirmed for Saturday at noon. If you could show up at the Santa Clara Police Station at around 11:45 in the lobby, that would be great."

She sounded a little worried, "Miranda, to be honest, I want to make sure I'm on the right track. Do you have some time to get together tomorrow night to review some questions?"

"Actually, one of the others, Margo Prentice, is coming up from Long Beach, and she'll be staying overnight. You can join us if you'd like. We're meeting at the Hyatt. Margo's got us a suite there."

She said breathlessly, "Seriously? I would *love* that, leaving the kids with my husband. I wouldn't miss it for the world. And is that the Heiress Margo Prentice who's accused of killing her husband?"

It took a second, but I realized she thought I meant she was included in the rooms for 'us.' Figuring Margo wouldn't mind, I said, "Right, that Margo Prentice. And these two cases have some interesting similarities."

She continued, "Do you think I can get an exclusive with her?"

I laughed, "I guess that depends on how well she likes you."

I could hear a smile come to her face. "Fair enough, Miranda. Fair enough. I'll see you tomorrow. How's nine?"

I smiled too. "Perfect."

I wondered if I should invite Wanda. The four of us needed to have a good rapport when we met with Patricia. I punched in her number. "Marshall."

230

I hadn't thought about my angle with Wanda. "Hey Wanda, this is going to sound a little strange, but would you like to join Margo, Lyanne and me at the Hyatt tomorrow night at nine? Margo booked us rooms there. More comfortable than trying to cram us all into my small space."

She chuckled. "What are we, in junior high now, Miranda?"

I continued, "Well, I get it, but here's what happened. Margo has a long drive, so she's coming in tomorrow for the Saturday meeting. When I told Lyanne that, she saw an opportunity to meet Margo and be kidless for an evening, so it's already three out of four. So I figured, why not all of us?"

I could hear the gears grinding in Wanda's head. "Um." I guessed that she wouldn't want to be the odd girl out on Saturday. "Yes, I'll do it!"

Chapter 29

I decided we should keep the party limited to the hotel room so we could speak freely and concentrate on what we were doing. There was a microwave and fridge in the room, so I figured I could bring some wine and snacks. Since I had a diverse group of women to provide for and had no idea what they all liked to eat, I settled on a random selection of cheeses, fruit, crackers, and frozen hors d'oeuvres to pop into the microwave. Then I came across Belgian cream puffs which looked yummy, so I picked up a couple of boxes of those. Then I needed something to drink. Not everyone was a big fan of cabernet, and come to think of it, I didn't even know whether or not Lyanne drank wine at all. I opted to get a mixed case of cabernet and pinot grigio because I whatever we didn't drink I could take home. I also grabbed a couple six-packs of soft drinks.

The hotel offered a continental breakfast so we wouldn't have to worry about what to eat in the morning. The final bill nearly depleted me of all my cash, despite the reason for the gathering. It felt good to be spending somewhat irresponsibly for the first time in over a year.

When I got home, I put everything aside and the perishables in the fridge.

I finally collapsed into bed a little after eleven reminding myself that I still had to clean up the apartment either first thing before work or after I got home and before Margo arrived at seven.

#

The sun peeked through the curtain to start an exciting day. Like a chemistry experiment, I was bringing together three of the most interesting women I knew. I hoped it resulted in something amazing and gratifying instead of something hopeless and horrifying. That was one of the interesting things about people, which was why dating services and websites were only marginally successful. It was difficult to predict how two people would react to one another face to face in real life when their chemicals were bouncing off one another. And this was not only a male-female thing. These chemical reactions were true with all human beings and responsible for why we felt very strongly about some people and very wishy-washy about others.

I hoped work would fly by today. I had the feeling Jason wasn't completely happy with me right now. We hadn't spoken in several days, and even our texts had been short and impersonal, not even any cute emojis or adorable little hearts.

My desk had a new pile of orders, which suited me fine. Tea barely spoke to me as she passed my desk to get to hers. I figured I must have offended her in some way. I decided she would tell me if it meant enough to her. If not, her loss. I didn't have time for immature games.

Suddenly, I could feel Tea hovering over me, reading my screen over my shoulder. I minimized my screen because I had been checking for updates on Patricia's case. I bristled because she was in my space. "Can I help you with something?"

She gave me a fake smile. "I was just wondering how long we are going to have to put up with you coming into the office one day and taking off the next. It's getting pretty bad around here when people can't rely on other people. It's starting to remind me of what it was like before you got here, and that's pretty bad. I never thought you'd take advantage of dating the boss."

233

I felt like my head was going to explode. I turned around and glared at her. "Not that it's any of your business, but do you really think this had anything to do with Jason and me dating? That is really sad." I stood because my neck was getting sore, turning to glare at her. "My best friend and upstairs neighbor is this close to going to prison for a crime that several other people and I are convinced she didn't commit. Something just doesn't add up, and I'm doing everything I can to see that she doesn't go away to prison for a long time. I let Jason know a while ago what was going on and that it might require me to be out off and on, and he said he had it covered. Do you want me to let him know that you are having a problem with it, Tea?"

Tea glared at me and spit some words at me. "Yes, maybe you should, Miranda. We can't do it all. I understand you have stuff going on. Well, guess what. We all have stuff going on. I'm trying to hold together a relationship that I don't know is going to last until tomorrow—." She surprised me by bursting into tears.

My heart melted at the sight of her sobbing. I wanted to reach out but I held back, not knowing if I was welcome in her space. Unable to stand it, I approached her and she opened up to my hug. She cried for five minutes while I hugged her. I had no idea she was in this kind of pain.

Finally I said, "Please talk to me. If things aren't good, whether it's here or at home, let me know so I can try to help. I'm not always the most perceptive person in the world, so please talk to me. Okay?"

She sniffled then nodded. "Thank you. I'm really sorry." She forced a bit of a smile and walked back to her workstation and started typing. Another crisis averted.

#

I got home just after five, expecting Margo in just a couple of hours. I invited the other two to meet us at nine at the hotel so that Margo and I could have some time to ourselves to plan for the evening. I saw Margo as a critical person in the group. I felt that she could make or break the success of the whole evening, and I wanted to ensure that it went well. I knew that people sometimes perceived her as over the top. I loved that about her, but it could be a turn off for others.

I quickly changed into an old pair of sweats. My adrenaline was raging as I jetted around the apartment, vacuuming, sweeping, fluffing pillows, cleaning the bathroom within an inch of its life, dusting, washing dishes, wiping counters, and washing windows and windowsills. It made me realize how lax I had been in cleaning since I moved. I promised myself I would do better.

I looked at my watch as I rushed to the bedroom to change into something more presentable. It was ten of seven. I decided I could fit in a shower if I made good use of time. I flipped on the water while on my way back to pick out my clothes. I decided on pair of colorful leggings and an oversized t-shirt. It seemed perfect for the occasion, and I wouldn't even have to change for bed if I didn't feel like it.

I had just finished putting my hair up in a clip when the doorbell rang. I ran to the door to find Margo standing there, looking stunning in a magenta long-sleeved flounce top and free flowing wide leg palazzo pants. Besides her oversized white framed sunglasses, she had a feathery thing in her hair that matched the clothes.

"Margo, you look amazing!"

She smiled demurely. "Oh, I bet you say that to all the girls."

"Well, you're the only one here, so I can truthfully say, I'm only saying it to you."

She stepped in and looked around and removed her glasses. We hugged briefly.

"So, what's the plan for tonight?"

I sat knee to knee with her on the couch. "Well, you know I asked Lyanne and Wanda to meet us at the hotel at nine. Have you ever met Lyanne Melendez? She's a bit of a celebrity here on the local news."

She bit her lip. "I've definitely heard of her. Attractive late thirties? Very well-spoken. Impressive as far as I remember."

I smiled. "I think you'll really like her." I blushed. "Um, I sort of promised she could interview you if she came."

She hit my arm. "On TV? Girl! You're going to be the death of me."

I could tell she was thrilled with the attention. "Sorry." I winked.

She smiled. "And I had a chance to ask Willie Ames a bit more about Wanda Marshall, and he had nothing but nice things to say about her. I've got something I need to show her later. You put together a good group, Miranda. I'm impressed that the police and the court were willing to let us get involved in the case. That says something about the climate of fairness they have here. It seems like everyone is trying to accomplish the same thing, to get it right."

I was surprised Margo didn't have anything in writing with her. "Do you have a list of questions or anything to get us started?"

She looked at her hands and sprung up from the couch. "Oh. Of course. It's in my purse. It would have been a shame to have left that home after working on it for four hours."

I was relieved that we weren't starting from scratch. I had a couple of pages of hand-written questions in the bedroom tucked away in my overnight bag. I glanced at my watch. It was almost eight, and we hadn't reviewed any questions yet.

"Why don't we compare our questions now so we don't duplicate them and waste time tomorrow. We can check with the others later."

We retrieved our respective lists and I poured two glasses of wine.

We spent the next forty-five minutes comparing notes, laughing at the end that we'd thought of almost the exact same things to ask Patricia.

We left for the hotel at eight forty-five, each taking our own car. I left a message for Jason on his cell telling him where I would be Saturday. I pulled up at the front door of the hotel and let the doorman retrieve my overnight bag and the cases of wine and shopping bags of food.

Right behind me, Margo stepped out of her Mercedes and pointed at the trunk. The bellhop brought out two suitcases and a large picnic hamper.

Wanda and Lyanne arrived a few moments later while we were checking in. They were caught up in a discussion about a story Lyanne had recently done about how local law enforcement struggles with the issues brought about by undocumented immigrants.

Wanda said as they entered the lobby, "It was a really thoughtful piece that took everyone's point of view into account. I was impressed with your ability to see and report all sides of a story equally."

Lyanne smiled. "Well, thank you. That really makes me feel good coming from a law enforcement professional. I know you guys are out there dealing with these issues every day."

They both carried small overnight bags, which they set down near our bags. Margo stood beside me, waiting to be introduced.

I took the opportunity once there was a pause in their conversation. "Lyanne Melendez and Wanda Marshall, this is Margo Prentice."

They all shook hands. Margo, ever the socialite, spoke first, "I've heard such wonderful things about both of you. And before you say it, I know you've both heard things about me too. Well, I hope before this night is over, you'll figure out that everything you've heard wasn't necessarily true."

They both started to protest, but she waved them off. "It's the reality of being me—the myth and the mystery. The fact is that I'm probably not that much more exciting than any of you, day to day. I had an exciting beginning, but since Montserrat and becoming a princess, my life has been pretty much like anyone else's."

I figured that was her standard start of any interview, and it seemed effective. She left Lyanne's and Wanda's mouths hanging open then said to Lyanne, "We'll talk more later," and winked.

I struggled to get their attention. "Okay, let's take this up to the room."

"Just one minute," Margo said. "Can I have a quick word with you, Wanda?"

The two women stepped across to the lobby and exchanged a few words. Margo handed a cell phone to Wanda and then Wanda used her own to make a call. Lyanne tugged at my arm, anxious to get going.

We followed the bellhop to the elevators as Wanda went to reception and had a conversation with the manager before joining us. All talk stopped until we reached the penthouse suite Margo had reserved for us. Shades of my old life. Rooms like this were once on my daily menu. I had a brief moment wondering how I could think my current living conditions were so wonderful.

I pulled myself together and turned to everyone. "Okay, since we are a group of powerful, independent, provocative, talkative," we all chuckled, "sexy, gorgeous, beautiful, intelligent, successful, and I could go on and on about the kind of women we are. There is no doubt that we could talk all night and then some, about the questions we should pose to Patricia tomorrow about her guilty plea. It could become pretty grim so what I propose is we cover all our questions so we understand where each of us stands and who will focus on which topic when we talk to her."

Lyanne said, "Then can we have s'mores?"

Margo held up a hand in a regal gesture. "Wait, I have something even better." She strolled over to the counter where the bellhop had placed her picnic basket and opened one side. "Ta-da," she said with a flourish.

The rest of us went over and peeked in as Margo pulled out a small tin of something. "The best Beluga Caviar from the Caspian Sea. Not a lot, mind you, but I thought we all deserved a treat. And I especially need all the comfort I can get until *my* absurd trial is over."

In our anxiety about Patricia, I think we had all forgotten completely about Margo's dilemma. She continued to pull things out of her picnic basket like a magician with rabbits from a hat. "A little something to quench our thirst." She whisked out two bottles of Dom Perignon.

I was starting to feel really embarrassed by my supermarket wines and cheeses. I stepped back and waited for what other delicacies might appear.

While Lyanne and Wanda oohed and aahed over Margo's selection, I felt myself growing more and more quiet.

Next came a plastic covered silver tray of sliced rare filet mignon. "Because a girl cannot live on caviar alone." She had baguettes of French bread, a block of brie, another plate with tomato and hardboiled egg slices, crystal salt and pepper shakers. I didn't even want to look any more.

Once everything was out and on display, Wanda brought us back to the reason for our gathering. "It seems a shame but we have work to do before we can indulge. So, let's gather at the table and get started. Miranda, are you all right?"

Margo said, "She's fine." With the other two looking at me, she raised a box of Swiss chocolates and waggled them as she grinned and winked at me.

I smiled, recognizing with that impish grin, she was acknowledging our first meeting and also reminding me that life has its ups and downs.

We gathered at the table near the window. I was thankful Margo and I had discussed a few salient points earlier because she was ready to pull things together. She produced her cheat sheet. "Okay, here's what I have as the broad categories of questions we should ask. One, her relationship with the Surf Brothers. Two, whether she had anything to do with her and Miranda's abduction. Three, if the Surf Brothers kidnapped them for ransom from Charles White, they obviously didn't get any money, so who did that anger enough to get them killed? Four, whether it was Patricia who had them killed, and if so, was Tony Sansone the killer? Five, how does someone like Patricia know a hitman, and six, did she then kill Tony Sansone or have him killed."

The other three of us stared at Margo like she was a goddess.

Lyanne spoke first. "Why would you even consider that Patricia had anything to do with the kidnapping or killing anyone?"

Margo tapped her long fingernails on the tabletop. "Well, I wondered if Patricia was involved with them somehow, but then they turned on her and saw Charles as a cash cow, so she turned on them. It's a long shot, but only she can tell us what was really going on, and now that she's got nothing to lose, I suspect we may get the truth from her. From what I've seen on television and heard about from Miranda, I can't stand her father. It's a shame he's not the one on trial." She chuckled.

I spoke up. "Something has been bothering me about Patricia's adoption. The more I look at her and her parents, I'd swear she's not adopted. I know that sounds crazy because it's public record that she is. And she and I have talked about this, so I'm not sure we can learn any more about it from her. She asked her parents point blank to tell her the details of her adoption and they went ballistic. She and I then tried to get information about her birth parents online who are allegedly dead. Now, I understand wanting to protect your adopted child, but this was over the top, and if they are dead, what exactly were they protecting her from, except perhaps the truth?"

Wanda broke in. "The whole Patricia White case bothered me from day one. I was only allowed certain access to evidence. Whenever I got too close to answers, they reassigned me to another aspect of the case. It was almost like my superiors didn't want me to solve it. So why are they so magnanimous now? I have no idea. I'm just going with it and hoping for the best. All I know is when politicians get involved in the law, the outcome is never good."

We tossed around ideas, tried some role playing, speculated on possibilities, and even played good-cop bad-cop which turned into a ridiculous comedy. After a couple of hours we agreed on our approach.

I was thrilled that we had a starting point. I imagined that there could be many questions that could come out from this starting point, depending on Patricia's answers, but we had no way of knowing which direction things would go until tomorrow. "So you know what that means, ladies! Time to dig in!"

Everyone cheered.

Chapter 30

Margo volunteered to open the first bottle of champagne while I opened the caviar and a spread a little on several crackers. I topped them with crème fraiche and passed the first one to Lyanne who looked at it skeptically. "Really. This is fish eggs, right?"

"Eat it," I ordered. "You eat chicken eggs, don't you?"

She closed her eyes and shoved the entire cracker into her mouth.

"Chew it!"

She opened her eyes, looking much like a little kid and dutifully munched on the treat that cost more than an ounce of gold as if it might make her sick. We all watched as she chewed and swallowed. She grinned. "That was really good!"

Everyone laughed and we carried on eating and drinking our way through the evening. Even my cheeses, snacks, and wines went down well at three in the morning after which we retired to our respective rooms—Wanda and Lyanne to the bedroom on the right; Margo and me, the one on the left.

Eight o'clock came way too soon. Before I even crawled out of bed, and Margo still snored in the other one, I called down to room service for a large pot of coffee and fixings for four. I dove into the shower, enjoying the luxury of the spaciousness and fancy shampoos and soaps.

When I emerged, Margo was just opening her eyes. I let her know I'd already ordered the coffee, and the shower was free. She looked a bit worse for the wear but struggled out of bed.

I left her and joined Lyanne and Wanda who were already ensconced in the living room.

These were not the powerful and self-assured women who were on top of their game last night, just four hungover women who needed lots of coffee, showers, toothbrushes, and breakfast. I let them know about the coffee.

Margo shouted from the other room. "Order breakfast. Whatever you want. It's on me. It's going to be a while before I can go out in public. I need lots of repair work here."

Lyanne called back, "Bless you."

When the coffee arrived and breakfast ordered, we went about drinking the coffee and putting ourselves together for the day. Margo emerged, looking fresh and ready to go.

She and Wanda, having a mutual friend in Willie Ames, had plenty to chat about. It seemed the more they compared notes, the more they had in common despite their diverse backgrounds.

Then Lyanne brought up her background living in Puerto Rico so she and Margo compared notes about their common experiences there.

By eleven we were all ready to leave and agreed to meet at Wanda's office at quarter to twelve. I still had to dress.

I put on a mid-calf skirt, a silk blouse, and brown leather boots. It sometimes still came in handy, having the wardrobe of a millionaire, even though I had to scrape my monthly rent together.

I arrived at the police station precisely at 11:45, excited and nervous about seeing Patricia. I wondered what she was feeling. I couldn't imagine waiting to be sent off to prison. It had to be a hopeless and helpless feeling. I didn't know if she would view us as the last hope or just another roadblock to jump over before she could finally get this wait over with. We would soon find out.

I found Wanda at her desk on her computer, as usual. It was hard to picture her in her pajamas sipping champagne and eating caviar like some kind of playgirl just a few hours before. But now, she looked more like the cat that caught the canary and I wondered what she had up her sleeve.

I sat in one of the side chairs, sensing that she wanted to keep things a little more businesslike now that we were back at the station. "All set for Patricia?"

She scrolled through whatever it was she was scrolling through, avoiding eye contact with me. "As ready as I'll ever be. I think we've got some good questions. This could be productive or a waste of time. I have no idea." Why did I get the feeling she was toying with me?

Just then, I heard laughter outside her office. It was Margo and Lyanne. They quieted when they reached Wanda's office, realizing their laughter reverberated throughout the station.

Lyanne said, "Whoops, sorry." She put an imaginary key to her lips and locked it.

I stood, offering them the two side chairs.

Wanda said, "No need to sit. We need to get to the interrogation room. Everyone all set?"

We nodded. Wanda said, "You know where it is. I just have to make one more call and I'll be right with you."

Margo distributed each of our questions based on what we had asked last night. She was an administrative Godsend. Of course, we could always ask more questions, but we didn't want to forget the ones we came up with last night.

The room was only about thirty feet away, but my feet were starting to feel heavy. I hadn't realized how nervous I was about seeing Patricia again. I felt so bad for her.

When we entered the room, Patricia was in the middle of the table on the other side, looking gaunt, dressed in an orange jumpsuit. Much to my surprise, her mother Toni White was seated to her right. The four of us sat across the table.

I greeted them. "Patricia, how are you?"

She half-smiled. "I'm okay, Miranda. I'm okay."

I turned to Mrs. White and said as I hoped she didn't detect my hostility toward her, "And Toni, how nice to see you today. I had no idea you'd be here."

She responded, "Can you explain to me what's going on? Why do you all need to see my daughter?"

"Just a second. Detective Marshall will be right here."

Wanda entered a moment later and took control of the meeting.

As the law enforcement officer in the group, it was Wanda's job to preside over the event, or at least to get it started. "We are here to review the circumstances of Patricia's guilty plea in the case of Tony Sansone. We don't want to see you sent to prison for something you didn't do. Despite your plea, we know there is a lot more to your story. The truth needs to come out. The Santa Clara Police Department sanctioned this, along with the District Attorney's Office and Judge Richard Robinson, who presided over this case. And just so you know who *we* are, let us introduce ourselves, I am Detective Wanda Marshall, and I believe you know Miranda. Lyanne?" Wanda sat down.

"I am Lyanne Melendez; I am a news reporter from ABC 7 here in the Bay Area."

Margo raised her hand. "And I am Margo Prentice. I have a vested interest in this case as you may know. My late husband was a friend of Tony's."

Patricia's eyes widened slightly at that statement but she didn't say anything.

Wanda continued. "We have one more person joining us." She went back to the door and opened it. A young man in civilian clothes entered carrying a stack of papers and a cell phone in a plastic bag marked evidence.

"This is Carl, our IT guy. He's been doing a little investigating for me and has something to share with us. I don't know exactly what it is, but he promises that it will have a profound effect on this case and may change the direction of our questions here today." She looked directly at Margo and added, "I've already contacted your attorney like you asked."

Margo nodded. She folded her arms and looked like she'd rather be anyplace else than here.

"Okay, Carl. What have you got?"

"You want me to read it, or will you?"

"You can, please."

He cleared this throat. "This is a conversation between the late Malcolm Wilson of Long Beach, California and Charles White of Denver, Colorado, made on the sixth of March of this year."

I quickly calculated that would have been right around the time of the kidnappings and murders.

"Wilson: Malcolm Wilson here.

White: Mal, old buddy, Charlie White. I just wanted to thank you for your continued support.

Wilson: Right. Glad to do it. Is there something you want? I'm kind of busy here.

White: Anyone around right now? Can we talk in private?

Wilson: I'm alone in my office looking down on the ocean, enjoying the view.

White: Listen, I need a big favor.

Wilson: Sure. Name it.

White: There are a couple of punks trying to blackmail me and I want them taken care of.

Wilson: What's that got to do with me?

White: Word gets out. I need a name. Someone who might be able to make them go away.

Wilson: Give me the details and I'll see what I can do. Can I call you back on this number?"

Carl lowered the papers. "The next call is an hour later. From Mr. Wilson to Mr. White. Should I skip the introductions?"

"Go ahead," Wanda said. The rest of the group remained silent.

"Wilson: The name you want is Tony Sansone."

At this, everyone in the room gasped. Margo put a hand to her forehead and moaned. Mrs. White turned ashen.

Carl continued. "Wilson read out a telephone number and then continued. I don't want to hear about this again, Charles. And you never got this number from me. Keep in mind, this guy is the best. Whatever he wants, make damned sure you pay him. You don't want a guy like him angry at you.

White: I really appreciate this. I'd use my own guy but really need the distance from my organization."

Wanda thanked Carl and asked him to leave the transcript behind. He took the evidence bag and left the room. "Wow. He said there'd be incriminating evidence in there on someone. That was not what I expected."

"How does that change things?" I asked.

"It's the link between White and Sansone. Gives White motive to want Sansone dead so he can't ever hold the killing over him. Also gives him motive to get rid of Malcolm Wilson for the same reason."

Margo now had both hands covering her face. "Poor old Malcolm." Then she dropped her hands, her face angry. "I still don't understand what the hell was he doing cavorting with hitmen."

"Did you know Sansone was a hitman?" Lyanne asked.

Margo snorted then turned to me. "I did in a way. It's not like it ever came up in conversation. He was Malcolm's friend and his occupation was," she shrugged, "irrelevant to me."

After a momentary silence, Wanda turned her attention to Patricia. "We're going to take turns asking you questions and hope you'll answer them fully and honestly. If you are guessing at the answers, let us know that too. We all hope that you understand that it's in your best interest to answer them all. All right?"

Patricia looked resigned. "Sure. Yes. I guess."

Toni raised her hand. "Can I help her remember things or assist in answering?"

Wanda immediately said, "No. We prefer you don't."

Thank goodness.

Margo started the questioning. "Can you describe your relationship with John Blake and David Miller?"

Patricia looked around the room, took a deep breath and then spoke clearly and quietly. "I met John in Denver, although he was going by the name of James Rich at the time, which is how I knew him. I was running in the park, and I had stopped to rest, and we struck up a conversation. He was a really attractive guy. He asked me out for a drink, and I said yes. We really hit it off, and sometime during the conversation, it came out that I was Charles White's daughter. He seemed impressed but I confessed that I had no desire for my father to run for office, either governor or president."

She refused to look at me. "So we put together a plan that we thought would end his candidacy. I would show James where we lived. He would threaten my life. And my father was supposed to be so concerned about me being in the public eye, that he would drop out."

She *lied* to me. She'd told me James stalked and threatened her, but nothing about a scheme. That's for sure.

She laughed cynically. "Nope, that didn't work. So we amped it up. He got more and more aggressive until finally, I ran to California, telling my parents I was running from James. Shortly after I arrived in California, we arranged for James and his friend David to abduct me. I figured that would definitely be enough to get my father out of politics for good. Since Miranda and I were pretty much joined at the hip, they abducted her too."

I held up my hand. "Wait minute, can I interrupt here?"

Wanda nodded. "Go ahead."

"Why did you include me in your scheme? They might've killed me when they hit me over the head. What was the point?"

She looked down at her lap and shrugged. "I'm sorry, Miranda. I never thought they'd get violent and I didn't want to sit in an empty warehouse all alone all night."

Toni put her arm around Patricia and said, "My poor baby."

I gaped at the two of them and had nothing to say. How selfish and immature can anyone be? I kept my temper and signaled for Wanda to continue.

Before Wanda continued, Margo, as if reading my mind, blurted out, "My god, woman! I have done some pretty stupid and selfish things in my life but never have I put any of my friends in jeopardy."

Patricia kept her eyes down and went on as if Margo never spoke. "You see, we had a plan. I knew my adoption was a sham and that Toni and Charles were my birth parents."

Patricia's mother turned bright red. "Patricia! You knew? When—? *How* did you find out?"

Patricia glared at her. "Didn't you ever hear of DNA? I've known for ages, Mother." She shrugged away from her mother and continued speaking directly to us. "After Nate was born and the doctors hinted that he might have a genetic heart condition, I did a DNA test in the hopes of learning more about my family health history. After I received the results of the DNA test and couldn't believe what I read, I contacted Colorado Department of Human Services and learned the name of the family that fostered me. They were very kind and explained that my father paid them to stay quiet about the alleged adoption. Mr. Newcomb explained that I was born before my parents were married. My father didn't want his family to know because they were community leaders with friends in high places and an illegitimate child in the family would have been really awkward."

She looked at her mother who burst into tears. "First, he wanted me to have an abortion which I just couldn't bring myself to do. Then he insisted I give you up for adoption. You have to understand, my heart was breaking because he still insisted he wanted to marry me in two years as planned. He said I would make a perfect companion for his political aspirations. He made me swear to never tell anyone about your birth. It was easy enough for me to stay out of the public eye until I had you, so no one ever knew I was pregnant. A new birth certificate was issued when we adopted you three years later from the foster home where his parents had placed you."

Patricia's lips quivered, but she maintained control. "I'd told James all about the adoption. That was when he came up with the blackmail scheme. He said all we had to do was threaten to tell the truth about my adoption to the world. That was perfect. I couldn't get him to drop out of the race, but I could bleed him dry of what he loved most—money."

Toni pleaded to Patricia, "He never told me about the blackmail."

Patricia glared at her mother but said nothing. "But before James and David could collect the first million, someone killed them. That's all I know."

Since Patricia had already answered the first three questions, Wanda went right on to number four. "Patricia, was it you who had James and David killed." She paused and looked at the paper again. "Never mind, we can scratch that one off."

She laughed. "All right, I suppose it's not appropriate to laugh when talking about killing someone, but they were my ticket. I guess I forgot to mention this part. They promised me ten percent since it was my dad, kind of like a commission, so I was due to get a hundred thousand dollars for every million they collected. No, I did not have them killed. And besides, "she added with a lascivious grin, "they were hot."

I wondered who this Patricia was. I was flashing back to my experience with my former friend Heather before she left town. I wondered if I needed a new friend selection process. Then I looked at the other three ladies on my side of the table and realized I had done all right this time.

Margo was ready for her final question. "And Patricia, did you kill Tony Sansone or have him killed? And remember, you swore under oath that you did."

I wondered if it really mattered that you committed perjury when you were in the process of going to Federal Prison for killing someone, but I didn't comment.

She took no time to think about it. "I had never even heard the name Tony Sansone until they arrested me for his murder. No, I didn't kill him."

We all four asked simultaneously, "*Then why did you plead guilty?*"

She hung her head and, with her elbows on the table, put her hands on her forehead. She spoke barely above a whisper, "*To save my father. His lawyer told me if I plead guilty, I'd only go to prison for a couple of years, but if they convicted my father, he'd get the death penalty."* She started sobbing.

Wanda waited a moment, then asked gently, "So you knew then that your father was the perpetrator of these murders?" Patricia nodded. "His lawyer explained it to me."

There was no point in asking any more questions. Our job was done here.

Chapter 31

The four of us went to my apartment to debrief, decompress, and destress. Even though it wasn't fair, it would take some time for the court system to figure out how to handle the fact that Patricia had pleaded guilty to a crime that she didn't commit and that her father was the likely perpetrator.

Patricia could be in hot water for some of the shenanigans she was involved in with the Surf Brothers before they died. She might have been better off not admitting to those. I hoped the court would be lenient when sentencing her on her guilty plea to the conspiracy to kidnap charge and perhaps her parents would cut her some slack on the blackmail.

Margo, Lyanne, Wanda, and I sat, wine glasses in hand, watching the evening news when a special news report interrupted. Suddenly there was Toni White, facing us and a hundred microphones and news people.

She wore a suit similar to something Jackie Kennedy would have worn in the sixties, classic styling. She didn't look nervous but she did look determined.

"I need to let you know some things that have transpired over the past several hours impacting our family. As you may be aware, our daughter Patricia recently pleaded guilty to first-degree manslaughter in the killing of FBI Most Wanted Hitman Tony Sansone. However, she is retracting her plea because she made that plea under duress and evidence has surfaced that will clear her of the charges. She will likely be released. I can't comment on any other possible suspects. However, there is something else I'd like to explain. Over the years you may have heard Patricia referred to as our adopted daughter. The truth is that we were young and unmarried when I gave birth to her. My husband's parents arranged to put her into foster care and he went along with it. I insisted that I wanted my daughter in my life and told him I would never marry him and would leave him if he didn't go along with my plan to get her back after we were married. I even made him sign an agreement. Of course, we could never get back the years we had without her, but at least I could finally give her the love that she deserved. But now, recently, because of Charles' platform as the morality candidate, he did not want the truth of Patricia's birth to get out for the fear that his voters would not understand and not vote for him. We had put out the word that we'd adopted a child and that was the end of that."

She smiled broadly. "You also need to know he is a controlling, emotionally abusing, womanizing, person and I would never have married him had I known any of these things about him. I will be filing for divorce very shortly."

She then looked straight into the camera and whispered, *"And I believe when all is said and done, the courts will be able to prove that he killed Tony Sansone and Malcolm Wilson."* She walked off stage.

Seconds later, an announcer's voice came on, "We'll have more on this developing story as it becomes available. We will now return to the program in progress."

We all turned to one another with stunned looks.

"Did she really say that?" Lyanne asked.

"I can't believe she said that on national television," Margo added.

I switched off the TV and spoke to Wanda. "So, this has been bothering me since this morning. Why would Charles White go to all the trouble of hiring a hitman to kill the guys who were blackmailing him, and then kill the hitman as well as the guy who referred him? It seems like he was pretty much home free once he made the deal with Sansone. I mean there's not a hitman in the world who's going to go to the police."

Wanda took a sip of wine. "I've had the same question running through my mind. I spend a lot of time trying to figure out why criminals do what they do. I guess we may only find this one out in court if Charles confesses the details since dead men tell no tales. I wonder, though, if Charles White used his own hit man to remove Sansone and Malcolm Wilson to permanently insure their silence."

"That's pretty sad, when you think about it," Lyanne said. "Now, he still has his own hitman to worry about."

"A tangled web," Wanda said. "Well, he'll be arrested, that's for sure, based on the phone conversation with your husband, Margo. And his wife apparently has plenty to say. I think it's safe to assume he won't be anybody's governor or president in his lifetime."

Margo sat at the kitchen table with Lyanne and spoke up. "How about Sansone's mother, your landlady? How does she fit in with any of this?"

I had thought a lot about Sally Maureen Reddy or Sansone. "She doesn't. She's just a lonely old woman with a colorful background and an unfortunate son. Ancient history."

We eventually finished our last bottle of wine and hugged our 'goodbyes,' promising one another that it wouldn't take another dead body to bring us back together, but deep down knowing that it probably would.

Once they were gone, I settled on my sofa, curled my legs under me and called Jason. "Baby, the case is finished. My involvement is done. It's you and me time."

I heard the smile in his voice as he said, "I'll be right there."

Other Books in the Miranda Marquette Series

Blood in the Bayou
Murder in the Extreme
Death in Santa Clara

Made in the USA
Middletown, DE
29 June 2022

67544777R00146